Sebastien stepped closer and suddenly the laughter died and every muscle in Jamie's body tightened in awareness. "You so wish to disbelieve I am what I say?" Sebastien asked. "Would it be so bad for your friends to find love?"

Jamie shook her head, then swallowed hard when he lifted his hand to her hair.

He brushed the wisps of hair from her temple. "Perhaps it is because you fear what comes next."

"N—next?"

"Your heart," he said softly, his voice an even more potent caress than his fingertips. "You are the last of the three, my mistress. When I succeed in this match, yours will be next."

She swallowed hard. "Impossible."

"One thing I have learned. Nothing is impossible."

"Who are you?" she whispered.

"I am the man who will bring you eternal happiness. . . ."

Your Wish
Is My
Command

Donna Kauffman

Bantam Books
New York Toronto London Sydney Auckland

YOUR WISH IS MY COMMAND
A Bantam Book / February 2001

ISBN 0-553-58241-0

Published simultaneously in the United States and Canada

Bantam Books are published by Bantam Books, a division of Random
House, Inc. Its trademark, consisting of the words "Bantam Books" and
the portrayal of a rooster, is Registered in U.S. Patent and Trademark
Office and in other countries. Marca Registrada. Bantam Books, New
York, New York.

This book is dedicated to
The Tuesday Morning Runaways

Thanks for giving me something
to look forward to every week!

Shirley, your support is wonderful
and truly appreciated.

Your Wish
Is My
Command

Chapter 1

The last thing Jamie Sullivan was looking for when she climbed the staircase to the third-floor attic was true love. She was looking for an extension cord. One thing she actually had a chance in hell of finding.

The air-conditioning system had died less than thirty minutes ago, and it was already muggy and musty-smelling. Ah, the French Quarter in the springtime. And it was bound to get a whole lot worse, she thought, praying that Marta's managerial skills extended to sweet-talking a repairman out early tomorrow morning.

At least the damn thing hadn't conked out until their grand-opening weekend was over. She pushed several boxes out of her way and ducked under the Y-beams as she stumbled toward the tool bench she recalled seeing on her last foray into the attic.

"What a mess." She'd spent all of her waking hours for the last two months getting the ground-level bookstore and café ready to open on schedule. She'd taken only enough time to convert the corner room on the second floor to a somewhat livable bedroom. However, her Martha Stewart skills had failed at that point. The remainder of the nineteenth-century Creole town house still looked like the neglected piece of real estate the place had been for the past couple of years. But it was her home now. Not exactly home-y. Not yet. But it would be someday. She'd see to that. She was nothing if not determined.

Determined to lean on the A/C repairman herself, she thought grimly, as a line of sweat formed at the base of her throat and trickled down to form a small pool in her bra.

She was still getting used to the idea that she had a fixed address for the first time in over ten years. Well, longer than that, really. She couldn't count the apartment her father had rented when she was a kid, since the two of them had spent next to no time there. And boats didn't count as fixed addresses, being as they didn't stay . . . well, fixed. There was the time spent here in New Orleans, in college. But a dorm wasn't really a home.

This, she thought, staring up at the steeply pitched roof, was a real home. Or would be. She had to admit, it was growing on her. She sneezed suddenly, then laughed as she rubbed her itchy nose. Yeah, New Orleans did grow on a person. Literally.

She stepped over a large box heaped with stuff, then stopped mid-straddle and looked down to her right. "What have we here?" It wasn't a box. She tossed aside a stack of old newspapers. "Whoa." A trunk. A very old one, if the worn leather trim and tarnished brass finishings were any indication.

She could feel the newly designed store logo printed on the back of her polo shirt sticking to her skin. *Find the extension cord. You can come back and play treasure hunter later.*

But her gaze lingered on the chest, even as sweat dripped off the end of her nose. This was buried treasure, matey, and she had to know what was inside. She tugged at the latch on the front, wincing at the grinding squeal it made, then hooting triumphantly when it flipped up. It took another minute or two of tugging to get the lid open. Her shoulders slumped when she spied the contents. Beads. Strands of green, purple, and gold beads, and tons of other Mardi Gras foo-foo stuff. Like she hadn't seen enough of them at the endless parades this past season. Shoot. So much for hidden treasure.

Just then an image of her father's smiling face danced through her mind. *Playing pirate queen again, Jamie, me luv?* She heard the words as clearly as if he were standing next to her. She was five years old again, standing defiantly on the prow of her father's offshore racing boat with a cardboard sword in her hand and a red rag tied around her head. She commandeered the sleek vessel as would any good pirate queen worth her gold doubloons.

Jamie bent down and sifted her hands through the silk masks, feathers, and beads. "No pirate queens here," she murmured. "Not anymore. I'm all grown up now, Daddy. Promise."

She started to pull her hand free, intent on closing the lid, wishing she could shut out the memories as easily. But she paused when her fingers brushed against something hard and leathery. Digging back into the pile with both hands, she grabbed what had to be a basket hilt to a sword. She drew the scabbard and sword free, quickly disentangling the beads and feathers from it.

This was no Mardi Gras prop. It was heavy. And old. Old and very real. She straightened and shifted it from hand to hand. The weight of it balanced nicely. She wondered why something so valuable would be buried in an old trunk of Mardi Gras junk.

She'd never met Edgar Santini, the man who owned this exclusive corner of Royal Street real estate up until his death. She knew that he hadn't lived in the house in decades but that the place had been rented off and on. More off recently, she thought, since her friend Ree Ann had taken over possession of the unoccupied building. Mr. Santini had left it to Ree in his will. Jamie supposed the sword could have belonged to any one of the previous tenants.

Jamie looked closely at the scabbard and the hilt. She couldn't imagine forgetting she owned something like this. Grabbing the corner of an old blanket, she rubbed at the silver and ivory handle, which had a gorgeous scrolled pattern engraved on it. If this was a reproduction, someone had gone to great lengths to make it look like an original. But she was betting this was no repro. Jamie knew her eighteenth-century weapons. An offshoot of her obsession with studying ancient seafaring vessels—pirate ships in particular. But when a kid grows up on a boat, that's a normal obsession, right? She was pretty certain it had to be.

All that pirate play as a child had evolved into her adult hobby of building tiny replicas of various pirate ships. An excuse to continue playing pirate queen, her father had once teased. He was probably right. She hefted the sword into her other hand and sighed, realizing it had been years since she'd built one of her model ships.

Now that the shop was open, she would have time to truly settle in and organize herself. She looked around the attic, thinking that if she cleaned up the place, scrubbed at the dormer windows, and cleared off that tool bench—it might make a good workroom. She grinned. At age thirty, she'd finally decided to give up hydroplane racing and become a responsible adult, but that didn't mean she had to abandon the pirate queen who still lived somewhere inside her heart.

Impulsively, she placed the scabbard on her hip and struck a mock stance. She slid the sword free and stabbed the gleaming blade forward into the air. *"En-garde!"*

She gasped, a scream locked in her throat as she

barely missed skewering the man now standing, sud
denly, impossibly, in front of her. Mouth gaping, she
stared at him as he gently pushed the deadly tip away
from its resting point directly above his heart.

"Be careful, *ma maîtresse*, you could poke an eye out
with that thing."

She was suffering heat stroke. Hallucinating. She
had to be. Because she'd just conjured up the perfect
pirate.

His jet-black hair was pulled into a tight ponytail at
the nape of his neck. His shirt was white, open at the
throat, where a deep-blue handkerchief was tied. He
wore a long dark coat, cut in at the waist, with heavy
sleeves and big cuffs and lapels. His breeches—they
couldn't be called pants—were snug and showcased
well-muscled thighs and . . . and . . . other well-
muscled things she struggled not to notice. His calves
were thick and heavy, something the thin white
hosiery he wore managed to set off in an absurdly
masculine manner. The shoes were brown leather,
with a brass buckle, thick heel, and heavy flap turned
back over the top.

He had to be sweltering in that getup, but as she
looked up at his face, not a bead of sweat showed on
his formidable brow. Dear Lord, what a face. High
cheekbones, a sharply slanted jaw, dark slashes of eyebrows, and eyes as black as midnight. They captured
and held on to their prey with nothing more than a
glint of . . . humor.

Humor?

He winked at her, as if reading her thoughts.

Jamie snapped out of her stupefied shock. He was
no hallucination. She pulled the sword back and
rested the tip on the trunk, keeping her eyes solidly
on the intruder in front of her. "This area is off-
limits to customers. What are you doing up here?"
Besides playing dress up, she thought, still rattled.

He swept an arm across his chest and bowed gracefully at the waist. His eyes locked on hers as he straightened. "You have summoned me forth, madame. Sebastien Valentin, at your service."

He was undeniably French. His voice was rich and deep. And very sexy. His costume, although it fit him like it was tailor-made for his impressive physique, was obviously some sort of gag. Gag? Her eyes narrowed as she immediately realized who would play just this sort of joke on her. Her cousin Jack. Flamboyance was his trademark. It was what made him a highly demanded makeup artist for the drag queens performing nightly over on Bourbon Street. This kind of prank was just his style.

"Well, Monsieur Valentin, I appreciate that, but I'm afraid I'm going to have to ask you to leave. Tell Jack he really picked a winner this time. You've got the swarthy pirate thing nailed. And please relay a message to him." She smiled wickedly. "Paybacks are hell."

Sebastien—if that was his real name—stepped forward, and she raised the tip of the sword in warning. Jokes went only so far. She gestured with her other hand. "Exit stage right, buddy." She stepped around him and motioned again toward the stairs. "And keep your distance."

Instead of looking thwarted, he smiled. Flashing white teeth only made his dangerous good looks all the more . . . well, dangerous. "I do not know this Jack you speak of. Did you not understand me, madame?"

"Mademoiselle," she snapped, immediately wishing she hadn't when his eyes gleamed in appreciation. Not that he had seemed remotely as interested in taking her inventory as she had been in taking his. In fact, now that she thought about it, he hadn't really looked at her at all. And why did she even care?

She'd officially returned to "mademoiselle" status a year ago, marking the second time she'd done so in her short adult life. Given that she apparently made a lousy madame, she figured it would be mademoiselle from here on out. Swarthy, grinning pirates and quickening heartbeats notwithstanding. Life's little divorces had taught her she would have to be made of sterner stuff than that.

She squared her shoulders. "What I understand is that you're trespassing, and I'd appreciate it very much if you'd leave quietly. I'd hate to have to call the police."

Her threat did not put so much as a wrinkle of worry between his perfectly piratical brows. "I cannot take my leave. You have summoned me forth, and as such you must select three souls. It is my duty to find their soulmates."

A surprised laugh escaped her. "A pirate genie with a cupid complex? Well, Jack is nothing if not creative. But, you know, it's hot as hell up here and there's a champagne glass downstairs with my name on it. I've earned it. In fact, I've earned several. So let's call it a day, okay?"

His smile grew wider. The first whisper of alarm lifted the hairs on her arm. He stepped toward her again, this time not stopping when she swung the blade up. In a move so swift she wasn't exactly sure what happened, he disarmed her, flipped the hilt to his other hand, then stalked her until her back hit the nearest wall. The damp brick stuck to her shirt, and dust motes danced in front of her eyes as he stood there, hardly a pace away. She could see the gleam of amusement still in his eyes.

Well, she'd been on the wrong end of the joke where men were concerned once too often in her life. And dammit, it just wasn't funny anymore.

She was a tall woman, almost six feet. And a life

spent manhandling high-performance speed machines had made her strong, very strong. But he was taller, and the ease with which he'd just handled that heavy sword—and her—predicted great strength. She was debating whether to jam him with her knee, shout out for help, or both, when he stilled her with the light touch of one long finger against her lips. "I mean you no harm, but you must hear me out, *ma chérie*."

Jamie swallowed dryly, but she didn't move. She didn't so much as blink.

"I am Sebastien Valentin, and my spirit resides in the Sword of Hearts. I am summoned forth when the blade is unsheathed."

Jamie's eyes widened. "Either you're a really good actor, or you honestly believe what you're saying."

He cocked one brow, looking from the sword back to her face. "I thought you, of all my masters, would accept the whimsy of a . . . how did you call it? 'Pirate genie with a cupid complex'? You like to play pirate queen, no?"

"I am not your master." And just how long had he been spying on her? She felt her cheeks redden and she tried to tell herself it was just righteous indignation.

"Ah, yes, forgive me. You would be my mistress, no?"

He winked, and damn her if she didn't have a little loosey-goosey moment in her knees.

Enough already. Her eyes narrowed. "The truth. Did Jack send you here or not?"

Sebastien slowly shook his head. "Although I'm certain I will enjoy making this Jack's acquaintance at some future date." He said *Jack* like *Jacques*.

Jamie almost smiled at that. How her cousin would love *that* affectation.

"You must make your selections," he said.

"Selections?"

"The souls you must choose for me to fulfill my destiny. I will find their soulmates, then I will take my leave."

Now Jamie did smile. "Boy, did you come to the wrong place."

He tilted his head slightly. "You do not believe in soulmates?"

He seemed honestly surprised, and Jamie felt the power equation seesaw in her direction. "Let me put it this way: Life has taught my business partners and me that happily ever after really happens only in books. Of course, some of us have needed more lessons than others," she added with a touch of self-deprecation. "So we named the bookstore downstairs Happily Ever After as sort of a private joke."

"You name your shop Happily Ever After because you do not believe in them?" He shook his head. "American women."

"How did you know my partners were women?"

He merely lifted a questioning eyebrow.

"Okay, fine. But, I don't think the feeling is exclusive to women, American or otherwise. I'm sure men and women all over the world would get that particular joke."

He leaned away from her and folded his arms across his chest. "Allow me to prove you wrong."

"How?" She asked the question rhetorically, of course. She didn't believe a word he said, but if playing his game would get him to leave quietly, she'd play.

"Make your three selections," he said. "I will show you that there is a true mate for every soul." He held her gaze. "In fact, mademoiselle, if you are so certain of your friends' lonely fates, I will offer a challenge. Allow me to find their mates as a way of fulfilling the first two of the three required matches. That will be your proof."

"And then what?" She was not going along with this lunacy, but she was curious to hear what he'd say.

"If I cannot fulfill my promise, I will take my leave from you and you will have your moral victory for women everywhere."

He seemed not the least bit concerned that this might actually be the outcome of his challenge. "And if you do?" Not that she was remotely worried either. She only wished Ree and Marta were up here listening to this. Boy, would they have a good laugh over this later.

He stepped closer, and suddenly she found a distinct lack of air to breathe. A slight miscalculation, she assured herself. She was still in control. His eyes were just as black close up, she noticed, with no distinction between iris and pupil. And his lips looked incredibly sensual.

"If I succeed," he said quietly, his accent making a sibilant murmur out of the last word, "your soul will be the final one I will match."

Jamie realized too late that she'd been talked into a trap. She couldn't be encouraging this guy. Playtime was definitely over.

He tilted his head and stepped closer. He wasn't playing either, she realized with a dry gulp. "Do not be afraid, *ma maîtresse*. Love is not all pain and anguish." He placed a finger under her chin, and she found her gaze pulled to his mouth again. "I will show you."

Before she could react, he dipped his head down and kissed her. His lips were firm and sure and every bit as sensual as advertised. The whole thing was over before she could comprehend any more than a fleeting sense of being kissed by fate. Absurd.

"Kissing isn't love," she managed roughly. She should have been furious, slapping him or kneeing him, screaming rape, or yelling to get someone's attention.

She did none of those things. She told herself it was pride. As a woman who'd spent all of her life competing—and winning—in a man's world, she'd had to handle her share of aggressive men. She could certainly handle one sexy French guy in a pirate suit.

He grinned. "Ah, *chérie.* The kiss wasn't to show you love; it was to seal our bargain."

"We have no bargain."

"Ah, but we do." He stepped back and swept his arm out to the side as he bent forward in another gallant bow. As he straightened, he slid the sword easily into the wide sash at his waist, a sash she could have sworn he wasn't wearing moments before.

He blew her a quick kiss, then saluted her. "*Bonsoir,* mademoiselle." He winked as he added a slight emphasis to that last word.

"Good Lord, Jamie, what in the devil is taking you so long?" Ree Ann's Southern-belle voice rang up the stairwell. "My forty-dollar mascara is threatenin' to drip right off my chin. I don't need waterproof makeup; I need stuff that's heatproof."

Jamie turned toward the hallway. She could hear Ree coming up from the second-floor landing.

"Jamie?" The sound of her high heels clattered on the hardwood stairs, and her bracelets rattled against the wrought-iron railing.

"Here." The word came out as a dry rasp. Jamie cleared her throat. "Just a . . . just a second." She turned back, intent on making it clear to Mr. Sebastien Valentin that he was not welcome in her life or that of her friends.

But there was no one there.

Chapter 2

Ree Ann climbed up the last step. "Why, sugar, you're as pale as powder." She fanned her hand in front of her face. "Come on down before you have a stroke. The champagne is chilled to perfection and Jack finally got here."

Ree Ann Broussard was one of Jamie's college roommates and her cousin Jack's favorite person. And it wasn't hard to see why. She was flamboyant without even trying. Deep-russet hair, bright blue eyes, the face of a beauty queen—Miss Metairie three times running back in their college days—and a lush figure that had turned more than one intelligent man into a garbling pile of hormonal mush. Of course, what Ree didn't advertise was that behind that bring-traffic-to-a-standstill exterior was the gray matter of a summa cum laude scholar.

"People are confused by what they don't understand," she'd explained to Jamie early on in their relationship. "And they don't understand brains that come in a package like this." She defended her flirtatious, Southern-belle manner by saying it was simply easier to give people what they expected.

Jamie had long ago given up trying to unwind that bit of logic. Of course, she'd never stopped so much as a moped with her looks, so what the hell did she know?

Ree studied her closely. "Honey, are you okay?"

Well, that was a loaded question. Jamie cast a quick look around the attic. The trunk lid was still open, but there was no sign of Sebastien. Or the sword that had started the whole thing. "I . . . I found this ancient old trunk," she began. How could she even try to explain what happened?

"And you had to explore. What a surprise." Ree laughed. It was one of those full-bodied types that begged anyone who heard it to join in. But Jamie didn't feel like laughing.

"At least you found the cord, so come on already." Ree popped back down the stairs, her heels clacking on each riser. When Ree had walked the length of the second-story hallway, Jamie heard her call down the final curving set of stairs that led to the back of the shop. "Wouldn't you know, I found her diggin' for buried treasure. Don't y'all open that first bottle till we get down there, now."

Buried treasure? *If she only knew.* Then the rest of what Ree said clicked in. *Wait a minute, what cord?* Jamie looked down at her hand and sucked in a breath. She was clutching a dusty brown extension cord. "I'm hallucinating and I haven't even *had* a drink yet."

"Jamie?" Ree's voice echoed up to her.

"I'm coming, I'm coming." *Right after I find the sanity I apparently lost somewhere in the last ten minutes.*

Jamie grabbed a fan from the storage room on her way to the café area. Ree took it and went to set it up on the coffee-bar counter. Before Jamie could do so much as push the damp hair off her forehead, Jack's beaming face popped up in front of hers. Dressed in perfectly pressed polo shirt and khakis, every strand of his thick brown hair ruthlessly coiffed despite the million-degree humidity, he swept Jamie into his arms.

"Congratulations!" He swung her expertly around

in a smooth dance step ending with a dramatic dip, which he handled with great aplomb despite the fact he was a good five inches shorter than she was.

Jamie was breathless as she good-naturedly smacked his hands off her. "You're a danger to left-footed women everywhere."

"Nonsense. I make you look good and you know it." He kissed the back of her hand. Then he turned and motioned to the elaborate spray of exotic flowers now dominating the front counter. "A little surprise for you. I truly intended to have them delivered this morning, but Emil was late and the delivery I was expecting never showed and—well, you don't want to hear about *my* day, do you?"

Ree Ann laughed. "It's just as well, sugar. We'd have never seen the customers standin' behind this jungle." She smiled at him and lifted a small tray off the coffee counter. "And I wouldn't have been able to dazzle the clientele with my new recipe for cinnamon pecan sticky rolls. Here, try." She lifted one to his lips.

Never one to disappoint, Jack swooned dramatically.

Jamie rolled her eyes. "We'll move the flowers to the table just inside the foyer. They'll make for a grand entrance." She shot Jack a look. "And we all know how important that is."

"So, you have been paying attention. Very good."

Jamie studied him closely. "You wouldn't have had any other kind of . . . grand-opening surprises planned, would you?"

He wasn't listening to her. He was watching Marta Lewis, fellow Tulane grad and the third partner in the venture, come out of the office door at the opposite rear corner of the shop. She wove her way through the shoulder-high bookshelves, never once taking her eyes off her calculator. Her brown hair was piled in a slowly avalanching bun. She'd apparently tried to circumvent its imminent collapse by jamming a mechanical pencil into the tangled mass. Judging by the dangerous wobble that occurred with each step, it had been one of her few miscalculations. Her granny glasses had slid halfway down her nose, and she trailed calculator paper behind her, unnoticed.

Jack made a tsking sound. "Miss Marta and I definitely have to have a talk."

Jamie hushed him. "Well? How'd we do?"

Absorbed in her world of numbers, Marta continued tapping away. "Not bad, not bad. I'm printing the whole thing out in the back, but there were a few more calculations and, well, we're about seven percent over the gross I anticipated, but then Ree had to have those imported linen cloths for the tables in the café, which reduces the net by—" More tapping.

Jamie slid the register tape from under Marta's elbow and quickly scanned to the bottom line. Her eyes widened. "Hey, did we really do this? Just today?"

Marta finally looked up, the barest hint of a satisfied gleam in her eyes. "Happily Ever After is now fully operational and proudly in the red." A smile played at one corner of her small mouth. "But look out, black, we're coming. Someday."

Ree let out a surprised laugh, but Jamie pumped her fist in agreement. It was rare that Marta made bold pronouncements. Well, positive ones anyway. The quiet one of the trio, she was perfectly comfortable handing out dire predictions right and left, which was why Ree had long since dubbed her Eeyore. So this was doubly encouraging. It was the happiest Jamie had seen Marta in years, maybe since Dan had died. Even if that single look of hope was Jamie's only reward, every sacrifice she'd made was worth it.

"Well, let's not just stand around while there's perfectly good champagne to guzzle," Jack said.

The cork made a satisfactory pop, and the champagne poured out of the bottle. The chilled tickle of the bubbly had never tasted better. This wasn't the first victory Jamie had toasted with champagne, but sharing this one with the three people who meant the most to her made it sweeter than any that had come before. If only her dad could have been there, it would have been perfect.

As if reading her mind, Ree asked, "Did you hear from Sully yet?"

She nodded. "He called a while ago, when you were serving up your last latte of the day." Jamie smiled, though it wasn't as heartfelt as she'd have liked it to be. "He was sorry he missed the grand opening, but something came up yesterday on one of the boats he sponsors and he had to fly to Crete."

Ree propped a hand on her hip. "He's in Greece? I thought he'd retired."

Jamie's smile turned rueful. "Did you really think that just because he finally stopped racing that he'd truly settle down?" And yet wasn't that exactly what he wanted for his only daughter? "I knew when he decided to keep his sponsorships going he wasn't going to really slow down." Sully had told her it was too late for him to enjoy life in the slow lane, but it wasn't too late for her.

Ree came over and stroked a light hand down Jamie's arm. "Are you doing okay with that? Are you sorry that you're here, stuck in this sweat oven of a city, instead of hoppin' about the globe with your daddy, racin' those death traps of his?" She tenderly brushed Jamie's damp bangs off her forehead. "Tell me true, Jamie Lynne."

Ree Ann was a natural toucher, whereas Jamie was not. Ree would hug, pat, and fuss over people. And after all her mother-henning, she usually got a truthful answer to her question. She made a person feel he or she owed the truth to her. Her concern was sincere, so even Jamie ended up giving in.

"I'd be lying if I said I didn't miss the unbelievable rush of racing over the water, Ree. The need for speed is in my blood. You know that." She covered Ree's hand with her own, knowing Ree needed reassurance too. Lately, things hadn't been so easy for her either. "But I don't miss the rest of that life—the struggle to keep on top, the jerk-offs who try and push you down, the sheer exhaustion of it all. Right now I wouldn't be anywhere else on earth but here." She nodded to Marta, who was talking with Jack. "Did you see that look on her face?"

Ree answered with a warm smile. "Almost made me cry. This is so good for her, Jamie." She suddenly pulled Jamie into a tight hug. "It's good for all of us," she whispered fiercely before setting her back. "And don't you go forgettin' it!"

è

An hour and two empty champagne bottles later, Jamie figured she was doing well to remember her own name. She drained the last drop of her last glass and ceremoniously stuck the champagne bottle upside down into the bucket. "I think we've celebrated enough."

Jack shook his head. "Oh, no, sister. This is just the beginning. It's time to take this show on the road. Hit the clubs. Really celebrate!"

"It's Sunday night," Jamie argued. "Time to really go to bed and sleep."

"Oh, you're always the party pooper."

Jamie propped her hands on her narrow hips. "I out-partied you on five continents by the time I was eleven. I'm over it, okay?"

"True, true. We can't all be jet-setting goddesses." Jack tossed his head back and smiled devilishly. "But

I've been doing my fair share of catching up." He turned, swung Ree into his arms, and spun into a deep dip that he'd practiced on Jamie earlier in the evening. "What say I take you out and make all my straight friends jealous?"

"I say you have a date." Ree turned to Marta. "Come with us. Come on!"

Marta shook her head. "I've got a million things to do before we open tomorrow."

Jamie shook her head. "Oh, no, you don't. It will probably be quiet in here tomorrow, which is good since I'll regret that last glass of champagne, around seven A.M. when I wake up with a pounding headache. You'll have plenty of time to bury yourself in the back office while I tend shop. Go on. Or I'll make Jack annoy you until you say yes."

Jack shot her a mock wounded look but turned to Marta expectantly.

She sighed, then shocked them all by shrugging and nodding. "What the heck. Sure." She straightened her shoulders, as if going into battle. And for the seriously nonsocial member of their group, it likely seemed that way to her. "But I have to be home by midnight."

"Sure thing, Cinderella," Jack said. "We truly can't con you into joining us, cuz?" he asked Jamie.

Jamie was tempted, if for no other reason than to bolster Marta's commitment. But Ree could handle that. After all the frivolity and consumption of adult beverages during the past hour or so, Jamie realized she'd actually forgotten what had transpired in the attic earlier.

She wanted to tell them about it, but what exactly would she say? If it had been a joke from Jack, he'd have been bursting to share a laugh over it. No, she wanted to do a bit more exploring before she said anything.

If she ever did. It all seemed hazy and unreal now.

"I'm beat, and I have to find a way to blow some of that heat out of the upstairs so I don't swelter all night. Although maybe sweating the champagne out of me isn't such a bad idea."

"I already have a call in to the repairman and a note in my Day-Timer to follow that up first thing in the morning. Of course, that expense will set us back another—"

"Say good night, Cinderella." Ree took Marta's arm firmly in hand and steered her toward the front door. She grinned and waved back at Jamie. "You may owe me for this!"

And with a bang of the door and a clang of the brass bell attached to the handle, the shop was suddenly empty.

Jamie looked from the door to the rear stairwell, then back at the front door . . . and had the fleeting urge to run after them.

But she didn't. Instead, she sat back down at one of the café tables and tugged apart another chunk of sticky roll. She groaned as she chewed. Damn, but that girl could cook. *A few of these every day and I won't have to worry about racing again.* The boat would sink. The grueling pace of racing hydroplanes burned calories in a way that the grueling pace of selling books did not. She'd have to figure out something. Because she was not giving up eating. New Orleans might be hellishly hot and humid, but the food more than made up for it.

She licked her fingers and looked around the shop. It was an incredible piece of architecture. It had first been an apothecary, then—with many renovations along the way—a variety of retail operations, finally ending up as an antique emporium before falling into disuse. The first floor hadn't been used in almost ten years, so they'd had their work cut out for them when Ree took possession of it. And the battle hadn't ended there.

Edgar Santini had left a single heir, his grandson, Angelo, who had made out quite handsomely in the will but still hadn't been happy to learn of Ree's bequeathal. "Greedy bastard," Jamie muttered, picking pecan pieces from the remaining sticky bun and crunching them. It hadn't helped that Ree let the moron believe she'd been nothing more than a ditzy gold digger. The truth was that what Ree knew about cooking was rivaled only by what she knew about investments and business management.

Jamie felt the stirring of a headache and turned her attention back to the shop. A sense of awe filled her. The cypress floors shone, the elegant molding around the fourteen-foot-high ceilings gleamed with fresh white paint. The antique chandelier glittered. As well it should, she thought. Her elbows were still sore and she swore her fingers would forever smell of vinegar from cleaning the room. The walls were lined with oak shelves, with attached rolling ladders positioned on each wall to reach the higher levels. Browsers could select a volume or two, then make themselves at home in the café or in one of the overstuffed chairs tucked here and there around the shop. The coffee counter had come from a bar over on Bourbon Street, complete with brass counter and foot railing. Jamie's find had been the antique cash register. She smiled thinking of the major battle she'd had—and lost—with Marta over using the register day to day. But she'd compromised: She used the computerized one Marta had insisted on, positioned discreetly to one side, and kept lollipops in the antique one, giving their pint-size customers a thrill by making the bells ring when she gave them their "change."

She leaned back and grinned. They'd really done it. Happily Ever After was a reality.

You name your shop Happily Ever After because you do not be-lieve in them?

Sebastien's words blew a hole in her warm, fuzzy cloud. A small shiver raced down her back. She went outside and locked the slatted shutters that covered the ten-foot windows and closed the iron gate that covered the big double doors facing the corner. She could hear the raucous music and the crowds from one block over on Bourbon Street. Laughing couples and small boisterous groups drifted down the street. One of the things she loved about the Quarter was that it was like this every night of the week. But her mind was no longer on celebrating.

She stepped back inside and bolted the doors. All alone. She hoped.

I will show you that there is a true mate for every soul.

Sebastien's words continued to haunt her. Soul-mates. There was no such thing. Or at least there wasn't for her. Or Ree, or Marta. Well, maybe for Marta, but her happily ever after had been cut tragi-cally short and she wasn't willing to risk trying for an-other. Jamie couldn't blame her.

She shut off the lights, then closed the door be-tween the shop and the rear stairwell. She checked the side door to the alleyway and courtyard, then found her gaze drawn upward. Her hand lingered on the switchplate, not sure if she wanted to plunge the vestibule into darkness. "You're being silly." She flipped the switch but quickly flipped on the one for the second floor before climbing the stairs.

It was hot upstairs, and she wished she'd taken the time to open the transoms over the doorways and the windows. The heat made her think of the stifling closeness in the attic. Or maybe it had been Sebastien who had made it feel so stiflingly close. Had she really imagined the whole thing? She looked down the hall-way to the curving wrought-iron railing that led to the attic. It was either go up now and prove to herself no one was up there or toss and turn all night.

She climbed the last flight of stairs and pulled the chain for the light, belatedly thinking she should have armed herself somehow. But, then, she'd faced him once before. Of course, she'd had the sword. For a short time anyway. And there had been people downstairs then. Within screaming distance.

There was no one to hear her if she screamed now.

"Okay, I'm spooked." But she made herself enter the attic and look around. The antique chest still sat in the middle of the mess, open, with its glittery contents spilled out into the lid. But no sword. For all the junk piled in here, there wasn't much of anything big enough to hide behind, or in. Which made her shiver in a clammy, sweaty kind of way. Because if there was no place to hide, then where had Sebastien come from? Had she been so distracted that she hadn't noticed him walk up the steps?

Somehow, she doubted that. Sebastien was incredibly . . . noticeable.

Of course, the alternative was believing he was actually . . . well, exactly what he claimed to be.

"Yeah, right, sure. A pirate genie with a cupid complex. Not." She swore under her breath but took one more look before pulling the chain and retreating—quickly—to the second floor.

She headed to her bedroom. She loved this room. It was elliptical in shape and sat directly over the shop, with French doors opening onto a balcony that sat out over the corner below. It had likely been used as a salon in a former life, and she loved the unique shape and view of the Quarter it provided. Yet, rather than sit down at the small table and chair she'd put out there and absorb the sounds and smells as she'd done many nights before, she went directly to the chiffonier, opened the top drawer, and slid off her earrings and watch, dumping them in the small inlaid jewelry box she and her father had haggled for in a bazaar in Madagascar.

She unwound her dark-blond hair from the single thick braid she usually wore it in and brushed it out good and hard. When she was finished, she wound it right back up again. It was so damn hot. She debated fighting with the water pipes for a cool shower but didn't feel like losing, so she peeled out of her clothes, kicked the duvet off her bed, and flopped onto her cool linen sheets. It was going to be a long night.

She stared at the ceiling, then crawled back out of bed and put a thin nightshirt on. She hadn't hallucinated that kiss. No way.

She forced her thoughts away from Sebastien and his insane claims and began to plan her attic workshop. She drifted into a heavy sleep—where dreams of model ships, buried treasure, and hot, fiery pirate kisses took over.

≈

One pirate in particular stole into her room—and kept a watchful eye on his mistress through the long, restless night.

Chapter 3

Sebastien Valentin loved women.

Having dallied with a fair share of them over the ages, he considered himself quite the connoisseur. Of course, it was that very appetite that had gotten him into this eternal fix. Not that he was complaining. He had been in his prime when Oriane hexed him, and now he existed eternally as such, able to adore women for centuries instead of mere decades. Not such a bad destiny, all in all.

And matching souls was not such an arduous labor. He believed most heartily in love and living happily ever after with a soulmate. This was not the case for himself, mind you. He was an exception. Some men were meant to sample at life's bountiful buffet, never to be satisfied or satiated with the same meal twice. He was one of those men. But his experience with the fairer sex had afforded him an expert eye for the look of love. It had stared him down many times. He simply had never looked back.

He'd discovered on his very first mission how gratifying it was to see that initial spark between two people burst into flame. A flame, if properly fed, that would warm their hearts for the rest of their mortal lives. To know he'd been even partially responsible for such contentment . . . well, surely that was more a blessing than a curse.

Oriane, island priestess and protective mama—the latter being the more dangerous by far—had damned him eternally by forcing him to bring together and nourish in others that which he could never have himself. She'd fiercely punished him for the virginity he'd stolen from her only daughter. But Sebastien had only taken what was freely given. When Oriane had demanded to know if he loved the girl, he'd answered truthfully.

And ended up as he was now.

However, considering that his mortal exploits most likely would have landed him in hell at an early age, this was not a bad alternative.

He breathed the damp morning air in the Quarter and looked to the bright blue May sky. Ah, yes, this was certainly the better opportunity. And, ever the opportunist, Sebastien had made the most of his time when summoned forth.

He stopped and looked in a store window, examining the tailored suits that draped the mannequins in such dapper fashion. Not bad, this current style. Not bad at all. This had been his longest dormant period—just over fifty years, according to the morning papers. Edgar Santini had hidden the sword well, he supposed. More likely it had merely gotten buried in the clutter that seemed to flourish wherever Edgar lingered. Ah, Edgar. A smile crossed Sebastien's face as he pushed the door open and entered the clothier's narrow shop. As he was fitted for his new wardrobe, he recalled those weeks of reckless abandon with great pleasure. Yes, Edgar had known how to have fun. And New Orleans had never forgotten how to deliver it. Matching Edgar with the young and beautiful Lucille Bergaret had been one of his more brilliant achievements. A truer love had never blossomed.

With a smile of satisfied remembrance, Sebastien stepped from the shop an hour later and smoothed his hands over the crisp pleats of the trousers and lightweight linen shirt he now wore, cuffs rolled back in deference to the building humidity. Not bad, he thought, for off the rack. He'd requested the remainder of his custom purchases, along with the clothes he was forever wearing when summoned forth, to be delivered to one Jamie Sullivan on Rue Royale. He smiled in anticipation of seeing his new mistress once again. He doubted she'd appreciate the delivery. Or the bill. Precisely why he'd done it.

She was unlike any woman of his acquaintance. Something about her defensive posturing spoke to his mischievous side. And he was certainly never one to thwart his own impulses.

She was going to be a different sort altogether than Edgar. A shame, in a way. She was also far from his type, which was probably just as well. But she'd already provided him with a challenge. And he loved challenges. Thrived on them. He rubbed his palms together, a plan forming in his mind, then the pleasant tug of hunger in his belly took over his thoughts.

He found an antiques shop and made a terrible deal on one of the few old coins he had in his pocket when summoned, but he wasn't in the mood to haggle. He was in the mood to eat. He strolled toward the riverfront, pleased to see that the Café du Monde was still doing a brisk business. He ordered a strong cup of chicory-laced coffee and a bag of sugar-dusted beignets, then settled down with a copy of every newspaper sold on the corner. It was time to catch up on the world. He anticipated being shocked by certain advances after such a time lapse. But he also knew from experience that while the world continued its rapid growth and development, people, for the most part, stayed the same.

His packages would arrive at Happily Ever After in three or four days. He'd be as prepared as he could be by then. He'd make a swift trip to Barataria, praying everything was still where he'd last left it, then take care of financing this particular adventure. The remainder of his time would be spent doing research. True love didn't always come easily.

Ah, the thrill of the hunt. It never abated.

◆

The packages were delivered at noon on Thursday.

Jamie handed the bag containing two books to her customer. "Come back again." With a nod and a smile, the older woman departed, jingling the bell on her way out.

Turning to the deliveryman, Jamie acknowledged the three boxes and several thick garment bags he placed on her floor and shook her head. "I think you've made a mistake."

The young man checked the slip on the box. "Happily Ever After, right? You are Miss . . . Jamie Sullivan?"

Frowning, Jamie nodded. "But I didn't order any of this." She checked the suit bag, noting the name of a prominent men's shop in the Quarter. "Men's clothes?"

He nodded, then tore the bill from the box and handed it to her. "C.O.D."

Jamie laughed and folded her arms. "Oh, I don't think so."

Ree Ann came out from the back, her arms full of fresh-cut flowers. "Who are they for?"

"I have no idea. You didn't get the sudden urge to cross-dress, did you?"

Ree Ann laughed. "Not in this lifetime, sugar. Maybe they're Jack's?"

"I don't think he'd dare stick me with that bill."

"Maybe a gift for a new love in his life?" Ree teased, and Jamie lifted an eyebrow. "You're right.

He prefers to be on the receiving end of such magnanimous gestures."

Jamie turned to the deliveryman, whose eyes were glued to Ree Ann. She didn't even sigh, long since used to this particular genetic disorder. "Is there another name on the order?"

He reluctantly focused his attention back on Jamie. "Uh, let me see."

He read the name just as the bell announced another customer. Jamie echoed the name as the man himself stepped into the shop.

"Sebastien Valentin."

"*Bonjour*, Mademoiselle Sullivan." Sebastien's dark shadow filled the doorway. He made a short bow in her direction. The sunlight filtering into the shop seemed to bathe him in a golden glow, making him even more impossibly, devilishly handsome than she recalled. Which had been far more often than she cared to admit.

"I'd finally convinced myself that you were a hallucination," Jamie muttered. Apparently not softly enough.

"Oh, I assure you, I am quite real," he responded with a broad smile, earning a scowl from her.

Like the pirate he was, he'd plundered her dreams that first night and each subsequent one since. She'd awoken every morning tangled in her sheets, frustrated that he'd wormed his way into her subconscious. And worse, she'd had to start each day with the emptiness of a hunger gone unfulfilled.

She combated this sensation with a nice early-morning run along the Riverwalk coupled with one of Ree Ann's apple tarts—okay, maybe two. In the daytime, she'd been able to convince herself that she had the upper hand, since he wasn't really real or, at the very least, since he was gone for good.

Yet here he was. Larger than life. Despite herself,

she noticed his very nicely tailored street clothes and thought that they should have made him less imposing. Yet he crowded the room with that broad chest, those long legs, and all that thick shiny hair cascading to his shoulders. He almost looked more the marauder now than he had that night in full pirate regalia. He exuded sensual charm with that twinkle in his dark eyes and that smug, knowing smile curving those lips. God, those lips. Lethal lips. Lips that had touched hers.

"Did you miss me, *ma chère*?" Before she could guess at his intent, he took her hand and gallantly kissed the back of it.

She yanked it back and wiped it on her trousers. "No," she lied baldly. "I'd forgotten all about you."

"You blush, Mademoiselle Sullivan. A sure signal that the heart and head are speaking different tales."

There was a counter between them, yet Jamie felt as backed against the proverbial wall as she had been literally that first night. She pointed to the boxes and garment bags. "I believe this delivery is for you," she said, firmly taking charge of their conversation.

"Yes, I hope you don't mind. I do not as yet have a fixed address."

Oh, lovely, a homeless pirate genie. With his looks and charm, Jamie doubted he'd have any trouble finding lodging. But it wouldn't be under her roof. She took the bill from the deliveryman's still-outstretched hand and slapped it in Sebastien's. "Then you won't mind taking care of this." She walked to the other end of the counter and out from behind it. "Now, if you'll excuse me, I have some stocking to do." Another lie—she'd sold only three books so far that morning—but maybe if she hid in the back long enough, he'd take the hint and go away.

Before she could make her escape, Ree Ann opened her perfectly painted mouth and did the

Southern-hospitality thing. "Why, Jamie Lynne Sullivan, I'll tell your daddy what a poor hostess you've become." All flirtatious smile and curvy walk, Ree Ann turned the full voltage on Sebastien. Jamie had never seen a man yet who could resist her. Deciding she'd enjoy this particular dismembering, Jamie leaned back against the counter and folded her arms.

"Ree Ann Broussard, meet Sebastien Valentin. Ree Ann is my partner; she runs the café. Sebastien is a . . . magician," she managed. "Of sorts." Close enough.

Ree's eyes widened in real surprise. "A magician? Are you here performing in the Quarter? Or over at the casino?"

Sebastien shot Jamie a knowing grin, as if to say he'd play her game. For now. Then he bowed toward Ree with a gallant flourish of one hand. "A pleasure to make your acquaintance, Mademoiselle Broussard." He straightened. "Let me take care of this transaction, then perhaps we can better that acquaintance."

Ree fanned her face and goggled at Jamie as Sebastien turned to the deliveryman. "You've been hiding things from me," she whispered, waggling a ruthlessly manicured nail at Jamie. "Naughty, naughty."

Jamie sighed. Even Ree's killer instincts had gone haywire with nothing more than a gallant bow. "No secrets. He was . . . in the shop at the grand opening. I think he's a little . . ." She circled her finger next to her head. "So be careful."

Sebastien turned back to them as the deliveryman left, just in time to catch Jamie's actions. She quickly altered the motion, scratching her head instead. "I'll be in the back if you need me."

Ree laughed. "No worries, sugar. I'll be just fine."

Jamie grinned back. "Maybe I wasn't talking to

you." She stepped quickly away and studiously avoided looking at Sebastien. She had no doubts Ree Ann could easily handle their guest.

But, much as she'd like to see Ree Ann in action, she refused to risk getting caught up in any further shenanigans Sebastien might have in mind. That she'd been affected by him at all was as good a wake-up call as any. She'd sworn off impulsiveness where men were concerned. If and when she decided to indulge herself—and at thirty, she had no plans to become a nun—she'd choose someone safe, someone she could control. Someone for the occasional night out, maybe even till morning. But no head-over-heels, full-out affairs of the heart. Uh-uh. Those relationships were a thing of the past.

Sebastien's full-bodied laugh filled the front room, and Jamie's body hummed like an inboard motor.

Ree Ann ducked her head into the back. "We're going out for a little stroll. Will you cover for me?"

She managed a nod, quashing the ridiculous stab of jealousy that poked at her. Ree was more his type anyway. Jamie heard the bell clang against the door as they left. With a bit more strength than necessary, she ripped open a box of books that didn't need shelving.

❧

Sebastien guided Ree Ann along the Moonwalk toward Riverfront Park, the Mississippi rolling along lazily beside them.

"So, you never answered me," she was saying. "Are you performing locally?"

"You might say that," he responded with a small smile. He'd been doing a fair job of keeping the conversation focused on her. It hadn't been as easy as he'd initially expected. Most beautiful women he'd met were more than happy to pass away hours of time discussing themselves. There was far more to Mademoiselle Broussard than met the public eye, but she worked hard at keeping up this facade. He wondered why. The answer would be necessary information if he was to find her true match. "How did you come to open a bookstore with your friends? Royal Street real estate, especially a corner building, is still a scarce commodity, is it not?"

"Still? Have you been to the Quarter in the past?"

Sebastien silently cautioned himself. He'd never gone so long between summonses, and the time frame was a bit trickier to handle when dealing with other people. Rarely had more than a year or two passed without him being called forth. Though the sword had left New Orleans on several occasions, amazingly most of his matchmaking had occurred right here. He was glad to discover that Edgar had kept it in the Vieux Carré. With such a time lapse to deal with, at least he had the benefit of familiar territory.

"Often enough to know it takes more than a small business loan to realize a dream like your bookstore and café," he replied.

Ree suddenly stopped, the smile on her face hardening a bit. Her eyes lost their flirtatious twinkle, and all the fiery intellect that was buried behind came gleaming through. "I just figured it out," she said, the disgust in her voice self-directed. "Stupid me. Still a sucker for a pretty face, I guess."

Perplexed, but feeling rewarded for finding a chink in her heavy female armor, he said, "Figured out what?"

"You work for him, don't you? You probably tried to pump Jamie for information, and then you met the gold-digging bimbo herself and figured you'd go straight to the source."

"Bimbo?" He'd discovered the wonderful world of computers at the library. The Internet had proved to be a more magical discovery than any treasure trove he'd ever plundered. But this was a term he hadn't picked up during his crash course on the last fifty or so years.

She stepped in closer, her Southern accent deepening as the steel filled the magnolia. "Don't play dumb, it doesn't become you. Please tell Mr. Santini that he can come after my property until he draws his last breath, and I will make damn certain I hold on to it at least one breath longer."

"Edgar Santini?" Sebastien damned his loose lips as soon as the words were spoken. He'd assumed Edgar's building had changed hands several times over since his last visit. He hadn't had time to look him up, and hearing Edgar's name had surprised Sebastien. But, then, this woman was nothing if not full of surprises.

Her eyes narrowed. "You knew Edgar?"

Knew. "So, he has passed on," he murmured, feeling the pang of loss. This was the one downside to his eternal fate. Surviving, such as it was, beyond those he was summoned to match. "And his beloved Lucy?" The question just popped out.

Now Ree stepped back. "You knew about Lucy?" She covered her heart. "And yet you weren't aware of Edgar's death. Just how long ago did you know him? You can't be more than thirty."

He had to tread more carefully. He'd done some digging on Jamie, but he hadn't had enough time to gather information on her business partners. All he knew was that they were college mates. Could one of them be Edgar's descendant? She'd mentioned holding on to Edgar's property and that there was another Santini involved. A family squabble? He did a quick mental calculation. Edgar had been in his thirties back in forty-eight. Fifty-three years later . . .

"You wouldn't be his granddaughter, would you?" He didn't see any resemblance to either Edgar or Lucy, but one never knew.

"Where in the world did you get that idea?" She folded her arms, much as Jamie had back in the shop. "Why don't you tell me who you really are and exactly why you were in our shop?"

Perhaps she'd married into the family, then, he thought. A bitter ex-wife to this other Santini? He almost smiled. He didn't know Edgar's descendant, this other Mr. Santini, but he guessed the poor man had sorely mistaken his opponent if he'd ever referred to this woman as a . . . what did she call it? Bimbo.

"I was a friend of Edgar's a very long time ago, but we lost contact. I knew Lucy as well. I take it she has also passed?" The mournful note in his voice was not fabricated. As much as he had enjoyed the wilder side of New Orleans he and Edgar had avidly plundered, Sebastien had taken even greater pleasure in watching him fall helplessly in love with Lucille Bergaret. "They were so very much in love."

He was unaware he'd spoken the words until he felt Ree's hand on his forearm. "You did know them," she said softly. "You couldn't have been more than a child."

Sebastien said nothing, deciding to let her believe what she would.

Ree Ann went on. "He loved her until she died and every minute afterward until he passed as well. I don't believe I've ever witnessed a more vivid love affair, though I knew him only after she'd gone."

"After?"

She nodded. "Lucy passed away almost twenty years

ago. I met Edgar only six years ago. He was a private man. In fact, he didn't speak of her until I'd known him almost three years. We were close friends by then." She paused, as if waiting for a certain response from him.

Unaware of what that would be, Sebastien simply continued the conversation. "He never remarried, then?"

Something changed in Ree's expression, perhaps some of her wariness diminished. She shook her head. "No. He was still so in love with her. I was his . . . companion for the last several years of his life." Her voice became more forceful, prideful. "He was a wonderful man. I loved him very much."

She started to slip her hand off his arm, but Sebastien quickly covered it with his own. "I'm sure it gave him great comfort knowing he could talk of Lucy to someone who understood."

Ree laughed as she dabbed at her eyes with her other hand. The tension dissolved. "Oh, I don't claim to understand that kind of love, sugar. But it sure was reassuring to know it could exist. You know?"

"Oh, yes," he said quietly. "That I do know."

Her smile was natural and warm, minus the earlier flirtatiousness. He liked this Ree Ann Broussard much more. He would have to find a way to tell her that, show her that she was diminishing her life and wasting needless energy keeping up the ridiculous front. Or, better yet, he'd find the right man who would show her for him.

She linked her arm through his and smiled up at him. "Thank you," she said after a few quiet moments.

"You're quite welcome," he responded gallantly. "What deed has honored me with your gratitude?"

"It has been my experience that most men would form a, shall we say, less than favorable impression of my relationship with Edgar."

Now it was Sebastien's turn to laugh. "I am not most men, Mademoiselle Broussard," he said assuredly.

"No, sugar, you most certainly are not."

Chapter 4

Jamie plopped down on the stool and ran the back of her hand across her forehead. She took a long pull on a bottle of spring water, then surveyed the attic with satisfaction. She wasn't done, not by a long shot, but it was a start.

With the air working again and with strategically placed fans, it was actually bearable. All the boxes had been moved and stacked to the back brick wall. She'd started to go through them, but the first couple yielded nothing all that interesting—broken appliances, some old clothes, and a pile of newspapers. No swords or pirate genies. So she'd relegated future exploration to a rainy day and instead set out to organize the clutter as best she could.

She'd hauled up the boxes holding her tools and materials, along with several small trunks containing some of her earlier models. She looked over the table she'd fashioned into a makeshift workbench. She'd need to build some shelves and put up a Peg-Board before she could unpack everything, but she was already excited at the prospect of starting up her hobby again. She hadn't decided on the model yet, but she knew that whatever she chose would require a bunch of research first.

She swallowed another cool sip and found her gaze drawn to the antique trunk. She'd put all the Mardi

Gras stuff back inside and shoved it over to the short wall space between the two front dormers. Of course, out of sight was not out of mind.

It had been a little over a week since Sebastien had shown up to claim his clothing and take Ree out for a stroll. When Ree'd come back all dreamy-eyed over the man, Jamie had opted not to reveal the details of their initial meeting. Ree had pressed her on why she'd thought him a bit nutty, but Jamie just brushed it off as a mistake on her part. It was clear Ree wouldn't have been opposed to being paid some further attention by Monsieur Valentin. Jamie knew this shouldn't surprise her. Nor would it surprise her if Ree got her wish.

Wishes. Pirate genies. Soulmates.

She smacked the water bottle down on the workbench and jumped off the stool. She would be wise to forget she'd ever laid eyes—and lips—on the man. He was definitely not the type she needed in her life. Ree was welcome to him. He'd probably make a great boy toy for her.

Jamie, on the other hand, didn't play well with toys of that caliber. She always got emotionally attached. Then, inevitably, legally attached. So she was doing the wise thing. Which was to run screaming in the opposite direction.

She turned—and slammed face-first into a broad, well-muscled, linen-clad chest. So much for running in the opposite direction. She stumbled back, instinctively smacking him on the shoulder with her fist. "Don't ever do that to me again!"

Sebastien smiled, even as he rubbed the spot where she'd thwacked him. "What is it I've done?"

Her heart was racing, and it was only partially due to the shock of his sudden reappearance. Damn, but his chest was hard. And wide. And really—"You want it in alphabetical order, or in order of importance?"

Sebastien's lips quirked at her sarcastic tone but he politely replied, "Whichever suits you, mademoiselle."

"What suits me is that you don't just pop up like that. Especially right in my personal space."

"Personal space?"

She motioned with her hands in a small swirl around her body. "This space here. Mine. Do not enter. Clear enough, monsieur?"

His brow furrowed. "Clear enough. Are you certain you feel all right? You're a bit flushed."

"I'm fine. Fine," she lied. Knowing he sensed her panic did little to help her get a grip on it. "Why are you here? What do you want?"

He walked over to the side dormer. It was bigger than the two on the front of the building and she'd cleaned the windows earlier, so the sun gleamed through, shining on his dark hair and all-too-perfect profile. The slanting roofline only served to make him look more imposing as he prowled from one window to the next. She continued to study him as he paced. Even in a tailored shirt, pleated trousers, and Italian loafers, he looked the pirate. It was the way he moved, she decided. Silently, with intent. Like a good smuggler should. She couldn't tear her eyes away from him. Maybe if she looked at him long enough, the strength of his impact on her libido would finally diminish.

He turned suddenly and looked directly at her. Her knees did that little dip thing and her skin felt like it had come alive as a separate part of her being. She sat down on the stool. Well, so much for that experiment.

"I have some questions to ask of you," he said finally. "About your friends."

"I thought genies did their thing without any outside help."

"I'm not a genie."

She waved her hand. "Whatever. Why should I help you win our bet?"

"Because you'd like to see your friends find eternal happiness?"

She laughed, but it wasn't quite as heartfelt as it should have been. "I think my friends are doing just fine for themselves, thanks."

"But now you believe I am what I say I am?"

"I didn't say that. I'm just placating you."

"Ah." The teasing glint in his eyes reappeared.

She wasn't sure, but maybe he was less dangerous when he was serious. She didn't trust those twinkling eyes. "I'm on to you, you know. You just want the details on Ree Ann. She *is* pretty amazing."

"Mademoiselle Broussard is an intriguing puzzle, *oui*. This will make my job more complex, yet more rewarding as well. There is much to her that she chooses not to reveal." His smile deepened. "Ah, but the rewards that await the man who can plunder the buried treasures of her mind."

Those words were not what she'd expected. She'd expected drooling and panting. Serious contemplation of Ree Ann as a person was new. He *was* dangerous. Twinkle or no twinkle. She'd have to warn Ree.

"And that man would be . . . you, perhaps?"

Now it was his turn to laugh, and it was as full-bodied and sincere as hers should have been earlier. "I do not involve myself personally with those I am destined to match. At least, not in that manner."

"What manner is that?"

He looked directly at her. "Meaning I may well befriend them, but I do not bed them."

Jamie was pretty certain there was an appropriate reaction to that announcement. One that would prove she'd grown and learned as a result of her previous disastrous relationships. Crushing disappointment was probably not it. "So . . . exactly how does this whole genie thing work? I mean, what are your special powers?"

Another tactical error. His grin turned decidedly wicked in response, and she winced as her nipples went rock-hard.

"I am not a genie."

"Cupid, then. Your name is close enough to Valentine, right? That fits. Cupid with a sword instead of a bow and arrow."

He smiled at that. "I am just a man."

"A man on a mission," she said wryly.

He nodded, quite serious. "*Oui*. That is what I am."

Jamie honestly didn't know what to think about the whole thing. If he was just some nutjob on the loose, he at least seemed to be relatively harmless. Well, harmless in an I'm-not-going-to-chop-you-into-bits-and-toss-you-into-Lake-Pontchartrain-for-fish-food kind of way. In all other ways, he was totally dangerous. Yet she wasn't racing for the phone to call the cops.

And exactly what would she say if she did?

Hello, kind officer, I have a gorgeous guy in my attic, dressed in immaculate designer clothes, who claims to be some sort of cupid genie.

Who would look like the nutjob? Yep, that was the kind of publicity the new shop needed, yessirree Bob.

And there was still the little matter of the sudden appearing and disappearing act he'd pulled that first night. Speaking of which . . . "How did you get up here today? We keep the door between the residence and the store locked during business hours."

"Your cousin, Monsieur Jack Sullivan, directed me. An interesting fellow, quite personable. I'm not certain why you think he would have hired me to play a joke on you."

Jamie rolled her eyes. "You don't know Jack." She'd been given the luxury of a full day off when Jack had popped in that morning and begged to play the

part of shopkeeper. He was wonderful with the customers—young, old, male, female . . . and all the
variations in between—so she'd let him have his way
and headed up here instead.

She almost wished she'd been downstairs when
Sebastien had come into the shop. She could well
imagine Jack's likely reaction to such a specimen en-
tering his temporary domain. She had to stifle a
smile. She also had to stifle Jack. "He shouldn't have
let you up here without asking me first."

"He was about to turn me away, but Mademoiselle
Broussard, wonderful woman that she is, waved away
his concerns."

"Wonderful woman. Of course. Thanks, Ree."

"*Oui*, you are fortunate to have such friends to care
about you."

"Care about me by letting strange men into my
home?"

"I am no longer such a stranger, am I?" He paused,
then said, "You did not tell them about me. About
my . . . mission, as you called it. Why?"

"I didn't think that was really wise. In fact, this
whole thing is really—"

"Inevitable," he broke in. "You cannot undo the
summons. But I agree with your decision to leave my
true purpose unheralded. I should have mentioned
that the first night. Things tend to go much more
smoothly when only my master—or mistress, in this
case—knows who I really am."

"And just who are you?" He was very convincing,
and yet she knew it was utterly ridiculous to allow, for
even one second, that he was truly what he said he was.
Ridiculous and dangerous.

He walked over to the stool where she sat. Her every
muscle steeled itself for . . . whatever it was he
planned to do.

"You are in no danger from me, *mon amie*," he said quietly.

Had he read her thoughts too? Did he know she was remembering their kiss? The feel of his lips on hers, so confident, so certain. So damnably brief.

"That all depends on how you define danger," she answered. She scooted back and slid off the stool, slowly sidling away from him until she stood looking out the side dormer window. She needed distance. "What questions did you want to ask?"

"I want to hear more about these lessons you spoke of."

"Lessons?" She turned back to face him. Tactical error number . . . hell, she'd lost count. The sun seemed to track him, always bathing him in that golden, ethereal light. In that moment she could almost believe he was exactly what he claimed to be. If he vanished right then and there, she doubted she'd be surprised. Maybe she just wanted to believe.

Not a good sign at all.

"The lessons you spoke of that first night, when you summoned me. You and your friends have learned from them not to trust love. Who taught you this?"

Now she really wished he would disappear. He had this intent way of looking not just at her but . . . into her. But she didn't turn away. Another thought had occurred to her: Maybe this was a good way of testing herself. He was the one she could judge her recent life-altering decisions by. And Lord only knew he was a good measuring stick. She was absolutely attracted to him. He was totally and completely unsuitable for her. Perfect.

More than perfect, really. Her first husband, Chad—good-looking, three-timing, jerkface slime-ball that he was—had admitted he was a good-looking, three-timing, jerkface slimeball. Well, only after she'd caught him in bed with not one but two of the most unnaturally built race-circuit bunnies she'd ever had the displeasure to see. And she'd seen way too much. Even he, Chad of the Golden Tongue, hadn't been able to sweet-talk his way out of that one. Of course, he'd tried. There was a lot of money riding on her swallowing that Golden Tongue of his. He'd been pretty inventive too.

But never once had he claimed to be a genie.

If she dealt with her attraction to Sebastien and controlled herself, she would know for sure she'd really matured and finally gotten a grip on her biggest character flaw. And, at age thirty, it was about damn time.

Yeah, but what if you screw up and fall in love again? her annoyingly whiny inner voice demanded. Even more annoying, her inner voice was right. She should listen to it more often. Chad had been bad and Steve hadn't been much better. Which made Sebastien a risk that simply wasn't worth contemplating.

"Jamie?"

Okay. She loved the way he said her first name. And why not? So she nixed the experiment idea. It didn't mean she couldn't fantasize about the man, right? She could only imagine what he'd be like in bed, whispering naughty nothings in that French accent. She felt her skin grow even warmer.

"These lessons of love. Who taught them to you?"

She sighed. Fantasyland was much more fun than Harsh Reality Land. "What difference does it make?"

"Knowing where things went wrong before will help me with the matches I will make for your friends. And then for you."

"You seem rather confident about this."

He simply nodded, then waited with an expectant smile.

She blew out another, deeper sigh. He really was totally charming. For a delusional person. "And I should help you why?"

"That eternal-happiness thing?"

She laughed at his awkward, French-accented attempt at modern lingo. It occurred to her then just how un-modern he generally sounded. She'd chalked it up to his accent, but now her curiosity was piqued. "How long have you been here? In the U.S., I mean."

He smiled at the question. "I am from Corsica originally. I was pressed into service with our navy against the Ottomans by Napoleon when I was eleven years old. Over the next dozen years events transpired that resulted in my being taken on, not altogether willingly, by a privateer named Dominique You, who worked out of the Gulf. I ended up here when they began . . . trading out of Barataria Bay and the bayous of New Orleans." That mischievous twinkle surfaced. "As it happened, I took to their way of life rather quickly."

Their way of life was the pirate life. Jamie knew who Dominique You was. He had worked very closely with another famous "privateer"—Jean Laffite and his brother, Pierre. Which would have been in, oh, around 1810. Give or take a year or two.

"Napoleon," she repeated, still processing the rest.

"*Oui.*" His expression hardened somewhat. "I was never to see my family again. But he was not a man one said no to."

No, of course not. Especially at age eleven. Which meant, according to him, he'd been born—she did a little mental calculation—roughly two hundred ten years ago.

Right. "So. Okay." Jamie painted a bright smile on her face as she took a careful step backward. She'd purposely given up her high-speed, globe-trotting life for this run-of-the-mill, "normal" existence.

Her biggest fear was supposed to be potential boredom burnout, not being pursued by a guy claiming to have run around with his buddies Napoleon and Jean Laffite. She took another step, edging toward the doorway.

Sebastien didn't come after her, but the knowing smile on his face told her he was perfectly aware of what she was doing. "I will convince you, *ma maîtresse*. I always do."

She stopped, less than a yard from the door and safety. Well, she hoped safety. Lately, things never seemed to work out like she planned. "I'm convinced, okay? You are who you say you are." *Yeah, right.* "But, you know, maybe it's better if we just forget this whole bet thing right now. I don't want to make you angry or anything, it's just that this isn't something I'm interested in being involved with. I shouldn't have agreed to it. It's my fault, really, so don't take offense. But maybe you should go find someone else to do your matching-up-soulmate stuff with. No hard feelings. Deal?"

"Our deal has already been sealed, *mon ami*."

That kiss again. She'd known that was going to be trouble. "Really, I—"

"Our destiny was fated the moment you drew the Sword of Hearts, Jamie Sullivan. I am sorry that my appearance in your life has caused you concern. It is not my intention to bring distress." He walked closer, not stopping until he was just outside the line of personal space.

It didn't feel like he was outside the line, though. He consumed her space, even from across the room. And her air. There was a distinct tightness in her lungs. Probably that was why she couldn't move. "It's just that—"

"Shhh." He held up a finger.

She froze, half-praying he'd touch her, just one

more time, and half-praying he wouldn't. Just so
when this was over she could claim her dignity for not
having fallen at his feet in a puddle of aching hormones.

"It will be done, *ma chérie*," he said quietly. "There
is nothing either of us can do."

His words held such sincerity that it was almost impossible for her not to believe everything he'd said. It
was very clear he believed every word. But that was insane.

"I have never once failed. Can you not be satisfied
with the knowledge that you and your friends will find
lifelong happiness for putting up with my presence
for just a little while?"

"How—" The word came out sounding like a frog
croak, and she was forced to clear her throat. "How
long is a little while?" Damn her for asking that. She
should be politely yet forcefully making him understand that he could not stay and be part of her life or
that of her friends. Period.

He lifted his shoulders in that Gallic way European
men had. God, he even shrugged sexy.

"Each time I am summoned is different from the
last. I cannot say. Only that if you help me, it will go
as swiftly as is possible."

"And if I refuse?"

He did touch her then. His fingertip traced the
line of her jaw and came to rest just under her chin.
He exerted the least bit of pressure but brought her
chin up just enough so that her eyes directly met his.

"I will do my job anyway. I will not go away until
your destiny has been found. For that is my destiny.
Neither of us can escape it."

Chapter 5

Jamie sat down across from Ree with their second cups of coffee and two pieces of biscotti. Thunder rumbled across the sky, causing the windows to vibrate and the deep-brown liquid in their mugs to shake. Heavy rains lashed the tall storefront windows. They'd had one customer since they'd opened.

"This will let up soon," Ree predicted. "Morning storms always do. But it's going to be a muggy one this afternoon. Thank goodness Fred got his refrigeration units fixed."

Fred Bartelone, a retired *Picayune* reporter and Quarter favorite, owned Get the Scoop, the ice cream shop located around the corner from Happily Ever After. "Yeah. Maybe we'll get some of his overflow traffic. Preferably *after* they've finished their ice cream," Jamie added dryly.

"Shoot," Ree said, "I'm planning on *being* part of that traffic."

Jamie smiled, then started when a ripping bolt of lightning was followed by an explosive bang of thunder. "I'm not so sure this one is going to let up anytime soon."

Ree toasted her with her mug. "More time for ice cream, then."

"Yeah, well, when we've slurped up what infinitesimal bit of profit we made today on chocolate chip cookie dough, you get to be the one to tell Marta, deal?"

Ree settled back in her chair. "Just be thankful she is such a good accountant. I still can't believe she went up to the market in this mess." She shook her head. "Who would have pegged her as a thunderstorm junkie?"

"Yeah, and I thought I was the elemental one."

Ree nodded, then smiled. "I think this whole thing has been good for her. I'm glad she got away from that job in Baton Rouge working for that misogynist SOB of a boss. I don't know why she put up with that company. They used her."

"Well, she used them, too, Ree. She needed to be needed after Dan died, and they fit the bill."

"You mean they took advantage of her grief and worked her like a dog."

Jamie shrugged but nodded. "I know. I just wish we could pay her better here so she didn't have to take in freelance work on the side. She's doing Fred's books too now, you know."

"Yeah, she told me. I think she likes it, though. People needing her, being in charge of her own work. She told me just the other day that this is the most independent she's ever felt. I mean, she married Dan when we were all still at Tulane, then gave her whole life to Aaron Associates after he died. So this is exciting for her. It's the first time she's taken real control of her life. She's really enjoying this, Jamie."

Truth be told, Jamie was enjoying it too. More than she'd expected. "It's been good for all of us."

Ree laughed. "Amazing what a couple of old college chums can do when they put their minds together."

"I know. Hard to believe one lunch conversation six months ago could make us change our whole lives." When Jamie had turned thirty just before the end of the year, Ree and Marta had insisted she come and visit them for the holidays and a long-overdue celebration. She'd been somewhere else, racing around the globe, on their landmark birthdays. It had been a long time—too long—since she'd made the time to come back and visit. Marta had still been buried at Aaron Associates, and Ree had just buried her longtime companion, Edgar Santini, and come into possession of the piece of real estate in which they currently sat.

"I've said it before. We were all at a crossroads, Jamie. Each of us was ready to make a drastic change. Maybe it was destiny that brought us together at that same point in each of our lives."

Destiny. Jamie breathed a low sigh. She'd been putting off bringing up the subject of Sebastien all morning. But she had decided after his Napoleon speech that she had to tell Ree what was up. "Speaking of destiny, I need to talk to you about Sebastien."

Ree's bright blue eyes twinkled. "Oh, goody. I knew you wouldn't be able to keep all the delicious details to yourself."

"You're the one mooning all over him."

"Sugar, he's moon material if God ever created it." When Jamie rolled her eyes, Ree prodded. "Come on, come on. You have to kiss and tell. He's too good not to dish a little over."

"How soon we forget our pledge. No happily ever afters for us. We've learned that the hard way, re-member?"

Ree cast her an outraged look. "Oh, sugar, I may be perfectly happy to grow old and stay single with you two to keep me company, but none of us said a word about bein' celibate during that time. I mean, maybe when we're seventy—or eighty—we'll start taking in stray cats and be the crazy, bookselling cat ladies of the Quarter." She leaned forward. "But right now we're young and vital. We have needs. And if I know men, and you know I do, Sebastien looks like a man with a few needs of his own."

Jamie smiled wryly at that. "The funny thing is, I thought he'd sought me out yesterday to ask for more details about *your* needs."

"Me?" Ree seemed honestly surprised. "Honey, anyone with two eyes can see the man is clearly interested in you. You two have some sort of, I don't know, almost cosmic connection or something."

Jamie froze for a second. "What makes you say that?" Had Sebastien told her about his . . . mission during their walk along the river? He couldn't have. No way Ree would have held that secret.

Ree scooted forward and leaned her elbows on the table, clearly in her element. "I don't know. He just looks at you with this air of . . . connection. I can't place it. I just see it. You can't tell me you don't feel it too. It's downright palpable."

"A danger sign right there, don't you think? Given my track record?"

Ree simply shrugged. "Honey, you can't run away every time your hormones get in a twist. And I didn't say you were his soulmate or anything. I know you're over that." She paused and stared at Jamie. "What? What did I say?" She reached over and covered Jamie's hand with her own. "Oh, sugar. It's not too late, is it? You didn't do something reckless. I mean, you just met the man, you certainly haven't fallen that quickly, much less agreed—"

"No, no, of course not!" Jamie said quickly. "I mean, yes, he's immensely attractive and very charming, but—"

"You can say that again. That accent, sugar. Whew. The way his *T*'s sound like *Z*'s. And those soft *J*'s." Ree fanned her neck.

Jamie knew all about the effect of those soft *J*'s. "Yes, well, under other circumstances I'd be interested in him. I mean, any woman with a pulse would be interested in him. But we're not involved. We can't be."

"Because you thought he was interested in me? Well, rest your mind there. I know interest when I see it, and as much as I enjoyed his company on our little stroll the other day, he didn't come callin' for me."

"You don't understand. His interest in me isn't romantic. Well, not him-and-me romantic. But me-and-someone-else romantic. And I don't want someone else." She pulled her braid over her shoulder and picked at the elastic binding the ends together. "Not that it matters. He has this rule about not bedding his mistresses."

Ree gasped. "For heaven's sake. Mistress? He wants you to be his mistress?" Then she frowned. "But not in bed? What the hell kind of deal is that?"

Jamie shot her a warning look and dropped her braid. "Honestly, Ree."

Ree's eyes rounded. "Wait a minute, you said he wants to watch you with someone else? My God, who'd have thought he was kinky?"

This was definitely not going the way she'd planned. Not that Jamie had a concrete plan to begin with. She'd hoped to somehow just warn Ree about Sebastien without revealing all the weird details. But now that she'd started, she realized just how badly she needed to confide in someone. And who better than her best friend?

She looked Ree straight in the eye. "I have something to tell you, and you're not going to believe it. You're going to think I'm nuts. I think I'm nuts for even telling you. But I have to. And you have to promise to listen and not laugh at me, okay?"

Looking both concerned and confused, Ree

squeezed Jamie's hand. "Sugar, you have my undivided attention."

Jamie took a breath, then blurted it all out in one nonstop rush. "I found a sword in the attic when I went to get the extension cord that night. When I pulled it out of the scabbard, Sebastien appeared, dressed like this amazing pirate, which he is, or was, a couple hundred years ago. Only now he's a genie . . . in a cupid kind of way. I'm not sure how it happened. He said that, as his new mistress, I had to choose three souls for him to match with their soulmates, and naturally, I thought he was nuts, so just to placate him I . . . I sort of named you and Marta."

Ree's mouth, having already dropped open, opened even wider, prompting Jamie to rush on even faster. "It was a challenge kind of thing, and really, next to me, you two are the last people who want or even believe in soulmates, so it wasn't really an issue. Only it turns out he really believes this whole deal and he's bent on finding your eternal love matches. As proof, sort of, that he is who he says he is. And if he succeeds, then he plans to find mine for me. I tried to talk him out of the whole thing yesterday, only he's not budging. He says it's his destiny. Our destiny." She ran out of steam then, and in the face of Ree's open-mouthed silence, lamely added, "Help?"

Ree sat back, finally closing her mouth. "Dear Lord in heaven. What did you just say?"

Jamie rested her head on her hands, looking down at her cooling coffee. "I can't say it again. It sounded too weird saying it out loud the first time." Thunder rocked the building again, as if Mother Nature was putting in her two cents. Jamie peered up between her hands. "What am I going to do, Ree?"

"You really mean this, don't you?" When Jamie

nodded miserably, Ree went into mother-hen mode again. She took hold of both of Jamie's hands and tightened her hold on them. "What is it with our luck with men, huh? But this one beats all, doesn't he?" She laughed.

"I'm not finding the humor here," Jamie said woodenly.

"Oh, honey, he seems harmless enough. Well, in a nonserial-killer kind of way, I mean. He certainly is one sexy wacko, you have to give him that. Do you think we should call someone? Maybe call around to the local hospital psych wards and see if they're missing a man who thinks he's a genie?" She shook her head, laughing again. "It's going to take me a while to get used to that one." Then suddenly she stilled and dropped Jamie's hand. Her face went a little pale.

"What?" Jamie demanded. "What is it?"

"I just remembered something he said, something we talked about that day along the river." She looked at Jamie. "He claims he knew Edgar."

Jamie's eyes widened. "Your Edgar? When? How?"

"He said it was a long time ago. He knew all about Lucy too."

They both sat there, staring at each other as their minds worked separately. Jamie spoke first. "He told me it had been a long time since he'd been summoned. And the sword was in this building, which belonged to—"

"Edgar," Ree breathed, eyes wide. "He went on and on about how much in love Edgar and Lucy were." She covered her mouth with her hand. Lowering it, she said, "You don't really think that maybe . . . you know . . . he matched them?"

Thunder rumbled again, the rain pounding harder against the windows. The gray light cast eerie shadows across the room, setting a tone where it was possible to believe that maybe, just maybe, things like ghosts, witches—and pirate genies—existed.

But Jamie was already shaking her head firmly back and forth. "Not even for a millisecond."

Ree settled her direct gaze on Jamie. "Liar. You have thought about this." Then she smacked Jamie's hand.

"Hey!"

"And didn't tell me! What kind of friend are you?"

"One who didn't want her best friends to think she'd gone off the deep end. I mean, really, Ree Ann, what was I going to say? 'Hey, I just met this cute guy in the attic who says he's a genie. He's going to match us all up with our soulmates. Isn't that neat?' " Her fake smile vanished. "Get real."

"You're telling me now, though."

"Well, I didn't think he'd come back. And when he did, I thought I could handle it, find out what was really going on. But after yesterday I figured I had to clue you guys in, because I don't know what he's really capable of." She leaned forward. "He also claims to have worked for Napoleon and Jean Laffite."

Ree goggled. "Whoa."

"Exactly."

"Maybe we should call someone."

"I don't know. We'll have to tell Marta too. I mean, he's out there somewhere, dreaming up God knows what kind of scheme."

"You're right. But damn, what a disappointment."

Jamie actually found a thin smile. "Hey, never a dull moment in my life."

Ree laughed. "Yeah, and you've added a new category. All the good ones are either married, gay—or genies."

Just then the door blew open and banged loudly against the wall, making them both yelp and jump up at the same time.

"Sorry, it got away from me in the wind." Marta struggled through the door with her umbrella, which hadn't done too good a job of keeping her dry. Her hair was plastered to one side of her head, and her trim pants and shop shirt were damp and clinging to her thin frame. She grabbed at the door and turned back to look outside. "Oh, no, you're not following me in here too. Now get on home. You must have one somewhere. Go on, get!"

Their other worries momentarily forgotten, both Jamie and Ree went to the door. "Marta, what on earth—" Ree began, but stopped short when a small, wet, bedraggled dog came trotting into the store, stopping right in the middle of the trio and giving a good, healthy shake.

"Oh!" Ree jumped back as dirt and wet and grit splattered her crisply creased khakis.

Marta swore. "I'm sorry, guys."

Jamie laughed. "You find a friend at the market this morning, Mar?"

She snapped her umbrella shut and set her bags on the floor. "Hardly. He found me. He followed me all the way back here, no matter what I did to discourage him."

"No owner in the market?"

"I asked around, but no one knew him or remembered seeing him there before." She looked down at the now-shivering mutt and narrowed her eyes. "I guess we have to call the pound."

Jamie looked at Marta in disbelief. "We can't do that to this poor little guy." She leaned down to check for a collar, but the dog immediately shuffled closer to Marta, sitting on her feet. "It's okay, I just want to check your collar, fella."

He shivered harder and tried to climb up Marta's leg.

"Oh, for heaven's sake," Marta said with exasperation, trying to dislodge the clinging creature with her umbrella.

Ree had dashed over to the café counter and came back now, kneeling down with her hand outstretched. She had a broken piece of biscotti in her palm. "Here you go, sugar. Come on, now, that's a good boy." But the dog remained stubbornly attached to Marta's now wet and muddy pants legs.

"Since he's your buddy, why don't you check his collar for a tag?" Jamie said to Marta.

"I don't want a buddy," Marta replied through clenched teeth.

Ree laughed. "Oh, come on, now, he's sort of cute, or will be once he's cleaned up a bit." He was small, maybe twenty pounds or so, tops, with a mix of black, brown, and tan shaggy fur. Sort of a Benji-type mutt. "Maybe we could make him our mascot here."

Marta's eyes widened in horror.

Jamie frowned. "What do you have against dogs?" She'd known Marta for ten years, but she couldn't remember them ever discussing pets before. Jamie had never had one—living on boats most of her life made that kind of hard. But Marta had had a typical middle-class upbringing. "Didn't you have one growing up?"

"Yes," she said tightly. "We had a spaniel. From the time I was born until I was fourteen." She looked to Jamie, then to Ree, her fierce look crumbling. "I don't want to ever lose another living thing, okay?"

"Oh, sugar." Ree immediately went to Marta and would have hugged her except for the sudden weak snarls coming from the dog. Ree kept her distance but aimed a warm, comforting smile toward her. "Honey, I'm sorry. I should have guessed that you wouldn't want to get attached."

Marta's momentary hollow-eyed look hardened a bit. "Besides, he probably belongs to someone."

"Well, check the tag on his collar and we can start looking for the owner," Jamie said. Her heart had dipped, too, at Marta's stark expression. She was a quieter person than either Jamie or Ree, even more so these past few years. And she'd always had a huge heart, which was why Jamie had been surprised at her reaction to the dog. But Dan's death had left a gaping black hole in that big heart. She'd come a long way toward healing, but there were some boundaries Marta had made clear she never wanted to cross again. Falling in love was a big one, and that understandably extended to small, furry animals.

Marta reached down and patted the dog halfheartedly on the head. His wet tail immediately began slapping the floor, sending sprinkles of mud and grit all over them. The dog was oblivious, looking up at Marta with the adoring eyes of one looking upon his savior and queen. With a disgusted sigh, she untangled the fur around the collar and dislodged the metal tag. "It's his rabies tag. The number of the vet clinic that registered it is on here, though. Wait a minute." She freed another tag. "Just a name." She looked up at Ree and Jamie. "No number or address." At their questioning looks, she sighed again and said, "Baxter. His name is Baxter."

"Oh, how darling is that?" Ree asked, kneeling down again and calling to the dog. But he only had eyes for his self-appointed mistress. "Obviously there is someone out there who loves you, little guy."

Marta looked at them almost pleadingly. "Can you please get him off me now?"

They were saved from responding when the door opened again. And Sebastien walked in.

He had no umbrella. His shirt was soaked and clinging to his chest. His hair was dripping wet, yet he

had a broad grin on his face. Jamie gulped, easily en-
visioning him standing at the prow of a ship, and she
caught herself checking his waist for a sword. She
lifted her eyes and met his gaze.

"A glorious good morning to you all," he said, but
he kept his eyes on Jamie. "Nothing like a good storm
to get the day going."

She started to say something—what, she had no
idea—when Baxter snarled and drew his attention
away from her.

Sebastien crouched down but kept his hands carefully away from the dog. "What have we here?"

"Marta picked up a stray at the market this morning."

"I did no such thing," Marta said. "The stray
picked up me. And who might you be?"

Sebastien swept into a bow, elegant despite his
bedraggled appearance. "Sebastien Valentin, at your
service."

Marta looked at Erin, who could only shrug. "He's
harmless." She hoped.

"He looks quite thankful for the rescue," Sebastien
commented, ignoring her. "A good bath and a warm
bite would probably be welcome at this moment." He
looked to Jamie. "Can we use your facilities upstairs?"

Jamie opened her mouth to object—certainly she
was going to object—but Marta cut in.

"I am going to call the vet on his tag and track down
the owner. He or she can give him a bath." She turned
and stumbled over the dog but walked determinedly
back toward her office. Baxter dripped water after her,
resolutely following right on her heels. Marta stopped
abruptly after only a few steps. "Oh, for heaven's
sake."

Sebastien stepped forward and relieved her of her
purse and parcels, in turn handing them to a frozen-
in-place Ree before turning back to Marta. "Allow

me to assist you." He bent toward the dog, who made it clear he had no intention of being touched by anyone. Anyone other than Marta.

Sebastien grinned up at her. "You've made quite the conquest here, mademoiselle."

"It wasn't intentional."

"Be that as it may, I say we take the poor lad upstairs and at least get him clean and dry. If you'll unlatch the collar, I'm certain Jamie can locate the vet while we clean the fellow up a bit and make him presentable."

Marta looked ready to protest, then heaved a sigh of defeat. "Fine, fine." She looked down at the dog. "A bath, then you get your one phone call. That's it, you understand?"

Baxter thumped his bedraggled tail enthusiastically on the floor. Marta slipped the dog collar off and handed it to Jamie, then scooped the dog up. Her expression one of total disgust, she turned and walked to the rear door that led to the upstairs apartment, Sebastien in tow.

Jamie finally found her voice as they were unlocking the door. "I'd like to have a word with you, Mr. Valentin."

He winked over his shoulder. "Certainly, *mon amie.* As soon as we have completed our rescue mission."

Mission. Jamie's eyes narrowed in suspicion as they disappeared upstairs.

Ree clutched her arm. "Do you think that's wise? Lettin' the two of them go upstairs alone like that?"

"I didn't see you jumping in to stop them."

Ree let her go. "Well, I was still startled by his sudden appearance."

"He has a habit of doing that to people."

"I mean, I've barely had time to register everything you told me, then there he was."

"Big as life," Jamie muttered.

"Dear Lord, yes," Ree sighed.

Now it was Jamie's turn to sigh in defeat. "I don't think he means her any harm, but why don't you go on up and oversee the proceedings while I contact the vet and clean up the floor." She looked around. "It's not like we're having a traffic jam of customers today."

As if to punctuate that statement, another rattling boom of thunder shook the windows.

Ree nodded and crossed the room, then turned back. "You know, even knowing what you said and all, I have a hard time believing he's a bad guy."

"Yeah, well, that's what I said about Chad, and that was *after* I overheard him telling a pal he'd married me only to guarantee a sponsorship deal with my dad."

Ree wasn't listening. "He just seems so perfectly . . . sane to me."

"That's just your hormones wanting him to be sane," Jamie muttered, well understanding the condition.

Ree wasn't the least offended. "I saw your face when he was lookin' at you just now. You have to admit, Jamie Lynne, when he walked in that door and started in with that voice of his, we were both prepared to believe whatever he wanted us to believe." She fanned her neck. "Wacko or not, the man has presence. In spades. And diamonds, and—"

"Yeah, yeah, I get your drift. Go on upstairs and protect and defend, okay? Leave the door open and scream if you need me."

Ree winked at her and did a little shiver. "I'd sure like for him to make me scream, sugar. Okay, okay, I'm going." Laughing, she turned and left.

Jamie went to the desk and looked at the dog tag as she picked up the phone. She didn't believe Sebastien was what he claimed to be, but if she was honest, she also wasn't ready to believe the alternative. Otherwise, she'd be making a list of mental hospitals to call, and she hadn't ruled that out. Yet. She simply wanted another chance to talk to him. Just this one last time.

Chapter 6

Three days later Marta walked into the shop with Baxter trotting happily behind her. Ree Ann and Jamie smiled at the duo. Marta scowled and headed directly for her office. Just as she had the previous two mornings.

"I know we shouldn't be happy she's miserable," Ree Ann said. "But he is so cute. And you know, maybe it's not so bad for her to get a teensy bit attached to the little darlin'."

"I heard that," Marta called over her shoulder. "The 'little darlin'' ate my Etienne Aigner loafers this morning. I've had them since college." She turned and eyed them both. "The only thing I'm attached to right now is calling the pound."

Ree put her hand to her mouth. "You wouldn't."

"I talked to the vet again yesterday afternoon," Jamie said. "She said they've left messages with our shop number on the owner's answering machine. He's obviously out of town or something."

"Then he doesn't deserve the dog back," Marta retorted. "If he can't arrange better care for him than to turn him loose on the streets."

"Baxter deserves better than the pound," Ree countered.

Marta narrowed her eyes. "Then you take him."

Jamie smiled sweetly. "He doesn't love us. He loves you."

Marta opened her mouth to retort when—as if sensing his life was hanging in the balance—Baxter reached up and nuzzled her leg. She went into her office without saying another word.

Ree nodded in approval when Marta didn't close her office door until Baxter was inside with her.

"You may be right," Jamie said. "If she'd just stop fighting it, she'd realize she's already half in love with the little floor-duster."

Ree frowned. "Yeah, but Bax *does* already have an owner, even if he is unfit."

"Maybe we can convince the guy to leave him with Marta. Or we can get her another dog when Bax goes home." Jamie looked at Ree, who glared at her. "What? Just because she doesn't want to give her heart to a man doesn't mean she can't give it to an animal. I know there's a downside at the end, but that's years away."

"Precisely why she won't give her heart away. No guarantee on how much time she'll get. She refuses to risk having it broken again. Her heart is as big as the two of ours put together."

"So why did you say it was a good idea for her to fall for the mutt?"

"Because more than anything else, she needs to be needed," Ree said quietly. "And by more than just the two of us and a half dozen small-business owners." She walked back over to the coffee bar. "You're right. If we can't talk the owner into giving the dog a good home with her, maybe we'll surprise her with a puppy for her birthday." She opened a box of napkins and started to arrange them in fancy stacks. After a few moments she said, "So, have you made any decisions about you know who?"

Jamie wished they were still discussing Marta's love

life. Even if it was a canine affair. She didn't want to talk about Sebastien. Three days had gone by since she'd seen him, and she still hadn't come to any firm resolutions on how to handle his appearance in their lives. "No. I never got the chance to talk with him." A seniors group had chosen the bookstore as a refuge from the storm right after Jamie had called the vet. She'd been tied up answering questions and guiding everyone through the stacks when Sebastien had slipped out to pick up some dog food. He'd apparently met Jack en route to the shop and sent the food back with him.

"What else is there to talk about with him? Have you called any of the hospitals?"

Jamie nodded. "I figured I had to at least do that for our own protection."

Ree rubbed her hands. "Oh, I have to hear this. What in the world did you ask them?"

Jamie gave her a look. "I just asked if they'd released anyone lately, either voluntarily or involuntarily, who was delusional."

"And?"

"Nada. Zip. Zero."

Ree sat down on one of the barstools. "So what next?"

Jamie shrugged. "What else can we do? Call the cops and claim harassment? I don't really want to go that far."

Ree smiled knowingly, humming as she went back to her napkin piles.

"Don't you hum at me like that."

"Why, sugar, whatever do you mean? I'm merely enjoying my day's work."

Jamie muttered under her breath, then turned to the door when the bell announced another customer. The gentleman that came in was average height, with sandy brown hair and smiling brown eyes to match.

He was dressed in jeans, a pale blue cotton shirt, and a lightweight blazer. No tie.

Well, Jamie thought, at least he'd made some deference to the scorching heat. He had to be dying in that jacket.

"Good morning." His smile was as infectious as his understated British accent.

Jamie found herself smiling back. "Good morning, yourself. Is there anything I can do to help you?"

"As a matter of fact, I think you already have. Apparently you've taken over the dog-sitting duties my cousin abysmally failed at."

Jamie's smile fell. "You're Baxter's owner?" This guy didn't come close to the Snidely Whiplash type she'd envisioned. He seemed . . . nice.

"Yes." His own smile faded and he looked anxious. "He's okay, isn't he?"

"He's fine. More than fine," Jamie answered. No thanks to you, she added silently.

The man sighed in relief. "Good. I'm already not speaking to Jane. I'd hate to have to put a contract out on her for killing my dog."

Ree gasped. Jamie's mouth dropped open.

"I'm kidding," he reassured them, then, with a straight face, added, "I wouldn't have the first clue who to call to put out a hit on anyone." He shrugged. "Guess I'd have had to kill her myself. Such a bother."

Jamie and Ree just stared at him. Then Jamie turned to Ree and said, "What, do I have a sign on me somewhere that says, *Send me your tired, your wretched, your delusional*?"

Ree laughed. "You always have had a way with men."

"I really am terribly sorry," he offered, sounding sincerely contrite in a way only a Brit could. "I have a somewhat unconventional sense of humor. My family never understands it either. We writers tend to get weird from spending long hours alone talking to ourselves." He stepped forward and stuck out his hand. "Name is Bennett Graham. I write young-adult books. Possibly you've heard of me."

Jamie had heard of him. He wrote a popular, offbeat fantasy series for the young teen set. But that didn't automatically make him an okay guy. She very tentatively shook his hand.

He turned to Ree Ann and gave a small salute. The fact that he didn't do a double take or fall all over himself once he'd actually looked at Ree raised him a tiny notch in Jamie's estimation. A very tiny notch.

"That's why I need my dog back," he went on. "People are much more tolerant of one talking to one's dog than they are of talking to oneself."

"As long as the dog doesn't answer."

All three of them turned at the sound of Marta's voice.

Bennett laughed. "True." He stuck his hand out. "Hello, I'm Bennett Graham, long-lost owner of a small mutt about yea-high." He started to make a motion with his hand when Baxter came tearing out from behind Marta and bounded joyfully into his owner's arms. "Bax!"

The dog wriggled with joy, his tail thumping so wildly that Bennett could barely hold on to him. Laughing, he staggered back a few steps and cradled the blissful dog in his arms.

"Looks like he's glad to see you." Ree said this with a tone that almost sounded like disbelief.

Bennett looked a bit taken aback, but Marta stepped in before he could comment. "I'm just glad you two were reunited. I'll get his things."

"Things?"

Marta blushed. "Well, I . . . I was just trying to

make him feel at home. You know, until we could contact you." She hurried off to the back room, not waiting for a reply.

Bennett turned to Jamie and Ree. "Was she the one who took care of him?"

They nodded. "He was glued to her side," Jamie added. "Wouldn't let anyone else near him."

Bennett looked thoughtfully toward the spot where Marta had been standing. "That's . . . funny."

Jamie studied him. He didn't look amused. He'd sounded almost . . . melancholy. Another one of his deadpan attempts at humor? She didn't think so.

Then he turned to face them, his smile not quite as bright or natural as before. "It's just . . . well, he was very attached to someone else once. He's a pretty gregarious sort, but where Lara was concerned, he was like her private guardian."

"Exactly," Ree agreed. "He was just like that with Marta."

"Marta? Pretty name. Unusual. I like it."

"I'm glad for you," Jamie said, still not completely won over. "We like it too."

"Oh, I meant nothing by it. As a writer of fiction, I'm always interested in names. You know, for my characters. I didn't get yours, by the way."

"Jamie Sullivan, and this is my other partner, Ree Ann Broussard."

Ree smiled. "Lara is a pretty name too. Family member?" Jamie elbowed her not so subtly in the side, but Ree was undeterred.

Bennett's smile faltered the tiniest bit. "My wife. She passed away a couple of years ago."

"Oh, I'm so sorry to hear that. I shouldn't have pried. Forgive me," Ree said. But her sincerity was undermined a tad when she nudged Jamie back, nodding toward Bennett with an encouraging grin.

Jamie groaned silently. She recognized the sudden twinkle of matchmaking fervor in Ree's eyes. For the first time, she sympathized with the guy.

"He'd be perfect for Marta," Ree whispered as they watched Baxter's renewed kissing spree across Bennett's chin.

"I'd really like to compensate Marta for her time and trouble," he said, chuckling as he pushed the adoring Baxter's tongue away from his face. "My sister, Susan, usually watches him for me, but she was unavailable and this trip was sort of sudden. So I recruited Jane, who happened to be in town on holiday. She left Bax in her courtyard while shopping, and the rascal managed to escape. She's been looking all over for him."

"He followed Marta home from the French Market several days ago during a really bad storm," Ree explained. "Maybe the thunder spooked him. We put a call in to your vet, but Marta has been the one caring for him ever since. She's great with animals. She has a very big heart."

"Laying it on thick enough?" Jamie said out of the side of her mouth. Ree ignored her.

"I can't begin to thank you all enough. Thank goodness Bax has good taste in women."

Ree's expression brightened further. "Yes, well," Jamie interrupted, "we're just glad it had a happy ending."

"That is the name of our shop, after all," Ree added with her infectious laugh. "You should really save your thanks for Marta, though. She was the one that fed and bathed him and gave him a home. You two have something else in common—"

Jamie sent Ree a warning glare, knowing Marta would not be happy to have her past revealed to some stranger, but Ree shushed her with a pat to the arm.

"She lost her husband about the same time you lost your wife. So it was good for her to have Bax around, even for a few days."

Jamie sighed in relief when Marta finally bustled back to the front with a paper bag full of dog toys. She had to stifle a laugh at the size of the bag. She'd had no idea Marta had indulged the dog so much.

"Here, this is what I have in the office. I have a few more things at home, but . . ." She trailed off, suddenly looking embarrassed. Ree and Jamie laughed.

Baxter chose that moment to all but lunge from Bennett's arms into Marta's. She dropped the bag and clutched the squirming ball of fur close. Bax transferred his adoring affections to Marta's face.

Bennett laughed and extracted Baxter from her arms, putting him down on the floor. He took a leash out of the bag and connected it to his collar. "Behave, Bax. You've got better manners than that." He smiled apologetically. "He really does like you."

Marta pushed her bun back toward the top of her head, but it slid right back down again. Her glasses had lick marks all over them, so she took them off. "So I've noticed."

Jamie watched in admitted interest when Bennett gently took the glasses from her and cleaned them with his handkerchief. How many men actually carried those around anymore?

He handed the lenses back to Marta. "I . . . I want to thank you for all you've done for him."

"No need. Really."

"I want to repay your kindness. It means a lot to me to know there are one or two Samaritans left in this world. Most people would have carted him off to the pound."

Jamie coughed and Marta shot her a dark look. Her skin flushed as she turned back to Bennett. "Yes, well, I'm just glad it all worked out."

"That is your specialty, I guess." At her confused look, he added, "Happily ever after, right?"

Marta laughed, and Ree poked Jamie in the side again. They did seem to make a nice pair.

"At the very least, let me take you out to dinner."

Ree's nails dug into Jamie's arm. "See," she whispered in her ear. "Am I good or what?"

Baxter wandered away, exploring. Bennett and Marta both moved after him, stopping to talk near Marta's office, where Bennett retrieved the end of Baxter's leash.

"He'll talk her into going."

Jamie extracted her arm from Ree's grip. "She's not going to let him sweet-talk her—" Jamie was cut short when Marta laughed.

"That's more like it," Ree said. "We don't hear that often enough. Laughter is a perfect way past her defenses. My money's on Bennett."

Bennett came away from the office with a triumphant, boyish grin. "See you at closing time, then," he called over his shoulder. "Ladies." He nodded to them on his way out the door, Baxter right on his heels.

Ree shot a smug look at Jamie. "Not bad, sugar. Not bad. That's what I call trading up."

Marta scowled. "It was the only way to make him stop."

Jamie couldn't hide her smile. "Stop him from what? Making you laugh? What a cad he is."

Marta glared at them both. "Be serious. He's a nice guy with a somewhat warped sense of humor. He caught me off guard."

Both Ree and Jamie planted their hands on their hips and looked back at her.

She blushed. "Okay, okay, so he's a nice guy and we're having dinner. Sue me. It's the least he owes me for putting up with that dog of his."

Ree grinned. "And that Hugh Grant accent isn't too hard to take either. Just think, if you two get close, you don't have to give up Baxter. Not completely anyway."

"Don't go making plans, Ree," Marta warned. "It's just dinner." She headed back into her office.

"This is going to be good," Ree said. She pointed to Marta's retreating back. "Watch."

Jamie saw the little dip in Marta's shoulders when she paused at the door to her office, then remembered Baxter wasn't there to follow her into the room.

"See? She misses his dog. I'm telling you, this is a good thing, Jamie Lynne."

"He'd better be nice to her" was all Jamie said. "Or he'll answer to me."

Jack chose that moment to come bustling into the shop. "Good morning, all you lovely people. I've arrived. Life as you know it may now continue."

Ree laughed and Jamie just shook her head. "What's up with you?"

He popped up onto one of the barstools and helped himself to some biscotti. "Nothing much. I turned in with the moon last night and I'm up with the sun today. I thought I'd see if you needed any of my expert help." He feigned a dramatic swoon as he swallowed the first bite. "I'm in love." He blew a kiss to Ree. "Make me a cup of espresso to go with and I'm yours forever."

Ree ducked out of Jamie's grasp and went back to the coffee counter. "You missed all the excitement today."

Jamie sighed in resignation and went to the back room to get the magazine cart, leaving the two of them to their laughter and gossip. She arranged the stack, taking out the old issues and stripping the covers. Her attention kept wandering back to the closed office door.

Bennett, warped British sense of humor and all, seemed like a nice enough guy. His dog worshiped him. Always a good recommendation. And she knew he was gainfully employed. She just didn't want to see Marta hurt. Not that she didn't wish her friend to have some fun and frolic in her life, but of the three of them, Marta was the most fragile and least social. She'd always been like that.

Ree handled men like she was born to the task, which, considering her background, she basically was. Jamie, despite her reprehensible choices in husbands, had been around the world enough to hold her own in basic social situations. Marta, however, was the most sheltered of the three. She'd never dated much before she met Dan, and Jamie didn't think she'd dated much, if at all, since his death. Jack dragging her out on rare occasions didn't count.

Jamie hoped tonight's date was a positive step for her friend. Marta deserved some fun, probably more so than any of them.

She was so lost in her thoughts, she didn't hear the bell ring. She didn't even know that there was anyone else in the shop, until a bright orange gerbera daisy was brushed across her cheek.

She jumped back, only to find Sebastien grinning at her from across the magazine cart, a fistful of colorful flowers in his hand. He presented the daisy to her with a bow. "For you, *mademoiselle*."

Way too gallant for her peace of mind. He winked at her, making her pulse spike. She snatched the daisy. "Thank you. To what do I owe this . . . honor?"

He feigned hurt, but his twinkling eyes ruined the pretense. "You owe me nothing, *mon amie*. I come bearing flowers for Mademoiselle Marta. I understand she lost her four-legged beau today, and I had hoped to cheer her up."

Jamie's eyes narrowed suspiciously. "How did you know Baxter was gone?"

"Simple. I saw him and his owner—friendly chap—over on St. Phillip."

"You talked to Bennett?"

"*Oui*. Why do you frown? There is nothing wrong with passing some time in conversation with a friend."

"So now he's a friend?"

"I'd like to consider him so. Did you not like him?" He looked honestly concerned.

Jamie's suspicions grew. "Exactly what scheme are you cooking up? And where have you been these past few days?"

He brightened, his grin instantly turning sexy and knowing. "Ah, so you missed me, my mistress?"

"I didn't miss you. And stop calling me that. I was simply . . . concerned." She narrowed her eyes. "Not for you. For the citizens of the Quarter." She grew serious. "Where exactly do you go? I mean, what do you do with your days? Do you have a regular job?"

"You well know what my occupation is." He sighed deeply. "I see I have not yet convinced you." He recovered quickly. "But I will. Soon. You shall see." He abruptly turned and walked out of the storeroom.

Jamie followed him out front and watched him walk to the office and knock. When Marta opened it, he bowed deeply before presenting her with his bright bouquet. She ushered him inside. Seconds later she heard Marta's laughter once again. She sighed and shook her head. Maybe she was being too paranoid about everything. Bennett was most likely perfectly harmless, just a nice guy with a goofy dog. And Sebastien . . .

Well, she couldn't bring herself to say the same about him. She sniffed the daisy and stroked the petals along her jaw, much as he had moments ago.

What was she going to do about Sebastien Valentin? And why did he assume she'd be convinced now? Did he honestly think she thought he'd been responsible for fixing up Marta and Bennett?

She wheeled the cart to the front counter and laid the stacks of covers on it. Sebastien hadn't even met Bennett until after their date had been made. For Sebastien to have had any role in this, he had to be instrumental in getting the man to the shop in the first place. But Bennett had shown up only because of the dog. She paused. . . . No. No way. It was ridiculous to think Sebastien had somehow been responsible for hooking Marta and Baxter up. Besides, no one could have foreseen the conclusion to that mixup. And he couldn't possibly have known the dog would take to Marta the way he had or that she'd keep him.

She walked behind the counter and started stuffing the stacks of covers into marked manila envelopes. But he *had* shown up just after Marta arrived in the shop with the dog. And he had helped in getting her to take the dog in and make him feel at home.

Sebastien came out of the back room and made a short bow to Jamie before sailing out the front door. A moment later he tapped on the window.

"Believe in me, Jamie," he said through the glass.

Jamie stood staring out the window after him, still lost in thought long after he disappeared from view.

Chapter 7

Sebastien smiled at the waitress as she seated him on the restaurant balcony overlooking Royal Street. He could just see the bookshop two blocks down. Suzanne, his bountiful brunette server, had made it clear she was interested in serving him more than lunch. Sebastien watched her hips sway as she retreated, and he considered following up on the silent invitation.

He'd been "back" for almost a month now and hadn't found time to indulge himself in life's more sensual pleasures. Except food. The spicy scents of jambalaya and gumbo wafted through the warm noon air. Ah, but there were some scents even more delectable than those. Like the scent of an aroused woman. He shook his linen napkin over his lap and smiled to himself. Yes, it was time to enjoy the more positive elements of his eternal incarceration.

Jack bustled in moments later and took a seat across from Sebastien. "Sorry to be late. It's just been murder this morning."

"Not to worry. I've been enjoying the view."

Suzanne chose that moment to bring him his drink and a menu for Jack. Sebastien smiled at her.

Suzanne smiled in return, openly interested. "What will you have?" she asked Jack flirtatiously.

"Stick with the tall one, sweetheart. He and I order off different menus, if you catch my meaning."

Unoffended, Suzanne laughed and flipped her pad open. "Sorry to hear that. What can I get for you gentlemen?"

"The women in New Orleans must love you," Jack said after Suzanne had gone. "They're not used to men as good-looking as you who also happen to be hetero."

In the short time since he'd been summoned, Sebastien had educated himself on the changes that had taken place since his last visit. He'd learned that a rather substantial homosexual community now resided in the Quarter. He'd learned aboard ship how to fend off unwanted advances. The gentlemen here were far more polite about the whole thing. And, more to the point, it meant more women for him.

A happy set of circumstances for all, as far as he was concerned.

He nodded to Jack. "Yes, well, let's just say I hope to prove your assumption correct."

"You will. It's not called the Big Easy for nothing."

They were both still laughing when their food arrived. Sebastien's bowl of gumbo was half gone before he finally broached the reason that he'd invited Jack to have lunch with him. "It seems as if Mademoiselle Marta is having a fine time with her new beaux."

"Beaux? Plural? She's only seeing Bennett, as far as I know."

"Let's not forget Monsieur Baxter. Never underestimate the allure of the animal kingdom."

"She does seem happier than I've seen her in years." Jack sobered a bit. "So many of my friends have gone through the agony of watching their loved ones pass on. . . . It's brutal. Extending an invitation of the heart after something like that is very difficult. Some never get over it." He sighed. "I suppose once you've found your soulmate, there is no sense in looking again."

"You mentioned last time we spoke that Marta and her late husband were such a pair."

"Oh, definitely. Such a tragedy."

"*Oui*. But I do not believe that she is destined to be alone. Or that anyone who has known great love and lost it should be relegated to a life of pain and loneliness."

Jack tilted his head in consideration. "Go on."

"A soul who has known such sadness is irrevocably altered. That altered soul is destined to have another soulmate, one who would have, at any other time, not been the perfect match. Do you understand my meaning?"

Jack nodded thoughtfully, then toasted him with his glass of wine. "You, my new friend, are quite the philosopher of life and love."

Sebastien smiled and shook his head. "I am merely one who pays close attention to the travails of the human heart and spirit." He sipped his wine. "I believe Monsieur Graham might be just that new soul for your friend."

"I think you may be right." Jack lifted his glass again. "To old souls finding new mates."

Sebastien grinned and tapped his glass. "I will have to remember that one. *Santé.*"

They were lingering over coffee when Sebastien finally worked his way to the matter at hand. "I understand from Jamie that each of them has somehow suffered at the hands of love." He shook his head. "A shame, really. They are such young, vital women."

Jack waved a hand. "Don't I know. I've tried to fix them up, but, hey, even *I'm* not a miracle worker."

"I find them each intriguing. Certainly I am not the first to be drawn by their unique charms."

"*Their* charms aren't usually the problem, if you know what I mean."

Sebastien smiled and nodded. "I also marvel that they are so different and yet such close friends."

Jack sat back and crossed his legs. "They've been friends since college. Each of them was an outcast, in her own way. I think that's what drew them to one another. That and their love of reading. They met when Jamie started a book club on campus."

"And now they run a store together. Destiny, perhaps?"

"It's actually more surprising that they managed to hold on to their friendship this long, all things considered."

"Things?"

"Well, you know Marta's story. Thank God, Ree and Jamie finally talked her into joining the store venture. Ree even found her a place over on Esplanade and got a few people in the Quarter who needed a part-time bookkeeper to sign her on."

"A good friend, Mademoiselle Broussard."

"Amazing is what she is. And what a life she's led."

"I can imagine her leading a life as vibrantly rich as the color of her incredibly bountiful hair."

Jack eyed him with a knowing smile. "Ah, so you're just feeding my addiction to fine cuisine as a means to get closer to Miss Ree." He reached over and patted Sebastien's hand. "Well, you wouldn't be the first to try, old chap."

Sebastien decided it was best to let Jack think what he would. If Ree Ann hadn't been selected as one of his soul-matching missions, he might have very well pursued her. She was absolutely his type. Lush, sensual, and provocatively intelligent. He would merely concede defeat after matching her, and Jack would be none the wiser.

Her coworker, on the other hand, would take a bit more creativity on his part. She was not at all what normally drew him. Strong and sleek with no curves for a man to sink into, not to mention her quick wit and defensive air. All of which did little to explain why she was constantly on his mind. Naturally she would be, given that she was his mistress, but still . . . Maybe it was that glimmer of vulnerability he'd seen just after he kissed her that first night. And again in the bookstore the other day, after Graham had made his first appearance.

He forced his attention back to the conversation. "You were saying, about Ree's background?" Sebastien grinned, making sure it was just a bit wolfish. "You have me very intrigued."

Jack settled into his chair, and into his story. "Not many know this, and I suppose she'd be unhappy with me for sharing it with you. I have no idea why I am, actually."

Sebastien kept his gaze—and his smile—squarely on Jack. Perhaps his charms with women would stand him in good stead here as well. No harm in trying, anyway.

Jack's cheeks warmed a bit, then he went on. "Her mother was an . . . exotic dancer. On Bourbon, back in its heyday in the fifties. La Bamba was her stage name."

It took all of Sebastien's acting abilities to maintain an innocently interested demeanor. La Bamba? Mademoiselle Broussard's *maman*? He fondly remembered his nights spent carousing Bourbon Street with Edgar those many years ago. Some of their best nights had been spent observing and enjoying La Bamba's considerable . . . talents. He silently thanked God he'd never pursued the woman, though he'd certainly considered it. Edgar had also done his level best to catch the dancer's eye. However, once Sebastien had paraded the virginal Lucy in front of Edgar's once-roving eye, La Bamba had ceased to exist for him.

Another thought struck him. Despite the advanced difference in their ages, Ree Ann and Edgar had become an item of sorts, or so it appeared. Could Edgar have known? Had he purposely sought her out? Or was it coincidence?

"In the fifties?" Sebastien noted. "And yet, Mademoiselle Broussard is so young."

"Her mama made not only a name but a modest fortune back in those days. It was rumored that a friend of hers—a . . . client, perhaps—invested her income wisely, and she retired when she was in her thirties. She became quite a character—something the Quarter has a particular fondness for—and was well known for her Friday night salons."

"Salon?"

"Literary salons. Believe it or not. Somewhat more bawdy than highbrow, but all of society drooled over being on the invite list."

"So this is where Ree got her love of the written word?"

"Absolutely. Her mother had been hostessing most of New Orleans society for almost a decade when Miss Ree made her grand appearance. La Bamba was well into her forties by then. No one ever knew—including Ree, as far as I know—who her father was. Her mother had quite a reputation from the sixties through the early eighties for taking young lovers then casting them aside when she grew tired or bored." Jack lowered his voice. "And she had a very short attention span."

Sebastien nodded and considered everything he'd learned. It went a long way toward explaining Ree's personality. Flamboyant and willfully sexual, yet he'd bet a good portion of his gold cache that in reality she'd never let a man close enough to discover the real woman.

"So her daughter will never know true love for all her prejudices."

Jack laughed. "Exactly what I've told her for years. But I always thought that when the right man came along, she'd fall and fall hard." He looked at Sebastien speculatively.

Sebastien ignored the knowing assessment. "So, tell me about Edgar Santini. There was an interesting pair."

"You know about Edgar?" Wariness edged back into Jack's voice.

Not certain what Ree might have said after their first little stroll, Sebastien had to play it aboveboard. "Actually, I knew Edgar quite some time ago, but we . . . lost contact. Ree mistakenly assumed I knew the younger Santini—a son or grandson, I presume— and spoke of Edgar as well."

Jack snorted in disgust. "Angelo. Or Angel, as he's called. Though he's anything but. Grandson and major prick, if you'll pardon me for saying."

Intrigued, Sebastien pressed for more. "She seemed to have quite a different opinion of him than she did of his grandfather."

"Angel is miffed that Granddaddy didn't leave him every last penny. He was none too happy to discover Edgar had left some prime real estate to our Miss Ree."

"I take it Edgar died a wealthy man?"

"It was a rocky ride over the years, but, yes, he was quite well off when he passed on. Just how young were you when you knew him?"

"Very," Sebastien fibbed. He had no other choice. "He was in banking then."

Jack was too entertained by his own storytelling to stop now. "Yes, well, he did very well, which was an obvious progression after he married Lucy, since her family were all bankers. But he ditched it all after she died, went rather bohemian, or so his family thought. He shocked everyone when he opened up a restaurant. Something that apparently had been a dream of his before he married Lucy."

Sebastien had been aware of this but knew Edgar was too young and wild to make a serious go of such an enterprise. Lucy had been devoted to Edgar and was a stabilizing force in his life. And he had brought his touch of wildness into hers. One of Sebastien's finest matches.

"How did he do in business?"

"Not so well. He was a great lover of food and people, but despite the banking background, he was a lousy businessman. Too kindhearted, apparently. Forever giving jobs to unreliable help; anyone with a sob story could talk him out of almost anything."

"He must not have been in the loan department before."

Jack laughed. "No. In fact, I don't think he ever actually worked in the bank. More an instant board member or some such. Lucy had her father wrapped around her finger, you know."

Sebastien did know. Another reason he'd introduced to her to the strong-willed young Edgar. He'd be a match for her father and for her own headstrong determination.

"Well, it took him years to go through all of his assets," Jack went on, "but he was determined and refused to abandon a sinking ship. When he met Ree, she was barely out of graduate school and, thanks to a business degree and her mother, had a keen way with money." He smiled. "I think Edgar was a safe place for her. A powerful yet nonthreatening man, whom she could shower with affection while knowing without a doubt she would be admired for who she really was. And not what she appeared to be—a bombshell like her notorious mother. It was a love match of the purest form. One of respect and dual admiration. Totally nonsexual."

"And her mother? What did she think of all this?"

"She passed away just after Ree turned nineteen. Ree was in college then, and her mother's long illness had used up most of their personal assets as well. But I think she would have approved of Edgar. Their relationship was totally misunderstood by almost everyone."

"By everyone except you. And Marta and Jamie?"

"Exactly. And Ree refused to enlighten the narrowminded idiots of the world. Like her mother, she let them believe what they would."

"So you're saying that Ree turned Edgar's fortunes around? She could have known him for only a short time."

"No one knew how badly off Edgar was. Certainly not his only son or his only grandchild. Which is partly why he was so deep in debt. Keeping up appearances at all costs."

"He couldn't have been too concerned with that if he took up with someone as young as Ree."

"His son died several years before he met Ree. Angel's mother had passed on when he was a boy. So Angel was all that was left by then. Besides, where Ree was concerned, Edgar never had a chance. She doted on him and gave him a new sense of purpose. She aggressively invested his money in high-risk funds and restored a good part of his fortune in a short period of time. In return, he fed her interest—pardon the pun—in the restaurant business."

Sebastien lifted a surprised brow.

Jack shrugged. "The woman loves to cook, and let me tell you, she's an angel of God in the kitchen. But her mother refused to let her dwell on something so domestic, even as a business. She had far more lofty goals in mind for her only daughter. When Edgar died, Ree hit a point where she had to ask herself what she really wanted for herself and not for someone else."

"And so the bookstore and café became a reality." Sebastien finished the last of his coffee. "A happy ending."

Jack smiled, but somewhat sadly. "She thinks so."

"Tell me more about this Angel. She is very angry with him still. Surely he knows he cannot change his grandfather's will."

"He knows, but it didn't stop him from trying. He tied Ree up in court for months, to the tune of thousands and thousands of dollars. He tried to prove she seduced Edgar into changing his will when he was no longer of sound mind or body."

"The man must be blind, then."

"I do like you, my friend." Jack's smile faded. "Naturally Ree did nothing to disabuse the ass from his idiotic assumptions. He has no idea that if it weren't for Ree, he'd have ended up with nothing. Including his precious little four-star restaurant. She made sure she kept her inheritance without letting him find out that she was responsible for keeping his safe. The man could use a major reality check." He waved his hand dramatically. "But logic flees when those two get anywhere near each other. It's like combustible fuel. I swear you can see the sparks fly."

Sebastien sat forward. "Sparks?"

Jack misunderstood his sudden attention. He waved his hand. "Oh, please. You have nothing to worry about from that direction. Ree would rather have the man shot than let him within ten feet of her.

And I don't think after the court's last ruling that Angel will give her that opportunity. The two have retreated to opposing corners, and I doubt you could pay either one to have anything to do with the other." He fanned his face. "Thank God."

Sebastien smiled with satisfaction. And allowed Jack to believe what he would. In fact, he was so deep into his plans, he missed the waitress's pout when he left the restaurant without so much as a glance in her direction.

Chapter 8

his sheet isn't attached to the clew like that. We used a hook and thimble. And we used iron parrels on the halyard."

Jamie let out a small shriek and almost fell off her stool. Stumbling to an upright position, she turned to find Sebastien bending over her workbench, studying the sketches for her newest project; a nineteenth-century pirate ship.

She tried to tell herself that her heart was beating wildly only because he'd startled her. But the fact that her mouth was watering over the way his linen shirt pulled snugly across his broad back told the real story. "Nice of you to drop in." She hadn't seen him in a few weeks. Only now did she realize how much she'd missed him.

He grunted in response, his attention fixed on the plans, photos, and stacks of other resource material cluttering her work space. She folded her arms across her chest. "And to what do I owe the pleasure of another heart attack?"

He finally looked up, and she felt her heart squeeze just the teeniest bit at the boyish way his hair had fallen across his forehead and the somewhat lost look on his face. "What did you say?"

"What is it with boys and boats, huh?" she asked, then laughed when he looked confused.

He straightened then. "What are these drawings for, mademoiselle?"

"It's a hobby of mine. Building model ships." She shrugged. "Boats aren't just for boys, I guess."

"I see." That teasing light came back into his eyes, making her throat suddenly dry. "And your new project just happens to be a privateer schooner. Interesting."

She should have left well enough alone. The man was a walking Y chromosome. And her X's were all clamoring to get closer.

She cleared her throat. "Yes, well." She turned her attention to the plans. "You're wrong about the halyard. I do very careful research, and every source I checked specifies that it looks exactly like that."

"Then you have faulty resources. I sailed a ship just like her." He grinned wickedly. "And I've boarded one or two others in my time." He pushed several papers around and slid the plan showing the rigging profile on top. "Yours is the original design, but privateers have, shall we say, specific needs. We were quite innovative in rebuilding our ships to suit our own purposes." He pointed to a scale drawing at the bottom of the plan. "This actually goes here. Connects there. That way the captain can hoist the sails far more swiftly when he has to get underway in haste." He winked. "Something that came in particularly handy in my former occupation."

Right. As a pirate. With Laffite. She hadn't forgotten that part, really. She'd just . . . tucked it away for a while. Now it was untucked again, and she still didn't know exactly what to think. He sounded absolutely convincing. "I . . . I'll take it under advisement and do a bit more research." She took the plan from his hands, stifling a small shiver when her fingertips brushed his warm skin. "Thanks."

He turned back to the scatter of plans on her workbench and flipped through them. "There are some other design flaws here."

Bristling, she looked past his shoulder at the plans she'd so painstakingly labored over. "These are commercial plans, but after fairly exhaustive research, I fine-tune and alter them to make as exact a replica as I can. I take a great deal of pride in my level of accuracy. I know my ships."

He turned and pinned her with his dark, penetrating gaze. "So, *mon amie*, do I."

Jamie suddenly decided that maybe this was one argument she didn't really want to have. She might have daydreamed on occasion about Sebastien's piratical claims. Okay, so there had been one or two hot and sweaty night dreams in there as well. But maybe it was best to walk away from all that. Right now.

He took a step closer. She stepped back. He didn't move closer, but the oxygen was rapidly evaporating anyway. The man consumed space. This was no time to speculate about who he might really be. When he looked at her like that, she had no trouble whatsoever seeing him climbing the rigging of a pirate ship, muscles bulging, cutlass clenched firmly between two sets of white teeth.

He leaned back against the workbench and folded his arms. "You can hardly be held accountable for faulty historic documentation."

She narrowed her eyes but managed to refrain from a retort.

"Do you have any finished models?"

"They're still packed. I haven't decided where to display them downstairs. I haven't had much time to get my apartment in order yet."

"Yet you have time to work on a hobby." He bent over the ship again. "Interesting."

She made a face at his back, then quickly masked it when he whirled around to face her.

"I'd like to see them sometime." He wasn't playing with her now. His interest seemed very sincere.

She didn't know how she felt about that. Part of her felt suddenly shy at the idea, even though she was very proud of her level of craftsmanship. Another part of her wanted to sit down and go over every model, questioning him endlessly on what he knew. Whether it was from personal experience or not, she didn't dare to consider.

"You must spend a great deal of time planning a project as detailed as this," he said. "How long does it take, start to finish?"

"Depends on the model, my access to source material, and how much time I have to devote to it. Usually a year or two. I moved around a lot, so it was kind of tricky. I might be able to get this one done a bit more quickly now that I've settled in one place."

"And how do you decide which ship to build next?"

She tried not to flush, honestly. The knowing twinkle in his eyes proved too much. "I'm in New Orleans, so I decided to take advantage of the information available to me." When he continued to study her, she hurried on. "It just so happens that this is one place where I can gather a great deal of authentic detailing on this particular kind of ship." She shrugged again, suddenly self-conscious.

"An unusual diversion for a woman." He stepped closer. "Could it be you have private dreams of sailing the high seas? Romantic visions of life as a pirate queen?"

Jamie swallowed hard, remembering how they'd first met each other. "I doubt it was all that romantic," she managed.

"You would be correct." He ran his fingertip along the rigging lines of one of her plans. His expression took on a faraway look, his eyes reflecting a fond sadness. "It was adventure and danger and every dream a

boy could have of treasures plundered.". He turned
suddenly and looked at her, his dark eyes now reflecting far more than an adolescent high-seas holiday.
"But romantic? *Non*." He dropped his hand. "There
are days when I miss the taste of salt in the air and the
feeling of being rocked to sleep by the sea. I miss the
camaraderie of having crewmates." The barest hint of
the twinkle resurfaced in his eyes. "And coming into
port had its own special pleasures." The light dimmed
as he turned away from her. "But the rest? . . ." He
shook his head. "I do not miss the rest."

"How long did you sail?" The question just popped
out. So what if he was a phony? At that moment, for
just that moment, maybe she was a believer.

"As I told you, I was pressed into service for my
country as a young boy. Our ship was raided, and I
was given to the crew who boarded her. Several times
over the next year I moved from crew to crew. Never
at my own request."

Jamie could not swallow. Even if she could have
formed the words, she could not have asked him to
speak of what she saw in his eyes.

"Then Dominique took the ship I was on and I became part of his crew. We sailed to the Caribbean,
and it was there I found my home. I found the closest
thing I ever had to a family. I stayed with them
until—" He shrugged and once again his smile returned, but this time it didn't ignite that twinkle in
his eye. "Until fate guided me in this new direction."

Jamie knew this was insanity, but it was almost impossible to look in his face, hear the experience of life
color his voice, and not fully trust that this man spoke
of things he'd truly known. "What happened?" Her
voice was barely above a whisper. "How did you end
up . . . you know."

"I fell prey to the machinations of a young island
woman."

Jamie couldn't help but smile at that. "Yeah, right. I'm believing you as the innocent victim."

The twinkle returned, and Jamie felt herself relax her guard altogether. Foolish of her, most likely, but she was enjoying herself too much to care.

"I was never innocent, *ma chérie*."

Foolish, most definitely. "What happened? You seduced an innocent woman?"

"Hardly innocent, despite her surprising virginal state. Her *maman* was an island priestess of sorts. She was as believing in my innocence as you."

"Ticking off a priestess. Tsk tsk. Not good juju."

Sebastien laughed at that. "*Non.* Not good juju, as you say, at all. She thought me callous and insensitive to the ways of the heart. As punishment, she cast me into the Sword of Hearts and this eternal destiny of matching souls. I am forever a slave to the hearts of others."

"Doomed to find the love for others that you believed you could never have for yourself?"

She'd meant it as a joke, but the sudden stillness of his expression told her that she had hit a vulnerable spot. Surprised and strangely touched by the discovery, she wanted to apologize, but he spoke first.

"Oh, I believe in love, mademoiselle. Most heartily. I find great pleasure in locating that rare seed and nurturing that most delicate of blooms."

"But only in others."

He nodded. "*Oui.* True love is for others, not me. Not in my mortal life. And certainly not now."

He was smiling, but there was a dead certainty to his tone that Jamie found unsettling. And sad. She worked up a smile. "But you have certainly sampled a bouquet or two."

His grin surfaced, most devilishly. "A bloom or two, perhaps."

I bet, she thought, unfairly jealous. She wanted to

be one of his sampled blooms. It was foolish in the extreme, but at least she'd faced the truth. Now she just had to make sure she kept all her petals to herself. Not that he'd made an attempt at unfurling any of them. She swallowed a sigh of frustration.

"So, you believe now that I am what I proclaim to be?"

"I said no such thing. I was merely interested in hearing what *you* think you are."

"And my matching of Mademoiselle Marta and her beau, Monsieur Graham, has not swayed you in the least?"

She laughed nervously. Hadn't she thought that very thing? "You're claiming responsibility for Marta and Bennett? And how, pray tell, were you involved?"

"You don't believe I guided that match?"

"His dog followed her home. It was serendipity, nothing more." *Wasn't it?*

He smiled knowingly. "Ah, so it would appear. I do not toss souls together at whim with no forethought. It takes great planning and a sixth sense that, if I may be so bold, I have well developed over the years. I am not obvious in my work. For love should be serendipitous." He winked. "Or at least appear to be."

"I still don't believe you."

He didn't appear insulted. Instead, he switched tactics. "She has been a single widow for how long?"

"Three years."

"And in that time she has dated how many single men?"

Jamie glowered. "None. But that isn't the point."

"I claim I will find her soulmate for you, and in less than one week I do so. This is not proof?"

"Coincidence. And they're not exactly married yet."

"They will be." At her stubborn expression, he sighed but continued undaunted. He waved his hand in that Gallic manner of his. "Fine, fine. Believe what you wish. Perhaps this time I will forewarn you, as proof. I have already put into motion the events that will lead Mademoiselle Broussard to her intended."

Jamie raised her eyebrows. "And who is the lucky bachelor?" She had to warn Ree.

Sebastien tilted his head and studied her. "I'm none too certain I should share that detail. You would work to subvert my plans just to thwart me."

"If they are truly meant to be together, then nothing I do could change that, right?"

He said nothing.

"Okay. How about this: You tell me who you have in mind, and as long as I don't see Ree in any danger or get any weird vibes about the guy, I'll stand back and let life happen. Otherwise, if someone happens to come into her life and you just take credit, how will I know it's really you?"

"You will not interfere?"

"You're saying I could? What kind of cupid are you?"

"I'm not a cupid."

"That's right. You're a man on a mission of love."

Sebastien laughed. "A man on a mission of the heart. And to answer your query, you cannot stop them from discovering they are meant for each other, but you could delay their eternal happiness with the interference."

Jamie thought about it, then nodded. "As I said, I won't interfere unless something happens to make me suspicious about the whole thing."

"Then promise me you will bring your fears to me first. Allow me to allay them before you involve yourself."

"Deal." Jamie smiled and rubbed her hands. "This ought to be good. You've basically taken on matching the unmatchable."

"You do not wish for her to find happiness?"

"Oh, it's not that," Jamie said. "I'd love for Ree to find the right man. I just don't think she'd ever allow herself to see him, even if he walked right up and presented himself. She doesn't have the same attitude toward men that most women do."

"Women like you? How do you think of men?"

Jamie felt the heat creep into her cheeks again. "Let's just say we both relish our single state, but for different reasons, okay?"

Sebastien nodded readily enough, but that penetrating look of his did little to settle her jangled nerves.

"So who's the lucky guy?"

Sebastien smiled. "Monsieur Angel Santini."

Jamie's mouth dropped open and she howled with laughter. It took her a minute to recover. "You have to be joking. They hate each other."

"Passion manifests itself in mysterious ways."

"Maybe. But there is nothing mysterious about Ree's feelings for this guy." Jamie grinned. "It's the impossible match of the century. But I will say, you pull this off and I'll believe anything you tell me from now on."

"You don't sound overly concerned."

"Believe me, I'm not."

He stepped closer, and suddenly the laughter died and every muscle in her body tightened in supreme awareness. "You so wish to disbelieve I am what I say? Would it be so bad for your friends to find love?"

She shook her head, then swallowed hard when he lifted his hand to her hair.

He brushed the wisps of hair from her temple. "Perhaps it is because you fear what comes next."

"N-next?"

"Your heart," he said softly, his voice an even more potent caress than his fingertips. "You are the last of the three, my mistress. When I succeed in this match, yours will be next."

She swallowed hard. "Impossible."

"One thing I have learned: Nothing is impossible."

"Who are you?" she whispered.

"I am the man who will bring you eternal happiness."

Jamie had lost her mind. She knew it was true. Because right at that moment she wanted nothing more than to believe him. And worse, the man she wanted for all eternity—well, she couldn't even allow herself to think it. Insanity and beyond. "I don't know what to make of you, Sebastien Valentin."

"You need make nothing of me, Jamie."

Dear Lord, she loved it when he said her name. She wanted him to continue talking to her in that sexy whisper, continue touching her, continue—His chuckle brought her back to earth.

"I fear the heat up here is getting to you. You're flushed."

She did flush then, but in mortification. She stepped away from his touch, from the hypnotic aura that seemed to emanate from him. "Speaking of which, I really want to get back to work. I don't get much time off."

"How long have you been making these models?"

She wanted him to leave, to let her find her balance again. "Since I was a young girl." He gave her a knowing look, and she laughed. "Okay, so perhaps I had one or two pirate-queen fantasies. I grew out of those, but my fascination with boats remained."

"As I said before, an unusual diversion for a woman."

"Not so odd, really. I grew up on the water. My father and I are both maritime-history buffs. My grandfather built models. He and my aunt and uncle—Jack's parents—helped raise me until I was old enough to go off with my dad. I used to spend hours watching Granddad in his workshop. I was fascinated watching the ships come to life. He knew all the stories for each of them."

"And your *maman*?"

"She loved the water too. That's how she met my dad. But she died when I was only two." She smiled fondly. "My dad was a great parent to me, though. We traveled all over the world, just him and me. He was an offshore racer. Later on I got into racing too."

Sebastien's face lit up in surprise. "You raced ships?"

"Why do you sound so surprised? It may be a predominantly male sport, but I did okay."

"You sail, then?"

"Actually, no. I mean, I love the history of the high seas and all kinds of ships built over the years. Especially the tall ships. But for racing, sailboats aren't my thing."

"Your . . . thing?"

"Too slow." She waggled her eyebrows. "I have a need for speed."

Sebastien looked taken aback for a moment, then he tipped his head back and laughed. It was such a deep, resonant sound that Jamie felt the rush of it across every inch of her skin.

He grinned at her. "Speed?"

"I like the salt in the air and the wind in my face. But I want to fly over the water. I raced hydroplanes. Unlimited class. Up to two hundred miles per hour."

His eyes widened. "I am unfamiliar with that type of vessel. Do you have one still?"

A little of the reminiscent thrill dissipated. "My father has it stored. I don't race anymore."

"Ah, yes, you sell books now. Quite a change." His

expression turned contemplative. "Do you miss the water, Jamie? It calls to me still. Very strongly."

His quiet words brought her right back to that edge of awareness. She wasn't sure if she liked the common ground they seemed to have found. It screamed danger at her. Maybe because she found she liked that bond all too much. And hadn't she come back to New Orleans expressly to get away from men and their fascination with boats? "I don't miss the racing circuit," she answered honestly. "But I do miss the flying."

Sebastien's eyes lit up. He grabbed her hand. "Then let's go."

Jamie pulled back. "Whoa, whoa! What are you doing?"

"Do you have to work again today?"

She shook her head. "Marta is overseeing a signing for Bennett in the store this afternoon. We're having a bunch of kids in for a reading from his latest book. Jack is coming in to help Ree. Then we close early since it's Sunday. But I'd really hoped to get further with my model this afternoon. I won't have time off again for two weeks."

He took her hand and kissed the back of her fingers. "You have spent enough time with replicas. You need to taste the air. We must feel the sea spray on our skin."

"But—We? *Our* skin?" Her protestations died as he whirled her around.

"You work hard, Jamie. But you are accustomed to playing hard as well, no? This I understand." When she would have protested again, he pulled her closer. "Just because you no longer compete in this racing of yours does not mean you have to close yourself into an airless box of an attic." He stopped her protest with a finger to her lips. "You say you miss it. This is true?"

She could only nod.

"I want you to teach me to fly, *mon amie*. I want to know more about this need for speed." His eyes were shining with an excitement she'd never seen. She was helpless against it. And, in truth, she wouldn't have fought it anyway.

She wanted to fly again too.

Chapter 9

Sebastien stepped thankfully onto the dock and away from the death machine Jamie called an automobile. The gentle swaying motion beneath his feet brought him immediate peace of mind. Here he was in control. Or at least confident of his survival.

"Are you okay? You look a bit pale."

He shot her a look. "Let us just say that I am no longer in need of a demonstration of your need for speed."

Jamie laughed and punched him playfully on the arm. "I'm surprised. Big bad pirate like you. I'd think you'd love a good road-hugging sports car."

He looked back at the tiny red demon he had barely folded himself into. He had to admit, the power of such a conveyance intrigued him. "Perhaps if I were manning one, that would be different."

"You should have said something. I'd have let you drive."

Sebastien felt the heat rise toward his face. He was unaccustomed to being made to feel less than in command. Especially by a woman. But he was rapidly learning that Jamie was not a typical woman. "I have no license."

Jamie nudged him as they walked down the uneven planking. "I won't tell if you won't."

He shot her a dark look, then sighed.

"What, you're going to tell me that a man who flaunted the laws of the sea holds to the laws of the road?"

"No," he said through clenched teeth. "I'm telling you I have never mastered driving such a vehicle."

Jamie stopped dead, holding on to his arm so he stopped too. "You can't drive?"

Sebastien felt his muscles twitch. "No. It hasn't exactly been a necessary tool for me."

Instead of teasing him further, a sudden look of uncertainty crossed her face. He immediately felt better with her off balance. Perhaps it would be wise of him to keep her that way.

"My last few times in the city I rode the streetcar everywhere I needed to go. At that time the rails covered more of the city. Prior to that, I rode horseback. Now there are taxis."

Jamie said nothing. He continued toward the small boathouse at the end of the dock, her long legs easily keeping pace beside his. She was as at home on the swaying planks as he was. If he allowed himself, he could almost feel a certain kinship with her. That wasn't such a bad thing, he tried to convince himself. Knowing her better could only help him in his mission.

And yet he fought those feelings. They signaled a danger to him he couldn't comprehend, but he adhered to them all the same. His instincts were good, and he'd long ago learned to trust them without question.

She began to explain the type of boat they were going to be taking out that day, a twin inboard something or other. He wasn't paying the closest attention. He was too busy studying her, trying to fathom from where his odd feelings were originating.

Her hair was in its usual thick plait, swinging to

and fro across her back like a pendulum. Light wisps blew freely about her face. He wanted to reach out and smooth them back.

Odd, this wanting of his to touch her. Surely it could be explained away—it merely irritated him to have his view of her face and expressions obstructed. And he wished to view her unobscured face only so he could divine her inward thoughts. Aiding him in the process of eventually finding her soulmate.

It wasn't as though she was a raving beauty. Her skin, for one, was tanned by the sun's rays. There were fine lines fanning from the corners of her eyes when she smiled, similar to those on his own face. He knew she'd earned those lines just as he had, from years spent on the water, beneath the sun. They weren't feminine and certainly couldn't be considered flattering. They shouldn't have drawn his attention in a fond way. And yet they did.

Then there were her cheekbones and jawline, both lean and far more angular than he usually enjoyed in a woman. Her shoulders were broad, her arms somewhat muscled. Definitely not alluring. She didn't look as if she'd ever leaned upon a man for assistance in her life. And he liked to be turned to, needed. She was narrow of waist, but with no breasts to break the clean line of her body and lend it the soft curves needed to redeem her otherwise mannish physique. No, there was nothing about Mademoiselle Jamie Sullivan that called to him as a man. He was—could only be—interested in her as another mission to be accomplished.

So why his gait was presently being hampered by a persistent ache in his groin was beyond him altogether.

She had him wait outside the boathouse and emerged moments later with a small set of keys. "Off we go!" She motioned to what appeared to him to be a small white raft tethered to the dock on a neighboring pier.

"In that? It's no more than a dinghy."

She grinned. "A dinghy with two big beautiful Mercurys mounted underneath. It's not a hydro, but this baby will fly us fast enough. Come on."

She grabbed his hand and tugged him toward the boat. He admitted that the line of the boat was sleek, the prow narrow and proudly lifted. He motioned for her to step down. She jumped and landed lightly before turning and steadying the boat for him.

He untied the boat from the dock and followed her lead, landing just next to her. "Feels sound enough," he said, liking the balanced way it rocked in the water. There was a single seat covered in a marine shade of blue behind the console, which boasted a small wheel next to a silver lever.

"It's fiberglass," Jamie said, noticing his interest. "Don't worry, you'll like it fine once we're out on the water." She moved to the console and started the engine. "Go ahead and pull in the line."

Sebastien did so, which allowed him to conceal the shock he'd experienced at the powerful vibrations the engines had sent thrumming beneath his feet and throughout his body. He certainly was aware of the advances of technology—generally speaking—but in all his times back he'd never had reason or opportunity to go out on the water. And if he had, he'd likely have chosen a boat with sails. Something that would cut cleanly through the water and allow him to use the thrust of the wind to power his vessel.

But this . . . this powerful throbbing sensation of harnessed fury was nothing less than life-altering. And they weren't even moving yet.

He supposed it was quite possible that he could learn to enjoy this. Immensely.

"Hold on," she shouted. She expertly maneuvered

the boat out of its slip and into the main waterway leading away from the many docks and boats. They barely left a wake behind them as they took a leisurely pace out toward the open waters of Lake Pontchartrain.

"We are hardly moving," he said over the engine thrum and the light wind. "It seems like a great deal of work for such leisurely pace."

She grinned at him, her brown eyes more vibrant and full of life than he could recall ever having seen them. "Just you wait."

She looked back to the open water, but he found himself still staring at her profile. Her body might not have been the bountiful treasure he sought in a woman, but in that brief moment just now as their eyes connected, his body had leapt in response.

Absurd, he thought, turning to face the water once again. It was more likely the thrill of being out on the water again, combined with the new sensations the engines were providing, that had stirred his blood so.

They passed a small buoy and he all but felt Jamie's body tighten beside his. "Are you ready?" she shouted over the increasing wind.

He could only nod, but he tightened his grip on the console next to her, bracing his legs a bit farther apart.

"Hang on, baby! We're gonna fly!"

She pushed up on the silver handle next to the wheel, and the boat actually leapt forward in instant response. Sebastien let out a startled laugh at the amazing feeling it gave him, then leaned into the wind and let the sensation rush over him.

They went faster and faster, the boat barely skimming the surface of the water. Never in all his life had he felt anything so fantastical, so exhilarating.

Jamie let out a shout of glee and pushed the speed up even faster. "Hold on, we're going wake jumping."

She angled the boat sharply to the right, causing a surprised Sebastien to clutch on to her momentarily before quickly adapting to the new direction.

"Wake jumping?" he shouted.

She only nodded, her grin a permanent slash of white across her tanned face. There was no hair in her face now, allowing him an unhampered view of the unmitigated glee with which she attacked the water. And it was most certainly an attack, with this throbbing boat beneath her serving as both her war machine and her weapon.

Just then they hit what felt like a boulder. Sebastien immediately pulled Jamie against his chest and grabbed the wheel. He saw nothing in front of them as the prow of the boat lifted, then came smashing down.

Jamie struggled hard in his embrace. "What in the hell are you doing?" She pushed his arms back. "Let go of the wheel!"

She took back control of the boat and swung them smoothly around so they hit the other wake with nothing more than a mere bump.

"I'm sorry," he said, still a bit shaken. "I thought we'd struck something."

"We did—a wake." She pointed starboard to the boat rapidly disappearing from view, a big wake streaming behind it. "It's called wake jumping. Didn't you see it coming?"

He'd been watching her—again. "Is it supposed to feel as if all one's bones are being dashed against the bottom of the boat?"

She laughed. "Well, I've never heard it put exactly that way, but it's as good a description as any."

"And you find this sport . . . entertaining?"

She throttled down and brought the boat to a smoother cruising speed that allowed them to talk without shouting. "In hydroplaning, you get used to being dashed about. So for me, yes, I guess this is fun. Sort of keeps you used to the abuse."

Sebastien could only shake his head. "Abuse for the sake of entertainment."

"Oh, and I suppose you'll tell me now that you've never woken up stiff and sore and considered it payment due for the fun you had the day before."

Now he found a grin. "Well, there have been nights of sport that left me sore, if not stiff."

It amazed him how easily she flushed for a woman with such a degree of cynicism, especially toward men. He tucked that revelation away for later pondering. It was very likely a clue that would help him discern the type of man he would be hunting when the time came to match her soul.

The sudden vision of her laughing and soaring over the open water with another man gave him a very unpleasant twinge in the vicinity of his heart. He also remembered all too vividly how she'd felt in his hands, how her lithe body had arched into his when he'd tried to save her from certain death moments ago—even if she had been trying to get away from him at that moment. And yet his body had roared to life once again.

"Would you like to take a hand at the wheel?"

He nodded absently, not really paying attention. What he needed was to take a woman—any woman, at this point—to bed. His body was obviously so starved for the feel of soft, feminine skin that it was willing to react to any stimulation.

Yes, that was it exactly. As soon as they docked and returned to the Quarter, he'd seek out that lively little waitress from the other afternoon. There. He felt much better now.

Which made it only marginally easier to ignore the surge that rocketed through him when she took his hands and positioned them on the wheel and the throttle.

"Squeeze like this, then push it up like this to open her up. Down and release to slow. I think you can figure out the rest. She handles like a dream."

Pushing, squeezing, handling. He wanted to groan in frustration. Avoiding eye contact, he moved into position and took over the controls.

Moments later all his frustrations fled as he had them soaring across the lake. There was a deep rush of sound, and only belatedly he realized it was laughter. His own laughter.

He couldn't recall ever feeling such a rushing sensation of freedom. Of pure joy.

Just then he felt her fingers squeeze his arm, and when he looked into her shining eyes, something passed between them that he couldn't name. But he felt it. There was no denial crafty enough to avoid the simple truth: In that moment they forged a bond of understanding—of something even deeper, perhaps. She understood the elemental passion for the water that ran through him; it was a passion that coursed through her veins just the same.

He could see her, then, as the pirate queen she'd wished to be as a child. And a damn good one she'd have made too.

She turned back to the water. Reluctantly, so did he. Had she felt as rocked by their connection as he? He was afraid to look at her and find out.

He almost laughed at that. Afraid? That alone would normally have provoked him to do it just to conquer the fear. And yet he could not.

"Clouds are blowing up. We're going to have an afternoon squall. We'd better take her in."

He nodded and turned the boat around. They said nothing as he guided them back, and he silently handed the controls over to her as they neared the buoy marking their way to the docks.

She seemed to accept the silence, perhaps wanting it herself, and quietly maneuvered them to the rental slip they'd left what now seemed like another lifetime ago. At least to him.

He moved to the prow and grabbed the line, expertly catching the pulley as she moved into the slip. She shut down and leapt to the dock to finish tying them up. Sebastien pretended not to see her outstretched hand and levered himself up onto the dock. Touching her at the moment—any moment—would have ripped away his last pretense of self-control.

"Thank you for the ride." It was all he could do to get that much out. His voice almost shook, and no amount of tale-telling would make him believe it was some latent reaction to several hours of boat vibrations.

But there were no words to describe to her what their trip had meant to him. And if he so much as tried, he'd likely only disgrace himself somehow. He avoided looking directly at her and mentally willed her to begin the trek back to the boathouse.

Of course, she didn't. Irritating woman.

She tilted her head to one side. "You enjoyed it."

She'd made it a statement, so he felt perfectly within his rights to merely nod in agreement of her assessment.

"Would you like to go out again? Sometime?" Her straightforwardness faltered a bit on that last part.

The uncertainty surprised him. Good, he thought uncharitably. Then he wasn't the only one feeling a bit disconcerted.

"I think we'd better head for your automobile if we're to escape this storm."

The dark clouds had scudded very quickly inland, obliterating the sun. She didn't press him on her of-

fer. She seemed almost . . . relieved. He wasn't sure
how he felt about that either. Was she so relieved to
not have to be in his intimate company again? Naturally he should have felt similar relief. The confusion
arose because he felt nothing of the sort.

They made it to the car in record haste. She paused
at the driver's side door. "I'd offer to teach you how
to drive, but maybe we'll save that feat for another
day."

Another day. With her. *Yes*, his heart sang. *No!* his
common sense interjected. What the devil was wrong
with him? And yet the wicked smile rose to his lips in
blatant disregard of common sense. "If we yet survive
your defiance of death on the ride home."

She laughed then, and all felt right in his world.

Now all he had to do was fold his body into the tiny
contraption and survive the careening ride home
without allowing himself to come in contact with her.

Maybe he'd just walk. It would take him only the
better part of the day—and night. In a raging storm.

He looked at the car and at her, and actually had to
debate the choices.

But then she was in the car, flinging open his door
from the inside and smiling up at him in that way she
had. Part invitation, part challenge.

And he did love a challenge.

He sighed and shook his head—then folded himself
into the car.

Chapter 10

*J*amie arrived alone back at the bookstore and was stunned at the size of the crowd. The noise and confusion helped to take her mind off the disturbingly intimate afternoon she'd just shared with Sebastien.

She'd had fun. In fact, it was scary just how much fun she'd had with him.

Certainly this was not a good sign. He was either otherworldly . . . or a fruitcake who thought he was a compatriot of Jean Laffite. She wished she were firmer in her belief of the latter. But he was getting damn convincing regarding the former. Either way she shouldn't be grinning like a giddy schoolgirl fresh from a date with the prom king. Nor should she be wishing he'd touched her just once on their return trip. He'd been remarkably compact for such a big man.

She remembered watching him walk away from the car after she'd dropped him off at the French Market. She'd have likely watched as long as he was in sight, but she was afraid he'd turn and catch her gawking like the love-struck—

"Hiya, sugar. Where've you been at?" Ree Ann pushed her way through the throng and gave Jamie a quick hug.

Jamie felt a sudden stab of guilt and pushed all

thoughts of Sebastien away. Or tried to. With the Memorial Day rush come and gone, and now the summer season fast approaching, the shop had been busy over the past few weeks, thankfully. Though Ree had brought up the subject several times, they really hadn't had a chance to talk about Sebastien. Since he hadn't shown up at the shop in person during that time, Jamie had just let it drop. Obviously Ree didn't know he'd resurfaced. For now Jamie was ready to leave it that way. She wanted time to analyze her thoughts about Sebastien. Something had changed out there on the water. And until she figured out what, she wasn't going to share.

"Wow, this is quite a crowd," she said instead.

Ree smiled. "Bennett does know how to charm. And of course, Baxter has his own little fan club now."

"He brought the dog? Ree, if he so much as snarls at one of these kids—"

Ree patted her arm. "Bax was just protecting Marta before, sugar. The kids love him, and it's a mutual-admiration thing. He's a sweetie. And so is Bennett, despite the weird stuff he writes about."

Jamie surveyed the crowd. Mostly young teens, sprinkled liberally with adolescent preteens, along with a goodly number of parents. "Looks like a decent group."

"He did his reading earlier and I swear you could have heard the sweat beading on everyone's brows. And with his accent and all, he really has a wonderful speaking voice."

Jamie nodded in agreement, then flinched when Ree elbowed her. "Hey!"

"See? Look at Marta."

Jamie rubbed her side. She was just tall enough to see over the sea of heads, and she spied her friend quickly. Marta was opening the front covers of the books and handing them to Bennett, who was chatting animatedly with the young fan next in line for an autograph. "So?"

"Her face. Look at her face, Jamie. She's positively beaming. Don't you think so?"

Jamie nodded. It was true. A person could actually glow; Marta was living proof.

"I swear I never thought I'd see her like that again," Ree added. She clasped her hands together, making her bracelets jingle. "I'm so tickled for them both."

"They've been going out for only a few weeks, you know. Don't marry them off and give them babies quite yet."

Ree turned and gave her a look. "Don't be a wet blanket. Just because we're not doing happily ever after doesn't mean we should go making dire predictions about her shot at it."

"I just don't want to see her hurt. Bennett seems like a nice enough guy, but come on, what do we really know about him? Other than he writes like Stephen King on a really strange day. Not all that reassuring, if you ask me. And then there's his dog, Cujo Junior."

Ree laughed and patted her again. Jamie hated being patted.

"Bax is a pussycat. And Bennett's perfectly normal and nice. He's successful, doing something he loves. And more than that, he adores Marta." She squeezed Jamie's arm and sighed wistfully. "And he makes her laugh. Often." She grinned. "So they can wait awhile to make me an auntie, but I'm betting we hear wedding bells by the end of the year."

Jamie opened her mouth, then closed it. She could picture Sebastien's smug smile at Ree's proclamation. Had he really been the driving force behind their meeting and falling in love? Which reminded her. She glanced at Ree, who was mooning like a doting mother hen. Jamie chewed on her lip as she thought about her promise to Sebastien. She'd promised not to interfere with Sebastien's plans to put Angel in Ree's direct path.

Part of her still had the urge to laugh hysterically over the mere thought of that match. It would, quite simply, never happen. No matter how creative Sebastien was in trying to foist them off on each other.

But, on the other hand, Ree had spent a lot of energy, not to mention money, fighting off Angel's claim to her inheritance from Edgar. Now that Angel was going to pop up, somehow, someway, Jamie felt awful and disloyal about not warning her.

Well, she'd only promised to not interfere if things looked hunky-dory. And while Angel was most definitely hunky, in that swarthy Italian kind of way, he wasn't remotely dory. Not with Jamie, and most definitely not with Ree. So she consoled herself with the knowledge that she could step in about two seconds after they laid eyes on each other again. The bad vibes would be immediate. She wished she'd thought to ask Sebastien just when his little plan was to go into action.

Jamie nudged Ree's arm. "You're getting a line at the coffee bar."

She glanced over. "So I am. Wanna come help?"

Jamie shook her head. "I need a shower." And some time alone to think about Sebastien. "I'll come down later and help clean up. Jack seems to be handling his own at the front counter."

Jack was more than handling it. To him, the throngs crowding the counter were but an avid audience to be entertained. And nobody played a crowd better than Jack.

"I'm afraid we can't ever let Jack and Bennett out together, though," Ree said with a laughing roll of the eyes. "Can you imagine? Charisma overload."

Jamie nodded. "I can only imagine what kind of bizarre lyrics Bennett would write for Jack to sing." She left Ree laughing and made her way to the rear door leading to the stairwell, feeling slightly better.

Ree would handle Angel the same way she always had. Those two definitely had a pyrotechnic chemistry, but Jamie doubted it was the kind Sebastien hoped for.

So what would happen when Ree and Angel didn't hit it off? Would Sebastien just try again? Or would he admit defeat and be forced to come clean about who he really was?

Jamie rubbed her arms and shivered as she let herself into her bedroom. She flopped down on the bed and pulled off her shirt. Okay. So maybe she actually sort of wanted to believe that he was exactly what he said he was.

There. She'd admitted it to herself.

Which only meant more problems. Pirate genie or no, she did *not* want him to go matching *her* up with anyone. She was really serious about her commitment to remaining single. Two strikes were enough. She didn't need three. Which did nothing to explain those little fantasies she had about riding the high seas with Sebastien. But those were exactly that, she consoled herself—fantasies. Just like his whole being was a fantasy. And she was certainly allowed to keep her fantasies, right?

Right. Just as long as she didn't marry them.

She tossed her clothes in the vicinity of the hamper and stepped up into the bathroom. It had been converted from an old closet some decades ago. It was tiny, just enough room for a sink, toilet, and tub, but she liked the old-fashioned porcelain fixtures and spigots. She wasn't too crazy about the old-fashioned way the plumbing delivered a wide range of temperatures as it saw fit, but she was getting to know its little foibles. She turned the handles of the shower and winced as the pipes groaned and squealed.

Her thoughts drifted back to Sebastien. If only she hadn't taken that stupid bet. Maybe she could have wangled a different third choice, leaving her love life out of the whole soul-matching equation. But she *had* taken the bet. She brightened as another thought occurred to her. If Sebastien didn't make the love connection between Ree and Angel, then technically the bet was over and she'd won. There was no clause in there anywhere about giving him multiple tries at it. That meant no match for her. She immediately felt better.

Then there was the matter of the sword. She'd tossed and turned in bed the other night, trying to figure out a way to ultimately prove his claims, one way or another. And she realized she'd forgotten all about the sword. He had taken Ree's property, and she had no idea where it was. Or, for that matter, where Sebastien was when he wasn't intruding on her life at the oddest moments.

Although she was having a hard time being all that upset over today's intrusion. It had turned out to be a fun and exhilarating afternoon. With reluctance, she was also forced to admit that racing over the open water had been only a small part of that exhilaration.

She stepped into the shower. Yep, it had been so exhilarating she'd never gotten around to asking him about that sword or anything else. She worked a rich layer of lather into her skin as she contemplated just what it was about him that captivated her to the point of ignoring major danger signs and allowing him to remain not only in her life but in those of her friends. Jamie suddenly realized that her hands had slowed in their soaping motion and she was getting

lathered in a way that had nothing to do with suds.
"Oh, for heaven's sake." She rinsed, shut off the water, and stepped out, toweling off quickly.

Well, pirate or not, she had to know the truth for
sure. So while he launched Operation Angel, she
would launch Operation Pirate. She'd put all her research skills to good use—and see what she could discover about Monsieur Sebastien Valentin.

                              ❧

As it turned out, Operation Angel got under way
first. She had to hand it to him. He didn't waste any
time.

Her first clue that fireworks had been launched
came two days later when she was in the back loading
books onto a cart for shelving. Even with the Cajun
twang of BeauSoleil playing over the shop speakers,
she still heard Ree shouting. And using the kind of
language normally reserved for dockworkers.

What in the hell was going on out there? The shop
didn't even open for another ten minutes. Well,
whatever was going on, at least it wasn't going on in
front of paying customers.

Ree launched another volley, slowing Jamie's foot-
steps as she emerged from the back room pushing the
cart.

"Sugar, I don't care what you believe!" Ree went
on, her decibel levels drowning out Michael Doucet
on the fiddle. She stabbed a finger toward something—or someone—Jamie couldn't see.

Had some poor, misguided delivery guy stepped
over the line? Again? She shook her head. Ree most
definitely invited men to look and enjoy, but only the
truly foolish tried to touch.

"I believe what this paper says." This from a voice
much deeper—if not any quieter.

Jamie froze. Oh, God. She knew that voice. Angel.

What was Sebastien *thinking*, sending him right into the shop? It was like sending a lamb directly into the slaughterhouse.

Except Angel was no . . . well, angel. He could hold his own. And then some.

Jamie watched as Ree snatched the note and read it, her eyes widening until her lashes brushed the sculpted arch of her eyebrow. "What on God's green earth would ever cause me to send you a note like this? This is obviously someone's idea of a sick joke." She crumpled the paper in her fist. "And, sugar, I don't know anyone that sick."

"It was delivered to me at Santini's last night. I believed it to be your handwriting. I've certainly seen your signature on enough legal documents to recognize it."

She leveled a look at him. "Who delivered this? What did he—or she—look like?"

Angel shook his head. "I never saw the messenger. My maître d' brought it back to me."

Jamie was itching to see what the note said. Although whatever it said, it hadn't worked. A meeting set up by an anonymous person was too simplistic for someone like Sebastien. He had to know it was going to take more than a note to get these two to speak civilly.

She caught herself there. Was she actually wanting Sebastien to succeed? No. Nonsense. She just wanted more of a contest than this lame effort. That had to be it.

"Well, I certainly didn't write or sign this." Ree smoothed the paper, then frowned as she looked over the handwriting again.

Jamie found herself smiling. Nice touch there, she thought. Although how he'd managed to copy her handwriting she had no idea. At least it had stopped the shouting.

"Then I suppose I have no business here," Angel said. He nodded sharply and turned to the door.

Jamie caught herself opening her mouth. To do what? she thought, shutting it abruptly. Call out to Angel and get him to stay? Ridiculous. She'd promised not to interfere. And even if she did, it certainly wasn't going to be to *help* Sebastien.

"Wait a minute," she heard Ree say.

Jamie's attention was riveted to the door when Angel paused and looked back over his shoulder. He definitely had that whole Antonio-Banderas-does-Zorro thing going. Ponytail and all. He was a gorgeous man, no doubt about that. He wore his tailored clothes almost as beautifully as Sebastien did. The morning sun shone through the door, casting a halo around his dark hair. An archangel, she thought. Either that, or he looked like one of Sebastien's former compatriots on the high seas.

Maybe that was why Sebastien had chosen him. He'd seen a kindred spirit. Except that while they both had swarthy good looks and were fiercely intent on getting what they wanted, Sebastien went about it with gallantry. Whereas Angel filed lawsuits and threw money at it.

Jamie swallowed a snort of disgust. No way would Ree ever look at Angel as anything other than the supreme pain in the ass he was.

"Yes?" he asked at length.

"Why?" When he raised a puzzled eyebrow at her question, Ree added, "Why did you respond to this note? I'd have thought you would tear it up or spit on it."

"You don't know me very well then," he said quietly.

"I think I have a fairly good idea how you react to demands," she responded. "If I *had* sent you something like this, I'd have at the very least expected you to say that if I wanted an audience, then I could come to your castle."

"Castle? Is that how you see me? A pompous king who expects his minions to dance in attendance to his whims?" He turned toward her. "Or perhaps you thought I'd feel threatened by someone like you if not on my own turf."

"Someone like me?" She shook her head but smiled. "Now you're acting like I'd expect you to. You don't know me very well either. But, then, you never made an effort to look past your own narrow-minded preconceptions. In that respect you're just like every other man I've ever met. Except, of course, your grandfather."

Even from the distance where Jamie stood, she could see him stiffen, his eyes narrow, as that remark hit home. He said nothing but regarded her steadily.

Ree stood straighter and unfolded the arms she had locked defensively in front of her. "Why did you come, Angelo?"

"You surprised me." He nodded at the note. "It was unexpected. People rarely do the unexpected." He looked straight into her eyes. "You had my attention. For a moment, anyway." He turned and let himself out of the shop.

Ree stood there, mouth open, fists tight by her sides.

Jamie pushed the cart to the front of the store. "Pompous ass," she said.

Ree spun around. "Oh! That . . . that . . . rrrrrr," she spluttered, her eyes blazing.

Jamie was about to jump in with another two cents—after all, she'd kept her promise and not interfered—but stopped when she looked at Ree. Ree was hopping mad, no doubt about that. Given the fact that those two had tangled before made the whole scene rather unsurprising. But Jamie hadn't counted on the other emotion she saw in Ree's eyes. Hurt.

Had Angel hurt her? Ridiculous. Yes, he'd said some unkind things, but not even in the ballpark of the comments that had flown fast and nasty way back during the court hearings. Ree had staunchly defended Edgar but had refrained from responding to Angel's baser assumptions. She'd known the will wasn't likely to be challenged successfully, so she'd let Angel think what he would. Angel had dug up the information on Ree's unusual upbringing and looked no further. The daughter was obviously just like her stripper, gold-digging mother. Like she'd said, he certainly wasn't the first man to underestimate her.

Jamie had spent some time with Ree during the final hearing. She'd seen her friend spitting mad during the final probate process—but she'd never seen her hurt. Had she just not been looking closely enough? No. She'd have known. Angel had the capacity to incite fury, but Ree didn't care enough about him to allow him the rare luxury of being important enough to hurt her. She'd been angry only on Edgar's behalf.

So what had happened here just now? What had changed?

Damn, Sebastien!

"Ree?" She placed a tentative hand on her arm and patted her awkwardly. It seemed much easier when Ree did it. "Don't let him get to you. He's not worth it."

Ree snapped out of her sputtering anger. "No, he's most definitely not." But the hurt lingered around her eyes. "What in the hell was that all about anyway? Who would send him something like this? And how did they copy my handwriting so well?"

Jamie swallowed hard and knew she wasn't a good enough actress to wipe the guilty look off her face.

Ree's eyes narrowed and she gave Jamie a hard look, then shook her head. "No, no way would you do something like this. It's not your—"

She stopped when Jamie shook her head and said, "No, *I* didn't do it."

Ree's eyes widened in sudden understanding. "Sebastien?" The name came out on a hushed, stunned whisper. Before Jamie could say anything, Ree tipped her head back and hooted with laughter. In fact, she laughed so hard Jamie was afraid she'd pull a muscle or something.

"Hey, want to let me in on the joke? I'm surprised you're not jumping down my throat for not warning you."

That stopped her. "You knew? About the note?"

"No, I just knew he planned to try and match you with Angel." She held out her hand. "Trust me, Ree, if I hadn't promised already not to interfere, I would have said something. And really, it's not like there was a chance in hell of him succeeding."

"So you just let him put that guy in my path again? What kind of friend are you? Jamie Lynne, I'm shocked."

"I'm sorry, Ree. I said I'd let him try but if things didn't look good I'd step in. You handled him, though. I knew you would. He won't be back," she added, trying to make them both feel better.

Ree looked at her. "So you promised to give him a shot at matching me up, huh? I'm guessing he's taking credit for Marta and Bennett."

"I can't prove otherwise."

Ree brightened then. "Oh! I see. You figured that him failing to match me up was a way to end this whole genie charade once and for all." Ree's smile faded as she looked closely at Jamie. Her expression changed. "Wait a minute, you're beginning to believe this guy, aren't you?"

Jamie looked sheepish but didn't deny it. "I don't know what to believe anymore, Ree." She spread her hands. "I mean, my head knows this has all got to be some wacky make-believe fantasy."

"Uh-oh, sugar. I'm not liking the direction this is goin'. Your heart is tellin' you something else, right?"

Jamie tried a weak laugh. "I know, I know, don't say it. We all know what a great track record my heart has." Her tone was more beseeching than defensive. "I'm not saying I'm falling for the guy or anything." She scowled when Ree merely lifted one elegant eyebrow. "I'm not! But I gotta tell you, he's getting more and more convincing with this whole thing."

Ree smiled then, a bit wickedly if you asked Jamie. "Until today. He didn't exactly bat a thousand trying to match me up with Angelo the Hun."

Jamie didn't say anything. She couldn't get the memory of that hurt look out of her mind.

Ree tilted her head. "What? What's going on in that head of yours? Spill."

Jamie shrugged. "I don't know." She looked at Ree, really looked at her. "I know Angel made your life hell right after Edgar died. You were grieving and he didn't help that at all. So . . ."

"So? You're right, he was awful. Still is."

Jamie took a breath and just blurted it out. "So why did you look so hurt? Just now, when he left." At Ree's baffled look, she went on. "I know he's said far worse about you, to your face. All he did today was confirm what we already knew about him. So . . ." She shrugged, wishing she hadn't pushed it. "Why did he hurt your feelings this time?"

Now it was Ree's turn to look away and try on a

mask or two. It didn't work any better for her than it had for Jamie.

She finally looked back at her friend. "Maybe I'm just tired of being overlooked." Now she held her hand up. "I know, I know, I all but ask for it. It amuses me. Men are such dorks about women, you know? I get a kick out of playing them for the fools they are. Or I did. It's all just a game to me, Jamie, you know that. Except . . . for some reason . . ." She shrugged and looked to the doorway Angel had passed through a while ago. "For some reason, today it ceased to amuse me."

Chapter 11

Sebastien lowered the newspaper he was pretending to read and watched Monsieur Santini leave the bookstore. Well, that didn't last as long as he'd hoped for. But he knew this would be no easy match to make.

A slow smile spread across his face.

What fun would it be if they were all easy?

Some of the most enduring, passionate matches were the most difficult to achieve. He took special pride in those.

Matching the grandson of one of his favorite former masters would be a special pleasure. And he'd come to respect and admire Mademoiselle Broussard as well. Oh, yes, he would enjoy this.

He closed the paper as Angel sped off down the empty, early-morning street. Should he go into the shop? He really had no reason to. He had much to do this day, plotting and executing the next step in the dance between Ree Ann and Angel. Jamie stepped outside just then and went about opening the tall shutters that covered the windows. He stilled, not wanting her to spy him there but at the same time unable to duck back around the corner and out of sight.

He'd enjoyed their time on the water. *Mais oui*, he'd more than enjoyed it. He'd found a kindred spirit in her. He'd never known a woman to find such primal

joy on the water. He'd felt her every tremor of pleasure as if it were his own.

He scowled at his wayward thoughts. If the truth
were to be told, he'd spent more time than absolutely
necessary thinking about that day. Yes, he had to analyze information about her in order to make her
match. But this obsessive need to go over and over—

Jamie had secured the final shutter and moved back
to the front door, where she paused. Sebastien eased
around the corner behind him just as she glanced
over her shoulder and looked directly to where he had
been standing.

Too close for his comfort. He had to regain control, and swiftly. He had no time to waste explaining
his presence. Certainly she already knew he was behind the manufactured meeting this morning. Just as
certainly she was crowing victory, still believing this
was a match made in hell.

His composure returned, along with his smile. The
added incentive of proving her wrong gave him just
the focus he needed. With a light whistle, he turned
and strolled down St. Phillip toward the river, his
mind already turned to his next move. The dance had
begun.

&

Jamie smiled tiredly as the last customer stepped
out the door. She glanced at her watch. Five minutes
and she could lock the door. It had been a long day,
the first time since the shop opened when she found
herself constantly eyeing the clock. She didn't know
why she felt so restless.

Her gaze was drawn to the front door. Liar, she
thought, you've been watching that door all day, hoping Sebastien would come in. He hadn't.

She'd tried to talk to Ree several times that day, but
for once her friend was uncharacteristically silent

about her feelings. She'd smiled and charmed their customers, but Jamie couldn't shake the feeling that it was all a front. She knew it was because of Angel. Which was why, she told herself, she'd been hoping Sebastien would show his face. So she could tell him that she'd no longer sit back quietly while he plotted his little matchmaking schemes.

That is, if Ree didn't tear him up one side and down the other first. She'd been none too happy with his machinations on her supposed behalf either. Jamie found another smile. Maybe letting Ree settle this with him would be the best solution.

"I'm all done in, sugar," Ree called from the coffee bar. "I'm going to hand my bank and receipts over to Marta and head on home for a nice, long soak."

Jamie stepped around the counter. "Ree, listen, I—"

Ree held up one hand but found a smile of her own. "Jamie Lynne, if you apologize for that man one more time, I swear." She lowered her hand as her smile faded. "I'm fine, really. It was just a surprise. No harm done. I don't think Angel will be bothering me again."

Jamie opened her mouth to ask why she'd been in a blue funk all day if that were the case, but she closed it again when she spied that same hurt she'd seen this morning. Finally, she nodded and said, "If you want to talk, you know where to find me. Okay?"

"I just need a warm soak, a nice little glass of white wine, and a good book. I'll be good as new tomorrow. Promise."

Jamie wasn't so sure about that. But she did know one thing: She had to find Sebastien and tell him to back off. She didn't know what was really bugging Ree, but she did know that the last thing she needed was having Angel thrown in her path again.

Problem was, she had no idea where to find him.

But she did have an idea where to start looking: Jack. Apparently he'd gotten a bit more chummy with Sebastien than Jamie had realized. The two had shared several meals, she'd discovered. God only knew what Jack had told him. He was loyal to his friends and family, but he was also a notorious sucker for a handsome face. And Sebastien had that in spades.

Jamie waved as Ree left, then she stepped outside to close the shutters and lock up for the night. Jack would be down at Beaudraux on Bourbon, doing makeup for the drag revue that was opening tonight. He'd be frenzied, but Jamie didn't care. It might work to her advantage. One way or the other, she was going to find Sebastien. And, for her cousin's indiscretions, she would have no compunction about guilting Jack into covering for her at work tomorrow so she could track the pirate genie down.

੩ৎ

Jamie turned sideways and squeezed through the throng at Beaudraux, angling her way to the front. At least here she didn't have to worry about getting groped, she thought dryly. It was a lame attempt to keep her humor as she made it to the door and nodded to Bennie the Bouncer. Jack had been no help. Oh, he'd been willing enough. He was contrite, no doubt. But he'd known nothing more about Sebastien's living quarters or general whereabouts than Jamie did.

She sucked in a deep breath of sultry night air as she finally made it to the sidewalk. The street was packed with all varieties of humanity, as it was every night. The music poured out of the open doors of pubs, bars, and nightclubs, and people laughed and danced as they jostled by her. She moved along, lost in her own thoughts, hardly noticing the women who were giving in to the age-old tradition of baring their breasts for the colorful Mardi Gras beads flung by the bounty of admirers on the balconies above. Someone yelled down to her to take her shirt off, pulling her from her thoughts. She looked up at the hopeful young man, then after a wry glance downward, looked back up and with a laugh shouted, "You must be joking."

The man laughed and flung her a string of beads anyway.

"Wonderful. Now I'm getting pity beads." She did smile, though, and loop the beads over her neck as she made her way to the quiet end of the street before cutting back over to Royal and the bookstore. She was so caught up in her musings, she didn't see the man step from the shadows until he was right in front of her.

Her hands flew up defensively, then dropped immediately. "Sebastien." She blew out a shaky sigh of relief. "I'm going to have to start wearing a heart monitor because of you."

He smiled. "I beg your pardon, mademoiselle. It was never my intention to disturb your heart."

If he only knew, Jamie thought ruefully.

He raised a finger and lifted the beads from her neck. "Been enjoying the pleasures of Bourbon Street?"

Jamie stepped back so the beads fell from his fingers. There was something far too disconcerting about the innocent gesture. "Hardly." At his raised eyebrow she added, "I've done my lifetime's share of partying. Those days are over for me."

His wicked grin surfaced, making her skin ripple in a delightful shiver despite the blanket of humidity that still hung in the air.

"But once upon a time you would have played for the beads?" He shook his head. "You should never grow too old to play. It is what keeps us young."

"It's what got me married and divorced. Twice," she shot back, trying hard for friendly barb-swapping. But it felt different. *Friendly* didn't begin to describe how it felt. *Bad idea, Jamie. Don't even start in that direction with him.* "Besides, I'm not the type that bares it all for beads."

"And what, mademoiselle, do you bare it all for? If not for beads?"

Somehow he'd stepped closer without her noticing, because the oxygen had simply vanished again. As had all her personal space. He just filled it right up.

"I . . . I . . . um . . . don't bare it all, in general, for any reason. Like I said, keeps me out of trouble."

He lifted the beads from her neck again and slid his fingers around them and down until they rested just above the space between her breasts. "What a pity."

Jamie forced a laugh and winced at the shrill note in her voice. "Yeah, well, pity is what I'd expect if I did bare it all. Not exactly Pamela Anderson Lee here. Heck, I'm not even Tommy Lee." She backed away again, but this time he didn't let the beads go. Unless she wanted to rip them from his hooked fingers, she was more or less trapped.

She didn't pull away.

"Who is this Tommy and Pamela Lee?"

"No one you'd match up, trust me," she said, but her dry tone was suddenly even drier for lack of being able to swallow.

Sebastien's intent gaze left hers and traveled slowly down the strand of beads to where his fingers were poised, then directly up into her eyes. "I only find myself regretting the fact that I can't seduce you to find out for myself what treasures lie beneath my fingers."

Her eyes widened in alarm. Had he really just said he wanted to seduce her? "Sebastien, really, this can't—"

He dropped the beads and pressed his fingertips to her lips. "I'm aware of what this can't be. Just as I'm aware that for some unknown reason, I wish it to be."

She lifted her head just enough for his fingers to fall away. The soft friction made her body ache. "Unknown reason?"

His white teeth flashed in the corner lamplight. "You are not the type of woman who usually draws my attention. And yet you have a disturbing majority of it."

Stung by his summation of her womanly charms—or lack thereof—she found the wherewithal to step back and away from him. "Probably something you ate while dining with my cousin." It was ridiculous to feel insulted. After all, she was well aware that her womanly charms were generally directly related to her father's checkbook. That he couldn't figure out why on earth he could possibly want her was insulting enough. She wasn't about to give him the chance to enlighten himself.

"Something I ate?" he repeated, momentarily confused. "I am speaking of other . . . appetites. Appetites that, upon my return, I've found myself unwilling to assuage. Odd, isn't it?" He seemed honestly perplexed.

"Downright bizarre," she said tightly. "A man who looks like you, even a delusional one, should have no trouble sating any appetite he has."

"Agreed. Which is why I find myself here tonight. I didn't see any other solution."

Jamie's eyes widened and she laughed harshly. "Well, if you expect me to fall at your feet in abject appreciation because you couldn't find a more worthy entrée, then you can go find another menu. I'm not fast food." She pushed past him and unlocked the iron gate. "The kitchen is closed."

He stayed her with one surprisingly strong, broad hand. "I have insulted you."

"Give the man a free dessert. You bet your sweet cherry-on-top I'm insulted." She turned in the tight space between him and the gate and looked up at him. "You know, I find you very attractive. I'm sure that comes as no shock to you, since any woman would. But you may be surprised to know that I have a low tolerance for being treated like a charity case."

Sebastien frowned and started to speak, but she waved him silent.

"I realize someone who looks like you probably doesn't think a woman like me can earn real honest attraction, and you know what? I'm not so sure I can either."

"You question your charms? And yet two men have committed themselves in marriage to you."

"The only person who should have been committed was me. To an institution, for buying their slick lines in the first place." She talked over his response. "So you'll forgive me if I'm no longer willing to put up with being played with for the sake of someone else's needs. Whatever they are. I don't know what you hoped to gain tonight, but whatever it was, we both know it's not because you really wanted me. So you'll excuse me if I opt out in the early rounds of this match."

She shoved at the iron grate that led to the narrow alley into the courtyard. He made no move to stop her, and she clanged it shut behind her, hearing the lock click into place before letting her breath out.

Sebastien gripped two of the bars and leaned his face between them. "I've stated myself badly. I never intended to hurt or insult you," he said quietly. "You have my deepest apologies for doing so. You are an intriguing combination of strength and vulnerability and a woman I've come to admire. It is to my shame that I didn't make that clear. I realize coming here tonight was a mistake. A mistake I will pay for, I assure you."

Despite telling herself to just keep walking, she stopped and looked back. "What do you mean?"

He looked at her for the longest time, an odd expression on his face. "I never considered that making these matches would endanger my own heart. Now I'm not so sure." Before she could speak, he turned and disappeared down the street.

She was so stunned by his quietly spoken words that she simply stood there, staring at the empty space where he'd been. By the time it occurred to her to follow him, to find out where he was going, it was too late. The street was deserted.

"Damn!" She leaned back against the gate. Had he done that on purpose? Said something so provocative as a calculated move to confuse her, so he'd have time to disappear? Was he that crafty?

She honestly didn't know. She just couldn't figure him out. Had he come here tonight seeking an easy lay? Had he been stalking her for that supreme purpose?

No, that was silly. First off, he could basically have any woman he wanted. Why in hell go after her? Secondly, if he'd really wanted her, he could have come after her in the more traditional fashion. And likely succeeded, she thought ruefully.

So, that left . . . what? That he'd honestly been confused by his feelings for her and had come here tonight hoping to sort them out?

She shook her head and walked through the small courtyard to the rear vestibule entrance. She just couldn't believe that. Or maybe it was more honest to say she couldn't let herself believe that. Because her feelings for him were confused too. And she didn't want to examine them either.

But, dammit, she wished she'd been more on the ball. She'd missed a prime chance to find out more about him. And now she wasn't sure when, or if, she'd see him again.

The sharp pang that brought to her chest served as the most dire warning of all.

"Who are you, Sebastien Valentin?" she murmured into the hushed silence of the night. "And why do I care so much?"

❧

Sebastien sat down on a bench and watched the river as it flowed by under the moonlit sky. What had he been thinking? Well, he knew what he'd been thinking with. He swore under his breath. He'd never faced such a challenge as this.

He was unable to put her from his mind, and this disturbed him greatly. Try as he might, he could not deceive himself into believing his thoughts were focusing on her so incessantly because of the battle of proof they were waging. He honestly hadn't meant to insult her. He'd been perplexed, yes, by his obsessive pondering of her. Yet he'd never meant to imply that because she was not the type of woman who usually drew his attentions that she was unsuitable for any man's attentions.

It was simply that he enjoyed women who were more obvious in their charms, more comfortable with how to use them. It kept things uncomplicated. And generally a great deal of fun was had by all.

He scowled and leaned back against the bench. There was nothing uncomplicated about Jamie Sullivan. Nor about his feelings toward her. He'd learned more about her tonight. She'd been married.

And divorced. Twice. Crucial information he'd not elicited from Jack. And yet, as he sat there, it was not how this information would affect his selection of her soulmate that filled his mind. Two men had pledged their troth to her. What had happened? She implied they had somehow used her affections for their own gain.

He hung his head. And now she saw his appearance tonight and his remarks about his confused affection for her as similar attacks on her heart. Of course, she was right. He had no interest in her heart. He couldn't, other than to find its mate.

So why the desire to seduce? Why the need to see her eyes light with that flame of desire and know he was the cause of it? Insanity. And why in God's name had he spoken to her of this insane need of his? Surely he knew better than that. But she hadn't seemed vulnerable to his charms, he argued with himself. Perhaps he'd only mentioned his growing desire in hopes she'd dash them with an effectively aimed retort.

Instead, he'd been the one with the deadly aim.

He stood and made an attempt to roll the tightness from his shoulders. He still had much to do with Ree Ann and Angel. He must put Jamie and her role in his life into sharp perspective, and quickly.

There would be no more talk of seduction and need. As she'd baldly stated, there were other women all too happy to quench that particular thirst.

As he strolled off the Moonwalk and headed toward Jackson Square, he wondered why it was that they held even less allure for him just now.

Chapter 12

The following morning was sunny and mild. Jamie opted for a run through the Quarter and along the river. Then she strolled through the stands at the French Market. Jack had showed up to work for her today—his way of making up to her for the guilt he felt about talking to Sebastien. She really wasn't angry with him, but she took the day anyway. It gave her time to implement Operation Pirate. She planned to make the most of it.

She'd tossed and turned all night, replaying Sebastien's words, analyzing the honest confusion and contrition he'd seemed to feel. She had no idea what to believe, but she still wanted to know more about him. Maybe that would help her figure it out.

She stepped out of the market and sank her teeth into a bright green, bittersweet apple. There were all kinds of historical resources right here in the Quarter, and she intended to make use of them. Crunching thoughtfully, she headed toward the Cabildo in Jackson Square. Maybe a little research on Sebastien's supposed former boss, Jean Laffite, would be a good place to start. She didn't hold much hope of actually finding Sebastien's name listed on some historical document, but it wouldn't hurt to do a bit of digging and see what came up. There were several other historians in the area who might be able to help as well.

She was crossing Decatur, trying to decide how to phrase her questions, when she spied Ree Ann coming around the opposite corner. *What's she doing down here?* It was early still; the shop didn't open for another hour. Maybe she'd had the same idea as Jamie and was heading for the market. She started to call out, then came to a dead halt when Ree ducked into an open gate. The gate was to an alley that led to the courtyard of—

"Santini's?" Jamie whispered, then snapped her mouth shut. Ree was going to see Angel. *Oh. My. God.* Without thinking, Jamie crossed the corner at a diagonal and headed directly toward the still-open gate. She stopped only when her hand was on the latch. What was she going to do? Go in and rescue Ree from the evil clutches of Angelo Santini? She'd have laughed, except nothing about this was funny. Had Angel called her? Or had Ree just decided to confront him on her own? To settle, perhaps, the reasons why she'd let his words disturb her so much.

Whatever the case, it was none of Jamie's business. Ree hadn't called her last night and confided, so Jamie should just butt out. Ree would probably tell her all about it when it was over and done with, anyway.

Jamie resolutely turned away. Then Angel's voice carried down the alleyway from the inner courtyard, and she stopped. Telling herself she was doing this only for Ree's protection, she shamelessly eased herself inside the gate. And maybe just a few steps down the alleyway.

"I didn't think you'd come."

Aha! He had called her. Jamie folded her arms and settled in next to the wall.

"So this note actually did come from you," Ree said, followed by the sound of crinkling paper.

There was a low chuckle. "I am still trying to determine the origins of that other note, but no one here can recall who dropped it off."

Jamie strained forward, breath caught in her throat.

"It doesn't really matter, does it?" Ree said.

Jamie blew out a quiet sigh of relief. The last thing they needed right now was to drag Sebastien into this mess.

"Is that why you asked me here?" Ree continued. "To tell me that?"

"Maybe I just wanted to see if you'd come."

Jamie could just imagine Ree stiffening up on that one. She caught herself smiling when Ree said, "Well, then, I suppose you have your answer. However, I don't have time for game-playing. I'll let myself out."

Jamie plastered herself to the wall and began inching back toward the gate as she heard Ree's heels click in her direction. Somehow, she was much farther down the alley than those initial few steps.

"Why did you come?"

The clicking stopped. Jamie stilled too.

There was a pause, then Ree said, "You came when you thought I'd asked you to. I was merely returning the gesture."

"You say you have no time for game-playing, and yet what else would you call your relationship with my grandfather?"

Whoa. Jamie didn't know whether to duck from the shrapnel when Ree exploded or to run in there and drag her friend out before she committed a capital offense.

Her mouth dropped open in surprise when Ree answered him calmly.

"You have attacked my character and tried repeatedly to provoke me by making these veiled insinuations about my relationship with Edgar. I have not responded because, to this day, I still cannot discover what business it is of yours. Perhaps if you can answer that for me, I would attempt to enlighten you."

It was the longest speech Jamie could recall Ree ever making directly to Angel. Of course, most of their prior conversation had been conducted through attorneys.

"He was my grandfather," Angel said. "Family. I had a right to know if someone was taking advantage of him."

"If you cared so much about your grandfather— your sole remaining family, as far as I know—then where was all this concern when he was alive? If you cared that much, you'd have known exactly who I was long before the reading of his will and exactly what role I played in his life."

Jamie smiled and gave Ree a thumbs-up. Maybe this was a good idea after all. In all the time they'd spent in court, Ree had taken her counsel's advice to heart and steered clear of responding to anything personal Angel had said. But that had apparently left a great deal of pent-up frustration and anger inside her. Jamie thought she'd simply buried it and turned her attentions to opening up the store. But it had obviously been festering.

Jamie had never thought she'd say this, but maybe it was good that Angel had asked Ree here today and finally given her the opportunity—in private—to vent those frustrations.

Angel's next words riveted Jamie once again. This was better than *Days of Our Lives.*

"Do not mistake my absence from his life as a sign of lack of concern. I wanted badly to be a part of his life. As you say, he was my only remaining family."

"Then where were you?"

"Banished." There was a long pause, during which Jamie could feel the tension all but suck the oxygen from the air. "All contact with him was severed. By him. Because of you."

Jamie rubbed the goose bumps on her arms. Angel had delivered his pronouncement without a drop of venom in his voice. Somehow that made it all the more chilling.

"Me?" Ree's surprise was sincere. "I didn't even know you. The first time I met you was when the will was read."

Yeah, Jamie thought defensively. What did *she* do?

"He did not tell you?"

"I knew of you, of course. He spoke about his only grandson, about the restaurant he'd handed down to you. I knew there was friction, but he didn't talk about it. I didn't push it. I assumed he was hurting because you ignored him once you had the reins of the business in your hands."

"You assumed far too much, then."

"Looks like we are both guilty of that. But what could my presence in his life have done to alienate him from you? I never spoke against you. I didn't even know you."

There was another long pause. Jamie silently nudged Angel to reply. *Yeah, what do you have to say to that?*

"It was I who spoke against you."

"I see." Now Ree's voice held that world-weary tone that Jamie had heard so often. The tone that crept in when the current man in her life proved himself to be a moron like all the others. Of course, Angel had proved that long ago—apparently a bit longer than even they'd known.

"You never met me, but that didn't stop you from thinking you knew me or, more specifically, my 'type.' You made that clear enough at the hearing," Ree went on. "I'm guessing Edgar cut you off as a way of defending my honor." She laughed, but it was a sad one. "Had I known, I would have made it clear that I could fight my own battles." She paused, then said, "When they are important enough to fight for. Your opinion of me means nothing to me. That it also offended your grandfather, however, does mean something to me. If that is how people in your family treat one another, then perhaps it was best that he distanced himself from your version of loving support."

Again, Jamie heard heels click on the flagstones. Again, Angel stopped her.

"I'm beginning to think perhaps you're right."

Jamie laid her hand on her chest. Angel was agreeing? She didn't think she could stand much more of this.

"Meaning?" Ree asked quietly.

There was the sound of creaking springs. Apparently Angel had been seated and now he stood. Jamie strained to listen harder and heard the slight scuffle of his shoes on the flagstones. When he spoke, he was as close to her as Ree had been.

"Meaning I have a great deal to think about. And an even greater deal to apologize for."

Double whoa! Angel Santini apologizing? Jamie thought she could actually hear hell freezing over.

"I'm not certain that I care, Mr. Santini," Ree said.

Jamie pumped her fist. *Right on, sister, you tell him!*

"Although I'm certain your grandfather would want you to make peace with yourself in your own heart," she continued. "So I'll leave you to it. I don't believe we have anything more to say to each other."

"Wait. Please."

Did Ree huff out a sigh of frustration, or did Jamie just imagine it because she knew her friend so well? Either way, there was a distinct tone of weariness in Ree's voice when she responded.

"Why? I can't imagine we have anything left to discuss. The courts have spoken in regard to—"

"This isn't about the land or the will."

"Then what?"

"I—"

Jamie craned her neck toward the corner. Had that really been a note of uncertainty in Angel's voice?

"I'd like to know more about my grandfather. About the last years of his life."

"From me?" There was no doubting the surprise in Ree's voice.

"You were closest to him."

There was a sustained pause, then Ree laughed. "You have nerve in spades, sugar."

"I believe it's an inherited trait."

"Possibly. However, let's say that Edgar wielded his nerve with a tad more finesse."

"You're probably correct. Finesse was never one of my finer traits."

Jamie wasn't too sure about that. Ree had held her own beautifully, but she was still here, which was apparently right where he wanted her.

"Dinner?" he asked. "Privately here at Santini's or a restaurant of your choice."

"You'll have to take it on faith that I'm not playing coy. However, I'll have to think on this and get back to you. I'm not so certain I'm ready to discuss a past that is still a bit tender. A past, I need not remind you, that you have disdained at every turn."

"I just want to know more about my grandfather. No digs, no barbs."

"You'll forgive me if I don't wholeheartedly embrace this sudden change in attitude. Whatever my decision, one thing won't change: I don't trust you. I don't like or respect you either."

"Then why consider the invitation at all?"

Again, a pause. Then, "Because I believe Edgar suffered for putting you at a distance. Your grandfather was a wonderful, kind, courageous man, and perhaps, just perhaps, you'll be a better person for learning more about him."

"Does this mean you will talk with me about him?"

"I suppose it does. I'll have to get back to you on when. And where."

Jamie leaned back against the wall. In shock. In a million years she would never have believed this outcome. She moved quietly down the alley and slipped out the gate before Ree could see her. She kept going until she was around the corner from Santini's. Should she let Ree know she'd heard the conversation? Now that it was over, the guilt crept back in.

But she had to admit she wouldn't go back and change her decision if given the opportunity. It was about Sebastien, not Ree, though. What Ree and Angel did was their business. She'd love to know every detail, there was no denying that. But no matter if Ree confided in her or not, she had learned one important thing that made her less-than-aboveboard activities worth the risk: Sebastien was still in the matchmaking race.

Not that she believed anything romantic could ever possibly blossom between Angel and her best friend. She shook her head and absently finished off her forgotten apple. No way.

Jamie peeked around the corner and saw Ree's retreating back as she headed to the store. Jamie crossed the street and continued on her original course to the museum. She hoped Ree was okay. Perhaps finding some middle ground with Angel wouldn't be such a bad thing. For all her resilient demeanor, Ree also had a huge heart and it could be hurt. She'd endured far worse than Angel's verbal parries just growing up with a flamboyant mother like La Bamba. But Angel had somehow managed to penetrate that steel, perhaps because of the link to Edgar. Jamie wasn't sure.

What she was sure of was that Sebastien couldn't really take any credit here. Ree and Angel had already met before his appearance, and the reasons they were seeing each other now were also based in the past. Besides, declaring a truce of sorts was *not* the same as dating.

She tossed her apple core in the trash and stepped into the cool interior of the Cabildo. After talking with the docent, she headed toward the Cities of the Dead exhibit. New Orleans was well known for its above-ground cemeteries. The rows of white mausoleums did in fact look like a city in miniature. Jamie slowly walked through the photographic display. She stopped when she found the one the docent had guided her to.

"The burial site of Dominique You," she murmured.

"Yes. Sad he ended up here rather than with his compatriots, Pierre and Jean."

Jamie jumped at the deep voice in her ear, but she didn't spin around. Instead, she ground her teeth and ignored him. She made a mental note of the cemetery where the infamous right-hand man of Jean Laffite was buried, then she moved on toward the exit.

Sebastien's long-legs made it easy for him to match her pace without seeming to hurry. She forced herself not to run, though the urge was there. It would solve nothing.

The docent nodded at her and smiled like a mooning schoolgirl at Sebastien. Jamie nodded back tightly and rolled her eyes when Sebastien's wink made the older woman all but swoon. She walked back out into the morning sunshine.

Sebastien said nothing but kept pace beside her as she walked across the back side of Jackson Square toward her next destination. Then it occurred to her that she could hardly continue Operation Pirate with the damn pirate in question strolling along next to her. She stopped suddenly, taking small pleasure in the fact that he went on a step or two before realizing she was no longer beside him.

He turned back to her but still said nothing.

"Oh, for heaven's sake," she said, exasperated. "This is ridiculous."

"Taking a walk on a sunny day?"

"Don't be disingenuous. Your accent makes you too good at it." Jamie fought a smile when his grin surfaced. She would not let him charm her. Not after last night. "Why are you here? To gloat?" She knew that, somehow, Sebastien was aware of the little meeting that had just taken place. "Well, I wouldn't get too excited just yet. The only sparks that will fly between those two won't be sexual."

"Now who is being purposefully naive?"

Jamie propped her hands on her hips. "You? Those two may find a neutral zone, but only because Ree has decided to act like an adult, and a lady."

"When a man and woman strike sparks the way those two do, it is always sexual. At least in part."

"And this is the basis for your eternal matches? Sex?"

Sebastien laughed. "It is a good place to start, no?"

"Not in my personal history."

Sebastien sobered. "I'm sorry. I was not making light of your past wounds."

"Apology accepted." How did he do that? Always say just the right thing to defuse her defenses?

"There are more possibilities between them than sexual sparks," he said. "Just as Ree Ann has been underestimated by Monsieur Santini, there is more to Angel than you credit him with. I predict that this dinner will not be their only meeting."

"You know about the dinner? How? Spying on them?"

"*Non*. But apparently you were."

Jamie didn't need a mirror to know her cheeks were red. "I was merely checking up on a friend, making sure she didn't find herself in a situation she couldn't control."

"She asked for this support? A surprise. Mademoiselle Broussard strikes me as a woman who can control most situations."

"Okay, okay, I was spying. But my heart was in the right place. And I still say you can't take any credit for this . . . this . . . whatever it is. And it's not a relationship."

Sebastien merely raised his eyebrows. "I brought them back together again. I do not believe either one would have sought out the other without my guidance."

"An anonymous note. How original."

He shrugged. "Sometimes it takes only a small push to begin a great romance."

"Well, I don't see a romance, great or otherwise."

Sebastien smiled with full confidence. "Have patience. This is only the beginning."

Jamie jabbed a finger at his chest. "If Ree gets hurt because of this clown, I'll hunt you down. That's a promise."

Her threat didn't seem to concern him overly much. "I was under the impression I was already being hunted down."

Her cheeks were most definitely red now. She could only brazen her way through it. "I was taking in an exhibition. I happen to enjoy French Quarter history."

"Do you wish to see Dominique's grave? I can escort you there."

"The cemeteries aren't safe these days. Even during the day. And I don't need to see it."

"I agree. Why waste time on research when the best reference resource stands before you?"

"Perhaps I need confirmation from a source other than you."

"Ah. My mistress is still unconvinced."

"Yes, I am. And I'm not your mistress."

That shrug again.

Jamie sighed. "And that brings up another point. The Sword of Hearts."

Now he looked wary. "What of it?"

"Where is it? It's not your property. It belongs to Ree Ann."

"I am afraid I cannot return it to her as of yet."

"What did you do? Hock it for cash?"

He looked honestly offended. "I will not dignify that question with a response."

"Then how do you support yourself? You don't seem to have a job."

"I am very much employed. An eternal occupation, you might say."

Jamie looked to the sky, seeking patience, then back at him. "Okay, fine. Let's not go there. How do you support yourself? Other than getting Jack to feed you, you have no visible means of support."

"I also take offense to your characterization of my meals with your cousin. I have always taken care of the payment."

Which admittedly sounded just like Jack. "But you do admit to feeding him in order to pump him for information."

"I admit that it is a proven way to help me in my mission, yes. Jack meant no harm, and none will come to anyone for his revelations. Quite the opposite, I hope. What we discussed remains between us."

"You're avoiding my question."

"Which is? I've lost count."

"Very funny. The question was, how exactly do you

live? What do you do for income? Where do you stay when you're not haunting my every step?"

"You see me as a ghost?"

"I see you as a pain in the rear."

Surprisingly, he laughed. "No one will accuse you of tempering your true feelings with false niceties."

"As I said to you last night, I don't play games any longer. I find it best to get straight to the point."

"Then why don't you?"

Now it was her turn to be confused. "I believe I am."

"You set out today to research me, did you not?"

That stopped her for a moment, but she made the connection. "Oh, so you had breakfast with Jack this morning? I swear, when I get a hold of him—"

"Do not blame Jack. He thought he was doing you a favor. He merely told me you'd come to him, looking for me. I thought I'd save you the trouble of tracking me down."

"You thought you'd protect yourself by stopping me from tracking you down, you mean. You don't want me to find out what or who you really are."

"I have never told you less than the truth."

"But you've never told me everything either."

He spread his hands. "You have never asked."

"I'm asking now."

He said nothing but studied her closely. Jamie had no idea what was going on behind those dark eyes of his. He'd made no mention of what was said between them last night. She'd thought that when she saw him again she'd feel uncomfortable, at the very least. But she felt as she always did. Irritated, confused, and aware. All too aware.

He walked to her and held out his hand. "Come, then. And I will give you your answers."

Awareness leapt between them as his eyes met hers. The danger warning clanged loudly inside her head.

But once again her heart won the battle of wills. She wanted to know more about him. Had to know, if she was ever going to figure out what to do about him.

But she prided herself on at least being smart enough to ignore his hand and step past him. Touching him was definitely off-limits. She didn't need to know more about him to know that—she knew enough about herself.

"Okay." She swept her hand in front of her. "Lead on."

Chapter 13

*A*nother mistake. Sebastien was sure of it. He'd rarely, if ever, shown one of his masters his living quarters. Of course, no one had shown that much interest in him. Most of his masters, once they'd come to believe he was what he claimed to be, were interested only in what he could do for them. Jamie was different.

But, then, he knew that. Perhaps he'd known since that first night in the attic when she'd wielded the Sword of Hearts like a pirate queen, born with steel in her hand.

He led her to the small town house he'd rented for his current stay. It was at the residential end of Bourbon, only a few blocks away from the bookshop. It didn't look like much from the outside. It wasn't much more exciting on the inside. His demands for creature comforts were minimal. His indulgences had little to do with decor.

"Here?"

"You were perhaps expecting a mystical cave requiring a secret password in order to enter?"

She blushed but laughed. "Not entirely. I just wasn't expecting anything this . . . ordinary. Guess the open-sesame thing I was practicing won't be necessary."

Sebastien smiled but forced his gaze away from hers.

He was very attracted to the way the light danced in her eyes when she laughed. Too attracted. He unlocked the gate leading to the courtyard and rear entrance.

Jamie stopped just inside the courtyard and turned slowly. "This is beautiful."

Several trees along the outer walls provided shade. Gardens filled with portulaca and greenery dotted the edges of the tiled interior. There were ferns and pots of bougainvillea and impatiens spilling from the arched gallery openings on both the first and second floors.

Sebastien glanced over the lush vegetation. "I can't take credit for it; it was here when I rented the place. It rather tends to itself. A bit ungainly." He turned and grinned at her. "But I've always been one to enjoy abundance."

"A gross understatement, I'm sure," she said dryly.

Sebastien laughed, but he didn't miss the fleeting expression of discomfort on her face. She might want him to believe that being here with him wasn't affecting her personally, that she was merely an observer, here to obtain information about him. But he knew different.

He'd changed things last night. He would have to work hard to put that behind them and reassure her that he was quite in control of himself now and that she had no reason to fear he'd make any untoward advances.

Even if he didn't quite believe it himself.

He motioned to the wrought-iron table and chairs arranged by a small water fountain. "Why don't you have a seat and I'll go prepare something to drink as we talk. Are you hungry?"

This time the momentary flash in her eyes discomfitted him. Pleasurably so. He stepped away and turned toward the loggia. "I'll prepare some cheese and crackers."

"That's not necessary," she said. "I'm fine, really."

Sebastien was already retreating. Not running, precisely, just taking the wisest course of action. "I'll return momentarily. Make yourself comfortable."

"Would you like some help?"

He paused then and looked back. She was clearly disappointed not to be invited in. Her curiosity all but filled the air between them—the air that wasn't already humming with other, more-vibrant sensations.

He was tempted to invite her in. For some reason it was vital to him that she believe fully in him and what he truly was. If he were honest with himself, he'd admit it went deeper than merely advancing his cause with her to fulfill his obligations. It bothered him that she was so resistant to believing in him.

It was an issue of trust. And that disconcerted him most of all. For the last thing he'd ever expected from a woman was trust. And why should she trust him? In his extended life he'd always sampled freely from life's bounty. His loyalty was to the cause, whether it was with the Laffite brothers or his matching of souls. Never to something as fleeting as the pleasures one could find with a woman. Which was why he generally dallied with women who preferred a similar arrangement. Neat, tidy, and mutually satisfying. Trust and loyalty never entered into it.

Until now.

Her charms commanded his attention in ways he'd never anticipated. Which brought up the matter of having her in such close proximity to himself. This courtyard was intimate but not nearly as private as the interior. Given that, it was wise to answer her questions while keeping her at a distance. Perhaps their talk today would enlighten him as well, help him find some logic in the surge of emotions he was feeling.

"I can manage," he said. "Look around if you'd like." He forced a smile in the face of her obvious disappointment. "Why don't you formulate your questions? I'll answer them all as soon as I return."

"I have them all lined up." She smiled sweetly. "And yes, you will."

He left, smiling to himself. She was quite the match. A beguiling sauciness underscored with that thread of uncertainty that always caught him so off guard. This should be interesting. Very interesting.

≈

Jamie nosed around the small burbling fountain while waiting for Sebastien to return. There were several fat koi meandering lazily through the water. Her thoughts weren't on them, however. She was none too happy at being held at bay out here. She was dying to see the inside of the small row house. How would it be decorated? Was he a slob or did he tend toward the compulsive? Did he have any memorabilia of his supposed former life? Tables and mantels cluttered with plundered antiquities?

Or, worse, would the interior only prove that he was a regular guy, with dirty socks strewn about, men's magazines in the bathroom, and some delusional problems he kept swept under the rug?

Maybe it's better to stay out here, after all. Which meant she wanted answers but only if they were the ones she wanted to hear.

Then he was back, looking incredibly male in his pleated trousers and white linen shirt. The cuffs were rolled up, exposing tanned forearms with crisp curls of black hair sprinkled lightly over them. She wondered briefly if he had hair on his chest, then immediately yanked her thoughts away as she found her eyes drifting speculatively in that direction.

She half-rose to take the tray from his hands, but he shook his head and lowered the platter to the table. Two icy glasses of lemonade and a small plate of cheese and crackers, along with a small bowl of sugar and some napkins, filled the tray.

"I wasn't sure if you liked your lemonade tart or sweet," he said, explaining the sugar bowl.

"No sugar for me, thanks."

"Tart, then," he said with a smile. "Like your tongue."

Now, why did he have to go and say words like *tongue*? Didn't he know what kind of images that would instigate in her way-too-fertile brain?

It was all the jungle flora in this courtyard, she decided. Way too earthy. Perhaps being alone with him like this had been another tactical error on her part.

She studiously focused her attention on taking her glass and a napkin. She could feel the heat of his smile like a ray of sunshine beating down on the top of her head, but she resolutely refused to look up. She went about choosing her cheese and crackers as if it were a life-and-death decision.

And perhaps it was. She hadn't felt such a moment of consequence since she'd made the decision to leave racing.

He settled across from her. "What would you like to discuss first?"

Jamie decided she'd question him from the stance that he was what he claimed to be. Perhaps he'd slip up. Perhaps not. She wasn't sure which result she'd rather have, but she didn't have to worry about that right now.

"Where do you go when you're not here?" She waved a hand toward the town house.

"It depends on what my goals are for the day. Some days I spend doing research, some days—"

"No, you misunderstood me. I mean when you're not here—as in, on earth. Alive. Living, breathing. Where are you between assignments, as it were?"

"Ah." He leaned back and rested his icy glass on his

knee, heedless of the trickles of water sliding onto his trousers. "I'm not sure I can explain that to your satisfaction."

She smiled. "Try."

"I do not have any real cognizance of when I'm not here. It is as if, when I complete my work, I go to sleep."

"And you wake up when the next person draws the sword?"

"*Oui.*"

"So when the final match is made, what do you do? Go poof?"

"Not exactly. I retrieve the sword and present it to my master. Or mistress. Once they take hold of it, I disappear. Much in the manner I appeared before you when you drew the blade out."

"And if that same person draws the sword again?"

He shook his head. "I will not appear. You can summon me only once." He shrugged. "Beyond that, I do not know much of how or why the curse works. Only that it does."

"Wait. You're saying you don't even know the rules?"

"I can only explain my existence. When I am here, I am as human as you are. I do not feel as if any special powers have been bestowed on me." He smiled and lifted his shoulders. "Perhaps doors always seem unlocked to my touch—" He lifted a hand to stall her question. "I conduct myself as a gentleman always, mademoiselle."

"A gentleman who takes pleasure in giving me a heart attack by popping up unexpectedly. But at least I can stop locking the bathroom door now when I shower. Why bother, right?"

His eyes glittered with amusement.

Jamie glared back at him, not at all comfortable with the direction in which this was headed. "So that's it?"

"I seem to have a heightened awareness of when two people belong together. Perhaps my powers of persuasion are more highly developed." He grinned. "My rate of success speaks for that."

"So you've never failed?"

He held her direct gaze. "Never."

Jamie took a sip of lemonade but found it difficult to swallow. He was far too confident, and she was well aware that she was next on his list. She shook that off. It wasn't like she believed this. Not really.

"Some matches take longer to make than others," he conceded. "But every match I have made endured until death claimed one, the other, or both." He lifted a shoulder. "And who can say of their afterlife together, yes?"

"Do you check up on them? When you come back?"

"*Mais oui*. This time it has been somewhat more difficult, in that my time away was much longer than ever before. It is more usual for months to elapse, occasionally a year or so, but this time it was decades. Edgar must have tucked the sword away so safely that no one ever came across it during the remainder of his lifetime."

"Yes, he did. I suppose at one time he lived in the building he left to Ree, but no one had lived there for some time. I guess none of the people he leased it to ever snooped around."

Sebastien grinned. "Unlike you."

He had an uncanny way of making her blush. She couldn't recall ever having that particular problem before. When she was with him it was almost a chronic condition. "Yes, well, I think we've already discussed my love for buried treasure."

The sudden flash in Sebastien's eyes was far too intimate for her comfort. The sense of connection she felt with him at times bordered on the spooky. She turned her attention to the cheese and crackers, and back to the conversation as well. "So, how many couples would you say you've matched up?"

"Hundreds."

She choked on her bite of cracker but forced it down. "Hundreds?"

"That is a fair assessment, *oui*." He said it matter-of-factly, without false modesty or arrogance.

This whole conversation wasn't doing much to re-assure her. Yet. "Is it unusual for a woman to summon you?"

"It is true I have had far more masters, but you are not my first mistress."

"I imagine you enjoyed those . . . liaisons." She'd meant to sound wry, but it had come out a tad more accusing than she'd hoped.

"I have found some pleasure in each of my summons." He sat forward, looking more closely at her. "Ah, that is not what you meant. I see. Well, perhaps I can set your mind at ease. Just as I do not bed those I am destined to match, I do not dally with those who mistress me."

Jamie wanted to ask him what in the hell last night had been all about, then. She was both mistress and match. But she wasn't ready to go there. She did real-ize, however, that this was exactly why she was here to-day. To make some sense of what he'd said last night. To make sense of her attraction to him, a man who was so completely wrong for her that even she could see it. And to make sense of his attraction to her, a woman he'd made it clear—in more ways than her ego specifically required—he would never normally "dally" with.

Sebastien had apparently taken her rejection rather easily, since he'd had no problems reverting back to a more platonic mode with her. She had only herself to blame for being so ridiculously disappointed. After all, she'd told him no way, no how.

"Yes, well, I can see where 'dallying' could complicate things." She hurried on. "So is your mistress or master always one of your matches?"

"Many times, to be certain, but no, not always. In fact, I recall one elderly mistress of mine. Arabella DuPrais. Delightful woman. Very witty. She had me match up her three grandchildren." He grimaced. "They weren't so delightful."

Jamie found herself laughing. "So I'm not alone in being less than overjoyed at the prospect of being saddled with someone for life?"

He tilted his head and studied her in that disconcerting way of his, but only said, "These particular souls had been searching for their mates for some time. Let us just say there were some obvious reasons why their attempts were not meeting with success. Some souls must overcome many obstacles before their mates can be found."

He shifted his attention to the crackers and cheese, and Jamie took advantage and studied him. If this were merely a role he was playing, he was a brilliant actor. Of course, if he were merely delusional, then he truly believed he was his character. Either way, his role was picture-perfect—and very convincing. Her forehead began to throb.

Sebastien shifted his gaze to hers, catching her unaware. She didn't look away. "You still do not believe."

She shook her head, then shrugged. "Honestly, I don't know what to believe." She tried for a laugh, but it came out sounding a bit hollow. "You have to admit you're asking for a lot. I suppose everyone else just leapt at the opportunity to have their own personal genie and didn't bother to ask questions?"

"No, you are not the first unbeliever. As long as I can get my masters and mistresses to name their souls for matching, it is not imperative that they believe."

"But most end up believing, don't they?" She knew the answer before he nodded. "So why do you care what I believe?"

Now it was his turn to shrug. "I have asked myself that. Many times. The logical response is that, because you are one of my matches, it is to my benefit to have your assistance."

"But that's not why?"

"It is part of it, to be sure."

Jamie's muscles tightened up and she sat her glass back on the table. That inescapable magnetism was heavy in the air between them. She wanted to back away, to shift the conversation to some other path. A path without her right in the middle of it. But maybe that was the real problem. Maybe it was time to be done with it, one way or the other.

"And the rest of it?" she asked. "Why do you really care?"

He sat his glass down as well. "Do you really wish to discuss this?"

"No," she answered honestly. "But I think maybe we'd better."

"The rest of it is this: I am attracted to you. I told you this last night."

A shiver of excitement that was totally unacceptable raced over her skin. Foolish. "You also told me you couldn't figure out why in the world you were." She raised her hand to stall his response. "But you're telling me this has never happened before?"

He held her gaze captive. "Not like this."

Her ego had taken a beating last night. That one sentence made up for almost all of it. Her throat worked, but it remained dry. "And what . . . what is 'this'?"

"Attraction is usually a fleeting thing, a physical thing. For me, anyway. If the woman is unattainable for some reason, I generally don't waste time pursuing her. I find another . . . distraction to meet my needs."

Jamie tried hard to ignore the images of Sebastien distracting himself with someone else. They flooded her brain anyway. And she discovered she really didn't like them at all. Not a good sign.

"And yet, this time . . ." He paused, then raised his hands helplessly. "I cannot seem to find a suitable distraction."

Jamie wasn't sure what to say to that. She knew what her body wanted to say. Her body wanted to fling itself across the table, into his lap, and tell him to dissipate his tension at will. And at great length.

"I—I—"

Sebastien lifted his hand to silence her. Which was good, since she had no idea what would have come out of her mouth just then.

"I will not pursue this attraction I feel for you. It cannot be. For many reasons. Not the least of which is my responsibility to find your match. I apologize again for not keeping this disturbing development under my own counsel."

"Out of curiosity, what would happen to you if we . . . you know, dallied." Had she really asked that? When his eyes flared and her body reacted accordingly, she wished she could've retracted the question.

"I've never become involved in any way with any of my mistresses or matches. Initially that was more by chance. I do not know what would happen if I did, only that I feel it is wrong. It is not my purpose."

"And just how do you know what your purpose is? I mean, you seem awfully accepting of this eternal curse of yours, you know?"

"Perhaps I was not all that accepting at first," he

said, his tone sharper. "But then I came to realize that as curses go, this one is fairly bearable. It is, in a sense, immortality. Have you not wondered what will become of people, of places, of things, beyond your lifetime? Because of this 'curse,' as you call it, I have been able to discover this."

"Of course, I think we all wonder what the future will be like, but it couldn't have been that simple for you."

"I never said it was a simple matter."

"Then tell me, that day you were cursed . . . well, what happened, how? When did you know your fate? Did someone explain it to you, or did you just appear the first time someone pulled the sword out and know in your gut you had to match three souls?" She was bullying him a little, but maybe she was doing it more for herself. A last-ditch effort to break through his facade, if this was one. Hadn't she set out today to find out, one way or another, just what and who he really was?

"These are not simple questions with simple answers."

She leaned back, terrified of what she might be about to hear, and yet she knew she had no choice. The look in his eyes was as steady as ever. But was there a warning there as well? Had she gone too far, pushed too hard? "In all this time, certainly someone has doubted you before."

"Perhaps once or twice. You would be surprised how unquestioning people can be when their good fortune is at hand."

"Well, you already know how I feel about my 'good fortune.'"

Now he sighed and leaned forward. "Jamie, perhaps it would be best if you simply—"

"Answer my questions, Sebastien. I want to understand."

When he spoke, his tone was expressionless. "Oriane was the one to place the curse, and it was she who explained, as she cursed me, what my fate was to be." He lifted a hand when Jamie opened her mouth. "If you wish to hear this tale, then you must let me tell it in my own way. If you still have queries when I am finished, you can question me further."

It wasn't until that moment that it occurred to Jamie how selfish her badgering was. He was always so charming and gallant, it was easy to believe that there was nothing dark in his life, that he was truly as affable and upbeat about his eternal fate as he seemed to be on the surface. "If what I'm asking will churn up painful memories . . . I'm sorry, Sebastien. I wasn't thinking."

"I am not concerned about the pain, Jamie. I don't see why the specifics of my past should matter, but obviously they do to you."

Jamie felt a shiver run down her spine.

"I do not recall what happened in the moments after Oriane cast her spell. She held the sword and muttered an incantation over it, and . . . the next thing I knew, I was floating in darkness. I heard her voice telling me what my mission was, what I was bound for all eternity to do." He stopped and sipped his lemonade. Staring at the glass, he continued. "I was not easily accepting of my fate. When I was first summoned, I was quite recalcitrant." A smile played at his lips. "I had cavorted with privateers most of my young life. We were not, in general, an acquiescent bunch.

"I quickly learned there would be no answers to my endless queries. My first match happened almost by accident. My master and I were out carousing in the Quarter, and, while in his cups, he told me the sad tale of the love of his life. Not thinking about my fate but rather happy to be alive at all, I laughingly told him a simple solution to his woes. He followed my guidance and was reunited with his love. I witnessed this reunion and I . . . I . . ." He shook his head, as if not believing his own story.

"What?"

He looked at her then. "I felt indescribable joy. It cannot be properly explained. It wasn't ownership of their love or even a sense of victory that I'd helped guide them to each other. It was . . . An epiphany perhaps is the best way to describe it, that Oriane's chosen fate for me was indeed real. Not that I didn't test it. I did, repeatedly, especially in the beginning. But I eventually learned, through a rather torturous trial-and-error period, that it was better for all, most especially myself, if I embraced my rather unusual future. I had plenty of time to contemplate it, and when it became obvious that there was no escaping it, I found it was easier to make peace with it rather than rail against it. After all, it was a far better one that I was likely headed for with my former compatriots."

"Did you miss the life you had with them? You said they were your only family."

"It wasn't the first time that I lost my family, Jamie. And we all had a rather fatalistic view of life. It went with the occupation." He said it simply, but there was a depth of emotion in his eyes she had never seen before. He was sparing her the darker details, she knew that. But because he was likely also sparing himself, she let it rest.

"You've never been tempted to find a way to end it?"

"You mean end my life? *Non*. That is for cowards. I will meet my final fate, whatever it shall be, straight on." He stood. "I have truly come to accept my life. It is not such a bad fate as all that, mademoiselle. You needn't look so sad."

Jamie hadn't been aware of her expression, but she

stood as well. Apparently their discussion was over. She'd never seen him quite this intense. "You really believe in what you are doing, don't you?"

He spread his hands, a beseeching look on his face. "*Mais oui.* That joy I mentioned—it is truly without description. But what I didn't add was that it is also addictive. Every time it is the same. Perhaps greater, though I can never imagine it to be. It is an honorable fate for one who led perhaps a not so honorable life, is it not? Perhaps one I did not deserve, but it is one I now embrace." He came around the table and stood just before her. "You need not believe, Jamie. I will do my duty regardless."

She looked up into his eyes. "I want to believe," she said. She had never been more sincere. "I want to."

He took her hand and raised it to his lips, pressing a warm kiss to the back of it before letting it go. "Then that will have to be enough. I will do my best to find you a match unlike any other. You deserve happiness, Jamie. I will see that you have it."

She wanted to shout that she didn't want anyone else. Correction. Anyone. That *else* made it sound dangerously as if she was about to say she wanted only him.

That wasn't going to happen. For so many reasons it was foolish to even contemplate it any longer, even fleetingly.

"I don't wish a match for myself," she said quietly. "Can I choose someone else for the third match? I mean, you win the bet. Pirate genie or not, it's clear that Marta is happy, and Ree—well, that remains to be seen. I still can't believe those two will have a romance, but then I never believed they could have a civil conversation and that's happened. So who knows."

"I cannot change what has begun," he said. "The choices have been made."

"But I didn't choose me. You did."

"Ah, but you agreed." He pushed some wayward strands of hair behind her ear. "You will have happiness, Jamie. I promise you."

"I already have happiness. Maybe for the first time ever. I'm better alone. I have my friends, my family, and a business that is challenging. And, most importantly, time to enjoy them all."

"And maybe because you have finally found your own happiness, you are ready to truly share it with another."

Jamie dipped her chin. "I don't know. I haven't had much reason to believe in that."

He lifted her chin and smiled into her eyes. "I will give you that reason. Believe me, Jamie."

And, in that moment, looking into his eyes, she did.

God help her, she did.

Chapter 14

The final numbers for our first month are pretty good." Marta handed printouts to both Ree and Jamie.

Ree sipped her coffee and looked carefully over the numbers. "These do look good." She smiled over the top of the sheaf of papers. "We're a hit, girlfriends."

"Hey, was there ever any doubt?" Jamie tossed her papers on the table after barely skimming them. She was great at mechanics and intricate design plans, but columns of numbers made her eyes swim. If Marta said they were doing well, that was good enough for her.

Marta smiled at Ree. She smiled a great deal more these days. "If we keep this up through the fall, we might be able to start making payments back to you by January. Spring at the latest."

Ree laid the papers down, already shaking her head. "I'd rather reinvest any profit back into the store. I'm doing just fine. We'll worry about paying me back later. For now my regular paycheck is enough."

Jamie knew, as did Marta, that Ree had long ago started building a portfolio. She'd made mostly modest investments but had also taken occasional risks, some of which had paid off pretty well. A chunk of that, along with Edgar leaving her this property, had made the store possible.

Jamie had stockpiled some of her winnings for that proverbial rainy day, most of which she'd used for her share of the start-up costs of the store. Marta had some of the insurance money from Dan's death set aside, which she'd put up as her share. But they'd agreed—or Marta and Jamie had—to pay Ree back two thirds of the store's market value as the shop made money. Jamie was already making payments to her for the upper levels.

"I keep meaning to ask you for some investment advice," Jamie said, then grinned. "But first I need to invest in a few other things. Like furniture."

"Just let me know when you're ready, sugar." She laughed. "I had a similar discussion with Jack."

Marta rolled her eyes. "He hasn't even started an IRA yet, much less a savings account big enough to bankroll a foray into the stock market."

Both Jamie and Ree laughed. It was true. Jack was amazingly adept at living off the kindness of others, but to his credit, he was willing to part with just about anything he had—even his paycheck—for those in need. And he often did.

"He's pathetically softhearted," Jamie said. "I'm pretty sure it's chronic, with no hope for a cure."

"Well, I'm not done working my wiles on him yet," Ree said, wagging her expertly sculpted eyebrows.

They all laughed. "If anyone can persuade him to a life of fiscal responsibility, you can," Jamie agreed.

Jamie studied her friend. Ree's visit to Angel had been only yesterday, but Ree hadn't mentioned the meeting or their prospective meal. Jamie had thought to keep her little spying foray to herself, but she was already busting to talk the whole thing over. Despite Sebastien's claims to a one hundred percent success rate, Jamie wasn't buying Angel's sudden about-face. There had to be a hidden agenda there.

She didn't want to bring it up in front of Marta. Not until she'd had a chance to talk to Ree. Marta was no fan of Angel's either, and Jamie didn't want Ree to feel as if they were ganging up on her.

Marta collected the papers into a messy stack and shoved her glasses back onto her nose as she stood. "I have to run over to Fred's and do his books, then make a quick stop at Bennett's. He's having problems figuring out his quarterly taxes. But I'll be back after lunch."

"Lunching with Bennett?" Ree asked with a knowing smile.

Jamie thoroughly enjoyed Marta's flushed cheeks.

Marta lifted her chin and tried to look innocent. "We plan to grab a bite or two, yes."

"Just don't forget to grab some food when you're done," Ree said.

Marta shocked them both by smiling slyly and saying, "Dating a man who sets his own hours does have its advantages." Then she turned and headed for the office, leaving her friends with their mouths hanging open.

Ree recovered first. "Well, I'll be damned." She clapped her hands together. "I honestly thought I'd never see the day when Marta would realize she's not a little mouse. Even with Dan she was pretty quiet and self-effacing." She grinned at Jamie. "I might have to move up my bet on the wedding date."

"Hey, let them be happy for a while before you sling the chains on them, okay?"

"Not everyone thinks of marriage as slavery, Jamie Lynne."

Jamie just looked at her friend. "And you are speaking from what experience?"

Ree laughed and waved her hand. "Okay, okay. But just because I've never envisioned myself tied to a man for life doesn't mean I can't appreciate the joy in such a union—for someone else."

Jamie caught the barest hint of envy in those last words. It was as good an opening as she was likely to get. She cleared her throat. "Listen . . . um . . . I have a confession to make."

Ree's eyes lit up and she slapped her palms on the table. "Oh, my God! Don't tell me. You and Sebastien—"

Jamie cut her off. "Not even. No, no, that wasn't what I was going to say."

Ree slumped back in her chair. "Shoot. You were looking so guilty I thought for sure it was going to be something good and juicy. Well, what is this big confession?"

Jamie took a breath and blurted the truth out. "I sort of spied on you. Yesterday, when you went to see Angel."

Ree's mouth hung open.

"I didn't mean to, really. I saw you when I was coming back from my run, and I was just about to call out to you when you ducked into the alley leading to Santini's courtyard." She raised her hand when Ree lifted an eyebrow and gave her a look. "I know, I know, I had no right snooping. I was just—" She stopped. "Okay, so I have no defense. I was shocked to see you there and I just couldn't walk away. I'm really sorry."

Ree reached over and patted her hand. "It's okay, sugar." At Jamie's dubious look, she smiled and added, "In the same situation, I'd have probably done the same thing."

Jamie breathed a sigh of relief, glad she'd come clean. "What compelled you to go there? He sent a note, I heard, but why respond?"

Now it was Ree's turn to shrug and look uncom-

fortable. "I really don't know. I can say I was just being polite and returning the favor. Even though I
wasn't the one to invite him here in the first place."

"But?"

Ree paused, then blew out a disgusted sigh. "But I
was curious, okay?"

"About what? The guy is cold and heartless and
thinks only of himself."

"I don't know, Jamie. Something about the way he
looked at me when he came here that day . . ." She
shrugged again. "I can't explain it, really. He just . . .
caught my attention, I guess."

"Uh-oh."

Ree narrowed her eyes. "Don't 'uh-oh' me, missy.
After all, you're the one seeing a delusional guy who
thinks he's a genie or something."

Jamie's own cheeks heated. "Touché, touché. But
Ree, we *know* for a fact Angel is not a nice man. And
the 'uh-oh' was because I'm worried that you're interested in him only because he's not your typical
conquest."

Ree arched one slender brow. "I beg your pardon?"

"No, listen. He assumes the worst about you, slan-
ders you all over the place, then months later he
strolls in all enigmatic-like and hints that you've gotten his attention. What I want to know is, if you
wanted his attention, then why didn't you set him
straight on what kind of person you really are back
during the will probate?"

"I had no interest in explaining myself then. Nor
do I now. And it's not some kind of revenge fantasy
here, where I get him to fall for me so I can ditch
him."

"Then what is it? Why did you agree to have dinner
with him?"

Ree studied her manicure. "He wants to know more

about Edgar. I think he's sincere. Edgar always felt bad about the falling out between them, and I feel responsible in a way. I mean, it was because of me."

"No, it was because Angel is an ass. You have no responsibility to him."

She looked up at Jamie. "But I do to Edgar. And I want Angel to know what kind of man he truly was, Jamie. As for the rest . . . I don't know."

That got Jamie's attention. "What do you mean, 'I don't know'? Ree, you can't be seriously attracted to that louse."

"I'm not saying I am." She shoved back the chair and stood. "But I'm not saying I'm not. Listen, Jamie, I don't know what's going on, okay? I'm just having dinner with him. It's not a crime. I wouldn't have told you about it for just this reason. I'll probably never see the man after next Friday."

"Friday?"

"Well, now the cat's out, isn't it." She sighed. "No following me, okay?"

Jamie pretended to look offended. "I wasn't actually following you yesterday."

Ree took Jamie's hands in her own. "I don't know what's going on with all this, okay?" she said quietly. "I just know I have to figure it out on my own. Do you understand?"

What Jamie understood was that Sebastien had somehow managed to work his magic. Again. All she could do was nod. "I just don't want you to be hurt. And I think Angel is capable of administering a world of hurt, you know?"

Ree nodded, then hugged Jamie quickly. "Thanks for loving me like you do, Jamie. I'll be fine. If anyone can take care of her heart, it's La Bamba's little girl."

And if anyone can find a way to make you lose that heart to Angel, it's Sebastien, Jamie thought. "Will you promise to at least give me the highlights?"

Ree smiled and nodded. "Now I've got to scoot up to the market. Sally promised me her sweet-potato cookie recipe this morning."

Jamie made a face. "There should be a law banning vegetables from bakery products."

Ree laughed. "You wait until you taste them. You'll be in heaven, sugar, I promise." She waved and sailed out of the shop, leaving Jamie to wonder just what was in store for her friend.

Which was a far more interesting—not to mention safe—topic to ponder than her own burgeoning relationship.

Relationship. There was no relationship. Except perhaps for an unusual friendship.

After they parted yesterday, she'd decided to stop worrying about whether to believe Sebastien was what he claimed to be and just accept his temporary residence in her life. She'd even decided to step back and not interfere with this new twist of events between Ree and Angel.

However, she wasn't all that blasé about the idea that Sebastien would now be coming after her with his matchmaking schemes.

Well, just because Sebastien was about to throw whoever he deemed the perfect man in her path, it didn't mean she had to fall at his feet. She'd make her own decisions.

Feeling only slightly more confident, Jamie went outside to open the window shutters and set about opening the shop for the day. She was rearranging the window display when her first customer walked in.

He was an attractive man in a nicely tailored suit. He offered her a sunny smile. "Would you by any chance carry out-of-town newspapers? I'm looking for *The Washington Post*."

Jamie stepped down from the window and motioned to the rack near the door. "As a matter of fact we do. We also have *The New York Times* and *The Wall Street Journal*."

"Thanks. I'm just looking for the *Post*." He shrugged in a way that was totally endearing. "A bit homesick, I guess."

Jamie found herself smiling. "Here on business?"

He scooped up the paper and headed to the counter. "Actually, no. I just moved here. I'm working for some law offices over on Canal, but I'm renting a place here in the Quarter. At least for the time being."

"You don't like the Quarter?" She heard the light, flirty tone in her voice. So what? When Sebastien had touched her yesterday, it made her feel all sorts of things that had nothing to do with platonic friendships. Maybe a little harmless diversion would help get her head back on straight.

"No, I like it very much. I'd like to buy something, though, make it a more permanent deal. But I want the time to scout around a bit, make sure I pick the right place." He paid for the paper but didn't seem in any hurry to leave. "Maybe you could show me around sometime. I'd be glad to toss in lunch or dinner." He grinned. "Or both."

Jamie had her mouth open to say, "Sure, why not," when sudden suspicion clouded her mind. He was cute, endearing, employed, and single. And he was taller than she was as well, making her feel all feminine and flirty. *Danger, danger!* Her eyes narrowed. "You haven't by any chance met someone by the name of Sebastien, have you?"

Surprised by her less-than-conciliatory tone, his smiled faded. "Uh, no. Not that I can recall."

"Think harder. He's a bit taller than you, wide shoulders, long dark hair. Has a French accent? Very charming."

The man was backing up now, clutching his paper under his arm. "No, really, I don't think so. Listen, I have to dash. It was nice talking to you." He all but barreled into Ree as he pushed through the door.

Ree laughed and squeezed past the man as he mumbled a hurried apology and took off down Royal. "Whoa, sugar. Why'd you chase that one off? He looked prime."

Jamie scowled and folded her arms. "Exactly. Sebastien sent him. I'm sure of it."

"So?"

Jamie slammed her hand down on the counter. "So? So I don't want to be all handily matched up, thank you very much."

Now Ree folded her arms. "Oh, and I suppose you think Marta and I are brainless twits or something?"

Instantly contrite, Jamie calmed down. "I didn't say that. Marta is blissfully happy, and you know I'm thrilled for her. What you and Angel do is none of my business either. I'm just saying I'm not in the mood to do the whole relationship thing. I'm still enjoying my freedom."

"I think you're already doing the relationship thing. I also think you don't want to be matched up with someone else because you're already enjoying the match you're in."

"He is not my match," Jamie said staunchly.

"But you want him to be," Ree said knowingly.

"It doesn't matter. It won't work, and even I have learned enough to know better than to pursue something as obviously wrong as any kind of relationship with him."

Ree dropped the sly look and instead appeared concerned. "You're not starting to believe the man is really . . . you know."

Jamie sighed. "Ree, I don't know what to believe,

and all I've decided to do is to stop thinking about it. But no matter what is going on, he's not right for me."

"Sugar, he doesn't have to be Mr. Right to be Mr. Right Now. I know that better than anyone."

"Yeah, well, if I want a Mr. Right Now, I'll take someone like that poor guy I just scared off. Cute but harmless."

Ree laughed. "Sugar, what is the fun in that?"

Jamie resolutely turned her back on her friend and went back to arranging the window display. "I just want to have control over who I see or don't see. That's all."

"No one has taken that away from you."

Jamie turned back to her. "That's just it. Knowing he's out there trying to fix me up is going to make me a neurotic mess. Every time I go to accept a date, I'll wonder, you know?"

Ree lifted her hands. "So? If you like the guy, who cares why he came into your life? What you do about it is still up to you. Right?"

Jamie grumbled, "I suppose. I just don't like feeling manipulated."

Ree came closer and patted Jamie's arm. "Sugar, you've grown up an awful lot since you and Steve divorced. I honestly don't think you'd ever let yourself be manipulated by a man again. Maybe you ought to examine the real truth here."

Jamie pulled her arm out of Ree's reach. "Which is?"

Ree moved around behind the bar and started setting up shop. "I think you don't like the idea that Sebastien wants to fix you up with someone other than himself. I think maybe you'd like it if he were a bit more possessive."

"That's ridiculous. I already told you we are totally unsuited. And if I learned so much from my failed marriages, then the very last guy I should be pursuing is Sebastien Valentin, pirate genie."

Jamie felt ridiculous just saying that out loud.

"Yeah, but he's such a cute pirate genie." Ree smiled enigmatically and turned back to her duties.

Jamie couldn't help but think about what Ree had said. Had she started to develop feelings for Sebastien beyond her infatuation with his sexy looks and swarthy confidence? Was she really upset about getting set up because she didn't want him manipulating her life—or was she hurt because he could so easily hand her off to someone else after claiming he was attracted to her himself?

Her forehead began to throb again. This was too much. She had to stop thinking about it all and just live her life. Right now she was interested only in working the shop and continuing to set up her new life. She had furniture to shop for and a model boat to work on. She scowled as thoughts of the pirate-ship model only led to thoughts about Sebastien. Perhaps she'd ditch her plans and do a schooner or something. Or maybe something completely different. "Like a Chinese junk."

"What was that?"

Jamie turned to find another customer standing at the counter. She'd been so lost in her thoughts she hadn't heard the bell on the door. This customer was blond and wearing khaki shorts, but otherwise he was a carbon copy of her first customer.

"Hi," he said with an inviting grin. "How are you today?"

"Fine. But I'm not going out with you, so don't even ask," she snapped.

His smile faded. "I—I just wanted to buy this book." He tentatively slid a popular *Times* list hardcover on to the counter. "I'm married."

"Oh, for heaven's sake," Jamie muttered. She was

losing her sanity. Red-faced, she rang up the sale and offered the man a smile. "I'm sorry, it's been a long morning. Please visit us again."

The guy smiled a bit unevenly and hurried out the door. Jamie was certain they'd never see him again.

Ree walked up behind her and put her hand on Jamie's shoulder. "Sugar, why don't you go in the back and handle the stock. I'll watch the counter. We're not in the black yet and you're scaring off the customers."

"Ha ha ha." But Jamie took her friend's advice and wandered to the back storage room. She had to do something. She had to see him again, somehow convince him to change the deal. Whatever it took, she had to get him to agree to leave her alone.

She had to get him to understand that it would be best if they never saw each other again.

Chapter 15

Sebastien sipped his wine and looked over the dinner menu. Santini's had a wonderful ambience. Small, intimate booths ran along both walls, with round tables for larger parties filling the interior. The decor was dark, plush, and comfortable. They took no reservations and filled up every night. The clientele was made up almost entirely of locals. All in all, a very successful operation.

Sebastien wondered if Angel knew how much of his initial success he owed to Ree Ann. He kept the menu in front of his face but sat at an angle that allowed him to keep an eye on the door. Ree hadn't shown up yet, and he expected Angel to take her to a private dining room once she was here. But Sebastien intended to stick around as long as possible. There was much he could learn from her face when she departed later.

If she departed at all.

He smiled to himself, imagining how stinging Jamie's retort to that thought would have been, had she been privy to it. He was well aware that she could not comprehend the attraction between Angel and Ree. But he could. He had felt the pent-up energy emanating from Angel the day he'd left the shop. Just as he could feel the same bottled-up need in Ree.

He'd done his research on Angel. Yes, the man had behaved appallingly toward Ree Ann. But Sebastien had discovered this was not typical of the way he treated others in his life. His employees—the ones Sebastien had managed to befriend—were consistent in their comments on his fairness and good managing style. His acquaintances murmured about his quiet philanthropy. Even the women he'd dated briefly—and none had been long-term—had nothing negative to say about the man. Except for the lack of his ring on their fingers.

Ree Ann, then, had been the only person to really shake him up. Sebastien saw this as a very good sign.

Like Ree, Angel had also proved to have an excellent eye for business. With Ree's guidance, Edgar had rescued the restaurant from near financial ruin, then turned it over to Angel. Angel had taken the reins and steered Santini's to an even greater success than Edgar could have imagined.

It was a pity the two had never reconciled, Sebastien thought. Both were stubborn, but Angel wasn't nearly as narrow-minded as his actions seemed to dictate. During the probate process, his behavior had been largely influenced by his own sense of failure where Edgar was concerned. There was also a personal history involving his parents that Sebastien hadn't been entirely successful in uncovering. But he knew it was somehow responsible for Angel's uncharacteristic attack on Ree that had caused the original rift with Edgar.

Whatever their past, he fully believed that now that Angel had finally met up with the sharply intelligent woman Sebastien knew Ree Ann to be, the combination could be downright explosive. They could forge a relationship that would be bold, passionate, and strong enough to weather any storm—that is, if they could lower their defenses long enough to see how right he was.

Sebastien ordered the first course of his meal and

settled in for the long, hopefully successful evening ahead. He imagined Jamie's expression when she realized that his second match was a success. However, rather than amusement, the oddest ache centered in his chest.

He sipped his wine. Nonsense. He was not pining over the affections of a woman. Certainly not when said woman was one of his matches. There were dozens—nay, hundreds—of other women in his future. Far too many for him to waste precious time and energy lusting after the one he couldn't have.

He carefully set the glass down when he realized his grip threatened to snap the fragile stem. He would match her and match her well. There was no other possible outcome to this chain of events. And yet he hadn't brought himself to even contemplate who that man might be. That he was tied up finalizing his work with Ree and Angel was a hollow excuse, and he knew it.

His appetizer arrived. It was perfectly presented and smelled heavenly. Yet he discovered he'd lost his appetite.

He wanted only one thing. The vision that came to mind stirred his hunger, but his belly wasn't what rumbled in response. *Mon Dieu*, had a man ever ached so supremely for wanting to taste a pair of lips?

Time passed, and still Ree didn't show up. His waiter replaced the half-eaten appetizer with his entrée. Sebastien was pushing his braised duck around on the plate when Ree finally made her entrance and snapped him from his malaise. And an entrance she did make. With nothing more than an understated black dress and her flame-red hair pulled into a sleek, sophisticated twist, she managed to reduce every gentleman in the establishment to drooling incapacitation. Much to their dining partners' dismay.

Sebastien shifted so he was not directly in her line

of vision and turned to watch as Angel stepped away
from a table where he'd been talking to several customers. He was rather striking himself, in a superbly
cut suit that had Sebastien making a mental note to
discover his tailor. His hair was slicked back and gathered in a queue at his neck, his face freshly shaven,
and his rather intense eyes focused entirely on his
guest.

Sebastien subtly shifted his attention to Ree and
had the pleasure of watching her step falter ever so
slightly when the two made eye contact. Good, good.
Everyone in the room had to be reeling from the
waves of sexual energy these two produced.

Her fiery looks were like an exclamation point to
his leashed intensity. Sebastien smiled. *Mais oui,* these
two will burn brightly together, he thought. And with
their intensity, the flame should remain strong and
bright for decades to come.

He watched as Angel placed a light hand on Ree's
back and escorted her to a private dining room in the
rear of the restaurant. He'd seen enough to be convinced that his match was the right one. But he admitted he wished he could observe them. Even in their
short time together, Ree Ann had won his affection.
What he'd learned of her unusual life had only underscored those feelings. He would enjoy witnessing
her fall in love.

He returned his attention to his food and put
thoughts of his next chore aside. He would have this
evening of victory. Then he would face Jamie's future.

ॐ

Jamie looked through the window of Santini's.
Damn, but she was good! Sebastien was right where
she'd suspected he'd be. Eavesdropping on Ree and
Angel's hot date. She marched to the door but paused
with her hand on the knob. She had come here to

confront Sebastien, but now that she was here, she realized Ree might see them together and think they
were both spying on her.

Jamie had to admit she was dying to be a fly on the
wall. Ree had been on an emotional seesaw at work for
the past couple of days. Which had been merciful only
in that it helped Jamie take her mind off her own
problems. She had stopped attacking every poor, unsuspecting male who entered the store and had put
her thoughts to work on helping Ree figure out what
she wanted. And Jamie was very much afraid her
friend wanted Angel. She still wasn't completely certain why, but there was no denying that Ree was like a
golden moth to his dark flame. At the moment anyway. Jamie trusted her friend hadn't lost all of her instincts. And if Ree's wings started to get a bit
scorched, Jamie trusted that she would fly immediately to safety. After scorching Angel's wings completely, of course.

Jamie took her hand off the knob and leaned
against the outside of the building. She didn't want to
intrude. Ree had made it perfectly clear she had to
handle this on her own. Fine. She'd just wait for
Sebastien to come out.

"Spying again?"

She let out a small shriek as she jumped away from
the wall. "No. That was your role tonight, if I'm not
mistaken. I was waiting out here to talk to you."

Sebastien was grinning at her from less than a foot
away. He raised an eyebrow in surprise. "Would you
care to join me for the remainder of my dinner?"

She was still glowering at him for making her jump.
Again. "No, thank you. Just tell me when you'll be
done and I'll meet you somewhere else. We have to
talk."

Now his smile faded. "Then we must talk. I'll be
right back."

Jamie opened her mouth to tell him to finish his dinner, but he was already gone. She swore under her breath. This wasn't going at all how she'd planned it. Not that she'd really thought it out that much. She had been working on rearranging her apartment, but her whirling thoughts made concentration impossible. She needed to talk to Sebastien, and until she did, she wasn't going to get anything else done. At least not well. And since it was her idea to force this confrontation, she thought she'd feel more in control of the situation. She didn't.

Sebastien reappeared and took her hand, weaving it through his arm. "Where to, mademoiselle?"

She slid her arm right back out and stepped carefully away. "Rule number one: no contact."

He nodded. "Agreed."

Jamie should have been relieved, but her stomach was too knotted up for the feeling to be noticeable. "I need to talk to you." Customers leaving the restaurant jostled by them. "In private."

"So you have said. Would you like to go to the courtyard?"

She knew he meant his courtyard. She shook her head. "Maybe along the Moonwalk."

"It is a Friday evening. We won't find much privacy there." He tilted his head. "Would you feel more comfortable on your turf, as they say? Shall we go to the shop?"

Jamie thought about it, but Marta was still there working on some of the other accounts she did on the side. And Bennett was supposed to meet her there later. She didn't want to interfere with that. Nor did she want Sebastien anywhere near her apartment. "Okay, we'll use your courtyard. But remember the rules."

He smiled at her, obviously amused, and motioned with his arm for her to proceed.

Fine, let him be amused, she thought. As long as he obeyed the rules. He wouldn't be smiling for long anyway. Not when he heard what she had to say.

≈

They were settling themselves at the wrought-iron table in his courtyard far too soon. She still wasn't entirely sure how she was going to handle this. Sebastien had been mercifully silent on the walk over, but her thoughts were a confused jumble. Anytime she got within three feet of the man, her mind turned to mush.

Well, that was about to end.

"Can I get you anything to drink?"

Jamie wanted to say, yes, and make it about one hundred proof, please. Instead, she shook her head. "Just sit down. I . . . I need to get this over with."

Sebastien frowned, but he sat. "What is the problem?" Then his face cleared. "If you are still disturbed about Ree Ann and Angel, please let me assuage your fears."

"It has nothing to do with them. Not that I'm thrilled with their liaison, mind you, but they're adults and what happens between them is ultimately their own business." She leveled a hard look at him. "Although if he hurts her, you've been warned. But that's not why I'm here."

"Then why don't we get right to the heart of it."

"Okay." She still had to take a deep breath. Then she blurted, "I don't want to see you anymore."

He lifted a dark eyebrow. "I wasn't aware we were seeing each other. Not in the current sense, anyway. In fact, I believe we both came to an agreement about why, expressly, that could never come to pass."

"No, that's not what I mean." She paused, then just said it straight out. "What I mean is, I don't want to see you at all. Ever. For any reason."

Now it was her turn to be surprised. For the blink of an eye, he looked stunned. And hurt. She almost doubted she'd seen it, given that in the next blink his expression became completely unreadable. But it had hit her too hard, too specifically, for her to be mistaken. She'd hurt him. Deeply. She was almost reaching across the table for his hand, half-ready to apologize, when he spoke.

"And for what reason have you come to this conclusion?"

Not once since the night she'd met him had she ever heard his voice sound so cold, so impenetrable. In fact, though she'd had glimpses of the man who might have ridden the high seas, pillaging and plundering, only now did she truly believe him capable of it.

A shiver crawled along her skin, totally out of place on such a balmy evening. "I . . . I simply can't live my life like this. Not knowing when you're going to pop in and out. And I'm hating this whole matchmaking thing. It's making me crazy. I don't need crazy in my life anymore. I left racing and came here to leave crazy behind."

"What is it I'm doing to make your life crazy?" His tone hadn't shifted one iota. He might as well have been made of stone.

Jamie had to shore up her confidence against his unrelenting stare. "You told me you'd find my perfect match."

"You know that I must."

"I know, and that's what's making me so crazy. Now every man who walks into my life is like some sort of bizarre game-show contestant, vying for the grand prize. Which is me! I look suspiciously at every guy who comes in the shop or passes me on the street and smiles. I'm always wondering if this is the guy you're going to try and foist off on me."

If her words were having any effect on him, he wasn't showing it.

She calmed down and quieted her tone. "I can't do this anymore, Sebastien." Her use of his name melted the wall of ice a tiny bit. She looked him directly in the eye. "If your purpose is to make me happy, then what will make me happy is to let me resume my life. Free of interruption or meddling."

He stared at her for so long, she wasn't certain that he planned to answer her. When he spoke, he sounded so distant, so detached, she couldn't help but feel a twinge of remorse for what she was doing.

"It was never my intent to cause you such distress, *ma maîtresse*. Or to disrupt your life to such an extent as to make you miserable."

She felt like an ungrateful slug. His calling her *mistress* didn't even annoy her as it usually did. In fact, it made her eyes burn with unshed tears. After tonight, she'd never hear him call her that—or anything else— ever again.

"Then—then you agree? You'll leave me alone?" Her voice was barely above a whisper. Her heart ached, and she honestly didn't know what answer she wanted him to give.

"I wish it could be otherwise, but *non*, I cannot leave my duty unfulfilled."

It was right then that Jamie knew she'd lost her mind. She was frustrated, yes. But she was also relieved he wasn't leaving her for good. What in the hell *did* she want?

I want him.

She absolutely ignored her immediate response. "Then can we please choose someone else to match? I know you said before that you couldn't, but you also said you didn't know all the rules of your . . . you know, your special powers."

"I have told you, I have no—"

"Yeah, yeah, I know. But you know what I meant. Why don't you just match up someone else first and see if that fulfills the deal? I'll even pick the person out. Then it will be all legal. Right?"

Sebastien continued his steady, unnerving appraisal of her. "Is it such a hideous fate, Jamie?"

Oh, sure, she silently groaned, say my name like that, why don't you. "For most other people, no, it probably wouldn't be. But for me? The prospect of going through another relationship is simply beyond me right now. I need more time on my own to figure out who I am and what I really need. If I don't know that, then how can I know what I need in someone else?"

"We discussed this before. I think you have discovered these things here. I think you are ready."

"Well, you're not me. You haven't walked in my shoes, or led my life, so you have no idea what I'm ready for." She wasn't getting through to him. Frustration curled through her, and she felt her fingers digging into her thighs as she grappled for control. "Can we at least try it my way?" She had a sudden inspiration. "Jack! You can match Jack! Lord knows he could use a calming influence in his life. And hey, if you enjoy a challenge, this could be the highlight of your career." Her smile was pasted on, her facial muscles tight as her eyes beseeched him to please, please agree with her plan.

Sebastien stood suddenly. Jamie watched his face, tension singing through her as the silence strung out. Finally he took a step forward and stood directly in front of her. Not liking the supplicant position he'd put her in, she rose, then faltered when she realized just how close together they were now.

The table was behind her and she couldn't back away. To his credit, he didn't try to touch her. But then, he was close enough that she felt his gaze like a caress anyway. Her breathing became shallow, and her heart started skipping beats.

"Wh-what?" she finally said, when he continued to look into her eyes.

"There is one repercussion to this request of yours that you might not have taken into consideration."

Did this mean he was considering her idea? Her heart was thrumming so hard now she could hardly hear his words. Somehow she managed to murmur, "What repercussion?"

He moved an infinitesimal step closer to her and managed to swallow up the remaining air when he did so. Still, he didn't touch her—although she wasn't so sure that was merciful at this point. Her body was beginning to clamor. She worked hard to ignore it. And failed miserably.

"If you are no longer my responsibility to match, then I am no longer forced to refrain from my feelings for you."

Uh-oh. Jamie's knees almost went liquid as his meaning slid home. "But . . . but . . . but—" *Oh, great defense there. That'll slow him down.*

Which was precisely the problem. She didn't want him to slow down.

"I . . . I . . . we . . . we—" He'd reduced her to babbling. "No dallying with your mistresses; you said that was a rule."

"I said it felt wrong. Suddenly I don't feel that way any longer." He took her shoulders in his hands and she lost all ability to make any sound at all. He stepped closer and tilted his head.

Dear God, he was going to kiss her.

And God help her, she wanted him to. More than anything she could ever recall wanting in her entire life.

To ache for something so badly that it was almost a physical pain couldn't be a good thing. Where she got the strength she had no idea, but just as his lips lowered to hers, she pressed her palms to his chest and pushed him back.

To his credit, though frustration was clear in his eyes, he heeded her silent plea. Just slightly. He merely stopped his downward motion, his lips still hovering just above hers, his gaze boring directly into hers.

"Sebastien, we can't," she managed, her voice a mere rasp of sound in the still courtyard.

"Why? Tell me you do not wish to feel my lips upon yours. Tell me you do not wish to feel my arms about you, my body pressed against yours. Tell me you do not imagine what it would be like if we were to come together. Tell me these things, Jamie, and then I will believe that this can't be."

"I—I can't claim any of those things." Her pounding heart made her sound almost breathless. "But this is wrong. We'll hurt each other. You won't be staying. And I am not willing to start something that can't be finished." She tentatively placed trembling hands on his chest. "Please understand. It would hurt too much. And I've been hurt enough. That's what I've been trying to tell you."

He slid his hands down her arms and covered her hands. His expression was a mixture of disappointment and need that made her heart ache, her body throb, and her eyes sting.

"I do not wish to hurt you, Jamie. As my mistress or my woman."

My woman. Dear Lord, what was she doing turning this man down? Somehow she managed to keep her mouth shut.

"You have done one thing that no other woman has managed."

Her heart stopped altogether. "What is that?"

He lifted one hand and placed a heartbreakingly

gentle kiss to the back of it, then stepped away from her. "I told you I had been given an honorable fate for such a dishonorable man. Well, you have just made me an honorable man." He turned abruptly and walked toward the house.

"Sebastien."

He paused, but it was a moment before he looked back at her. "Do not test this newfound honor, Jamie."

She shook her head but couldn't help wondering if she'd just made the biggest mistake of her life. Which, considering the whoppers she'd made, was truly saying something. "What happens now?"

"I will try your suggestion. We will see what fruit it bears." Then he left the courtyard without looking back.

Chapter 16

Ree leaned on the counter. "We talked until four this morning."

Jamie shot her a look. "Talked?"

Ree gave it right back to her. "As a matter of fact, yes. And we would have talked longer, except he was concerned that I not be late for work. You know, this is the first night I've spent with a man where he expended all his energies probing my mind—and nothing else."

Jamie cocked her head. "And yet, surprisingly, you don't sound entirely happy with that new reality."

Ree frowned and propped her chin on her hands. "I know. Crazy, huh?" She sighed deeply, and a slow smile curved her lips. "But he won't get away with that next time. I'm nothing if not successful when I put my mind to something."

"Next time?"

"Don't even start with me, sugar. I know this whole thing with Angel and me sounds too strange to be true, and I guess it is. But you certainly know me well enough to know that where men are concerned, I don't spend time unwisely."

"I know, Ree. It's just that—"

Ree grabbed Jamie's hand and folded it in hers. "Jamie Lynne, I can honestly say I've never been so attracted to a man in my entire life. And I'm not talking about his looks." She grinned. "Although, I have to admit, I cannot wait to get that man out of those designer suits of his."

Flashes of last night in Sebastien's courtyard played through Jamie's mind, and she felt her cheeks heat up. "Ree Ann, I really don't think I want to—"

But Ree was on a roll. "I know he was inexcusably cruel to me last year, but we've talked that all out too." Her eyes were bright and her skin was flushed.

Jamie didn't think she'd ever seen Ree like this. "So just like that you forgive him for being an asshole? For blasting you every chance he got?"

Ree didn't even blink, which made Jamie even more nervous. That must have been some dinner Angel fed her last night.

"I'm not so sure *forgive* is the right word," Ree said. "I understand a bit more where that all stemmed from. And I have to take some of the blame for not defending myself."

"Oh, now, wait a damn minute. Because you didn't bother to explain things to him does not make him less of an asshole."

"Sugar, I don't want you to be mad at me. But there's a lot in Angel's past you don't know about. Edgar never talked about his family. Lucy was the only person he spoke of. Of course, I knew he had a son, Anthony, Angel's father. He'd died some years before I met Edgar, when Angel was in his last year of college. I never really knew much more than that. Well, apparently Angel's mom died when he was real little, and his dad more or less raised him."

"That's terrible, but I don't see how it makes Angel a nice guy."

"Well, there was a lot more suffering than I ever knew. Edgar's son's death was fresh enough that he simply never talked about him, and I respected that. As Edgar's only son, Anthony had been well off his

whole life. Even after Edgar's financial empire started
to crumble in the late eighties, he had kept the money
flowing, not wanting anyone, especially Anthony, to
know how bad things were. Well, his son went through
money like water, and it only got worse after his wife
died. Apparently he had a major eye for the ladies.
They, I understand, mostly had an eye for his money.
Angel was left alone much of the time while his dad
spent his way through his money and then Edgar's."

"Speaking of Edgar, where was he during all this?"

"With Lucy gone, he doted on his only son, spoiling him. Knowing Edgar, he didn't approve of his
son's activities, but he was so overwhelmed and embarrassed by his own financial problems that he didn't
step in when he should have. I doubt he ever forgave
himself for that." She paused for a moment before
going on. "Anthony and his girlfriends managed
to go through everything they had left. Including
Angel's college fund. When Edgar found out, he offered to pay for it—even though I imagine he had no
idea how he'd manage it—but Angel took off on his
own and paid his way through school. Angel and his
dad had fought for years about his dad's spending
habits and the women he took up with. In fact, they
weren't speaking when his dad was killed. He died in a
crash. His current flame was behind the wheel of the
new sports car he'd just bought her."

Jamie shook her head, hating that she felt sympathy
for someone she'd spent a good long time not liking
very much. "And I guess when you popped into
Edgar's life not too long after that, Angel saw history
repeating itself."

"Exactly. He and Edgar had had some rocky times
before that too. The college thing was only part of it.
Angel had tried to get Edgar to stop giving his dad
money. But Edgar couldn't cut his only son off. And

he never let either of them know the truth about the
debts he'd racked up keeping his son in style."

"Stupid male pride. What is it with them?"

Ree smiled a bit sadly. "If I'd known half of this,
I'd have made him talk about it, made him deal with
it. But he never told me. When we got his various investments solvent again, he gave Angel one of them."

"Santini's."

Ree nodded. "It was his clumsy male way of trying
to mend their past. But by then it was too late. Angel
had made derogatory comments about me, and Edgar
split with him for good. Angel paid him back in full
for the restaurant. So they had no ties at all between
them." She sighed.

"Except the will."

Ree nodded. "It wasn't even about the money.
Angel just hated to see what Edgar had spent his life
working for given to—"

"A floozy. Like one of his dad's."

A small smile curved her lips. "Right. Now, I know
that this didn't give Angel total license to treat me the
way he did. But I got a goodly amount of what revenge
I needed when I informed Angel last night of Edgar's
past financial woes and my role in reversing them."

Jamie laughed. "I'd have paid money to see his
face."

Ree only smiled. "I am human, after all. He apolo-
gized for not giving me the benefit of the doubt. It
was just that Edgar really hadn't had any relationships
after his wife died, and considering his father's
lifestyle, Angel didn't exactly have me in mind for a
companion for his grandfather."

"Did you tell Angel you were just that? His companion, not his sex partner?"

"I didn't have to. He'd already figured that out. In a
way I wish I'd tried to explain all this earlier, but I was

so pissed at his automatic assumptions that I refused to give him the benefit. At that point I doubt he'd have listened to me anyway. We were both pretty raw."

Jamie shook her head. "I don't know, Ree. I hate to be such a stick in the mud, but it still seems an awful sudden turnabout."

Ree squeezed her hand. "I need you to trust that I know what I'm doing here. Even if I haven't a clue." She laughed and her eyes twinkled again. "He understands me, Jamie. Now that we're past all the emotional bullshit of his past and mine, I can't just walk away from what he's offering me."

Jamie's eyebrows went higher. "Offering you? Now he's offering you something?"

Ree shook her head. "Not in that way." She paused, turning more serious. "I know you won't believe this, but now that the emotional blinders are off . . . How can I put it? When he looks at me, Jamie, he sees me. He sees Ree Ann. Not the body, not the beauty, not even the brain. Just the person I am. And he's interested in getting to know that person better."

"What about him? Are you interested only because he's interested in you?"

"See, that's the scary part. Once we cleared the air, we really began to talk, to get to know each other. And, amazing as it sounds, I like him. He's a fascinating man. We share a lot of common tastes and beliefs. We've debated philosophy, movies, business management, and who was the better rock band, The Rolling Stones or The Who."

"The Stones, no question."

Ree grinned. "Naturally." She shrugged. "Who knows how long it will last, Jamie, or where it will lead? But I want to find out."

Jamie just shook her head, but she squeezed Ree's hand before letting it go. "Then I'll be here for you. I just want to see you happy, Ree."

Ree tugged Jamie into her arms and hugged her tightly, then set her back with her hands on Jamie's shoulders. "And that's what I want for you too."

The night before flashed vividly through her mind. Jamie stepped away. "Let's not go there."

"But sugar, you and Sebastien—"

"Ree, I've said I'll stand by you, but I need you to return the favor. Right now. I don't want to discuss Sebastien. Okay?"

She tilted her head. "You two have a fight?"

Jamie sighed in defeat. "No. Yes. I don't know. I just don't want to talk about him, okay?"

Jamie swore when she came back here last night that she was going to put it all out of her mind and concentrate on her life as if Sebastien weren't a part of it. Of course, then she'd dreamed about the man all night. Hot, sweaty dreams that she'd awoken from with full recollection of every seductive, drenching detail—and the knowledge that she could have had the reality instead of the dream. Except that she'd walked away.

Ree brushed a hand across her cheek, smoothing Jamie's hair back. "Well, when you're ready, sugar, I'm all ears." But Jamie knew Ree, and she was not capable of leaving that timetable completely in Jamie's hands. As if to prove her point, she added, "But I'm beginning to think that man might just be tellin' the truth about himself." At Jamie's gaping reaction, Ree raised her hands. "I know, I know. But, I mean, Jamie, he's two for two."

"Hey, it's not like you're walking down the aisle yet."

"I know. But soulmates notwithstanding, both Marta and I *are* doing the happy-heart dance." Just then Ree's eyes went wide and a look of understanding lit her face. She grabbed Jamie's arm. "And now that Marta and I are fixed up, he's going to go match you up with someone else. That's it, isn't it?"

"I don't want anybody else." Jamie raised a hand to stop Ree from speaking. "That didn't come out right. I don't want anyone, *including* Sebastien. I want to be on my own. I've just gotten used to it."

"Sugar, I'm not sure who you're tryin' harder to convince." She stroked Jamie's hair. "I don't know what advice to give you. It's all too supernatural for me. But, then, I'm truly falling in love for the first time in my life, and right now that makes me feel like just about anything is possible."

"Well, me being with Sebastien is not possible."

A sudden look of curiosity crossed Ree's face. She leaned closer and whispered, "Because of . . . whatever it is that he is, does that mean he can't . . . you know."

Jamie blew out a sigh of frustration. "Oh, no, he can *you know* just fine. In fact, he's made it clear he'd like to *you know* with me."

Ree's eyes went wide. "Well, then?"

"I just told you. I don't want a relationship just now. And one with Sebastien has disaster written all over it. It can't go anywhere, Ree."

"Maybe that makes it the perfect relationship, then. Did you think about it that way? You don't want to settle down, and he's a temporary man at best. So why not enjoy yourselves while it lasts?"

Jamie didn't answer for a moment. Not because she didn't know what the answer was—she did. That was what scared her. Quietly, she said, "Because maybe, just maybe, I've fallen a little bit in love with him after all. And maybe I can't take having my heart broken one more time."

"Oh, Jamie, I'm so sorry." Ree pulled her into her arms.

Jamie was a good head taller than Ree, but she hunched down and let her head drop down to her friend's soft shoulder anyway. "I think I convinced him not to match me with anyone else," she said softly. "So at least I don't have to go through that."

Ree smoothed her hair. "Well, that's one good piece of news. Who did you pick as number three, then?"

Jamie couldn't help the smile that curved her lips. She straightened and stepped away. "Jack."

Ree clapped her hand over her mouth, but laughter hooted out anyway. She dropped her hand. "Oh, Jamie, you didn't."

She nodded, laughing herself. It felt good, even if it was at her cousin's expense. "He's been looking for Mr. Right forever. This will just expedite things. And it will finish Sebastien's mission." Her smile faded. "Which means he disappears for good and I can finally get my life back under control."

"I'm so sorry it has to be that way, sugar, but you're probably doing the smart thing. Although I still say the two of you should just go ahead and burn each other out of your systems before he goes." She fanned her face. "I know I would have."

"Well, I'm not you. I can't handle that kind of thing. If I could, I wouldn't have been divorced twice."

Ree nodded pragmatically. "True, true."

"Gee, thanks for agreeing so quickly," Jamie said dryly, but she knew Ree was telling it like it was.

Ree patted her arm. "You're doing what's right for you, Jamie. I'm proud of you, even if I am sorry it didn't work out better."

"Yeah, me too." She pasted on a fresh smile and said, "Now, maybe we should get some work done?"

Now Ree did blush. "Actually, speaking of Jack, he should be here any minute to relieve me. I, um, have a lunch date."

"Oh? Well, I can certainly cover for you for an hour or so. No need to drag Jack in here."

Ree's lips curved into a rather wicked grin. "Well, sugar, if my plans for lunch work out, I won't be back this afternoon. Or evening."

Jamie rolled her eyes. "Why am I beginning to think this relationship is going to be harder on me than it is on you?"

Ree laughed. "I promise I won't shirk my responsibilities," she said. "Much." Jack bustled in just then. Ree gave him an exuberant kiss on both cheeks. "Hi there, sugar. Thanks for covering for me today. I owe you one." She sent Jamie a conspiratorial wink. "A really big one, if I'm lucky." Her laughter filled the air as she flitted out of the store.

Jack didn't bother wiping off the red lip prints adorning his cheeks; he merely waved good-bye and turned to Jamie. "Spill."

Jamie cut him off before he could get too excited. "I'm not going to gossip. You'll have to ask her yourself. I'll be in the back if you need me." There were no books to shelve, but she simply had to have a moment to herself. Several long moments, perhaps.

She'd meant what she said to Ree about why she turned Sebastien down. But those dreams crept back into her mind, making her all itchy and hot and uncomfortable. Doubt crept in right along with it. *No, no, no, Jamie. Don't let your hormones do the talking here. Stay strong.*

Sebastien found her there, staring unseeing at the stock cart. "Jack told me I might find you here."

She didn't jump this time when he spoke. She groaned. She'd spent too much time thinking about Sebastien's flesh to be seeing him in it again this soon. "Why are you here?"

"Good day to you as well, mademoiselle."

She rubbed the bridge of her nose, then took a deep breath before facing him. "I thought we agreed last night to not see each other."

"I don't believe that was the agreement we reached at all. I was under the assumption your fondest wish was for me to return to my sword as soon as possible. For that to occur, I must find Jack's soulmate. I thought, as his cousin, you would be the best one to give me guidance. Otherwise, my research could take me much longer." He stepped away and bowed. "But I will bid good day and go to his other place of employment." He turned with a graceful flourish that had her eyes attached to his—

"Okay, okay, don't get all dramatic."

He turned back to her, a smile curving his beautiful lips. Lips she'd spent most of last night dreaming about, lips that had—

She shifted her weight back and forth, suddenly irritable. "What exactly do you need to know?"

"Can we take a walk? I thought it would be best to have this discussion out of earshot." He nodded his head toward the front, where Jack was helping a customer.

"I can't. Ree is gone for the day and Marta won't be in till this afternoon. I have to help hold down the fort."

"Fine, then. Would this evening be more suitable?"

There was no suitable time if it meant time spent alone with him, Jamie thought. Her heart was beating faster and her palms were all damp—and he wasn't even doing anything but standing in the same room as she was. Seeing him alone, after hours—in the dark? No, not a good idea at all. "I'm . . . I'm busy tonight."

He cocked his eyebrows. "Oh?"

"This is so hard to believe? That I might have plans? I do have a life, you know."

"I do not question your desirability, mademoiselle."

The way he was looking at her—there ought to be

some sort of law. There wasn't a nerve ending in her body that wasn't on full alert. She turned her back to him and pretended to sort books on the nearest stock shelf. "Maybe some other time." She'd tried for nonchalant. She hadn't come close.

He said nothing for the longest time, and she wondered if perhaps he'd left. Then his voice came from a point far too close to her left shoulder. She stilled, unable to even pretend she was working.

"Is my presence so abhorrent to you, Jamie?"

Did he have to use her name? All dark and dreamy like that? "I . . . I said I have plans." She didn't dare turn around. "It's impolite to question a lady's word."

Again a pause, then, "Perhaps you've mistaken me for a gentleman."

"You said last night I'd turned you into an honorable man."

"I also warned you not to test my honor."

"I didn't come to you."

A long moment passed. "I know. It would have been easier on my conscience if you had. I told myself I came here merely to expedite the matter of my return to the sword. Now that I am here, I realize that for the lie it was."

Well, there went what was left of her oxygen. She swallowed hard against a parched throat. "Maybe . . . you should leave, then. Now."

He put his hand on her shoulder and turned her slowly to face him. Jamie knew she was a goner when she looked into his eyes. The desire she found there was hot enough to melt the polish off her nails. If she'd been wearing any.

"Maybe I'm not so honorable after all." He leaned closer. "Because leaving now is the very last thing I plan to do."

And he tilted his head down—and kissed her. It was

no tame meeting of the lips either. True to his background, he plundered her mouth. He took with abandon and reveled in the treasures he sought out and found.

For her part, Jamie surrendered without a whimper. A moan or two, and a definite shudder of desire, but once his mouth was on hers, she did nothing to fight off his invasion. In truth, she'd never wanted anything so badly in her entire life. And the reality was proving to be so superior to her limited imagination, she wouldn't have stopped him now for any amount of wishes granted.

She gripped his shoulders, which prompted him to slide his arms around her waist and—dear God, he felt good—pull her tightly against his body. This had to be wrong, wrong, wrong. In her experience, anything that felt even a fraction this good could only be really, really bad for her in the long run.

It didn't say much for her emotional growth that she cared not one whit about her dismal learning curve. He'd pressed his tongue inside her mouth and pulled her hips tight against his. Learning curves be damned!

His hand slid up her waist and cupped beneath her breast. Jamie instinctively started to pull away, not wanting to spoil the moment by having him realize just how little that particular foray was going to reward him with. But his fingers were strong, his mouth even stronger. He took her mouth more deeply, demanding she rejoin the attack. Her hand fell limply to her side as his thumb slipped up over her nipple and wrenched a low moan of total acceptance from somewhere very deep in her throat.

"I don't suppose someone would like to assist me in running this business." Jack's voice entered her brain about one second before the man himself entered the back room. She broke away from Sebastien's kiss in time to see her cousin's surprised expression turn to one of approval.

"Well, now, we are woman, hear us roar." He gave a little golf clap of approval. "It's about damn time. Don't you worry, I'll handle things out front. You handle . . . well, everything you can, sister." With a little wink at Sebastien, he sashayed dramatically back out front.

Turning more shades of red than she knew were humanly possible, Jamie disentangled herself from Sebastien's arms and stepped away, clearing her throat in a desperate attempt at reclaiming a shred of her dignity.

"Jamie—"

She put up her hand to stop Sebastien's advance. "Really, you have to go. Now." She stared at him. "Please."

Sebastien swore under his breath. It was mostly in French, but Jamie didn't think she needed a translation book to get the gist.

"I will return here tonight. We will talk. And not about your cousin." He muttered something about "if I let him continue to draw breath," then walked to her and lifted the heavy braid from her shoulder before she could back away. "I want to see this hair unplaited and spread across my pillow. Perhaps across my bare chest."

She trembled as the air left her lungs completely.

"This cannot end here," he said quietly. "We will finish what we've begun." He dropped her braid and ran the backs of his knuckles along her breast, making her shudder despite herself. "And I believe you understand how successful I am when I put my mind to something."

Jamie found her voice, shaky though it was. "I am not a victory to be claimed."

He smiled then, and it was so wickedly carnal that

Jamie just might have stripped naked and offered herself to him right there on the shelving cart. Had he asked.

"This victory will be shared by us both. That I promise you."

When he was gone, Jamie leaned weakly against the closest shelf and fanned herself. Dear God. She should be really sorry she'd let that happen. Really, truly regretful. After all her carefully built-up resistance, she'd crumbled under the first real assault on her defenses.

This could only lead her down the path of destruction. Again. She absolutely knew that to be true.

Which did nothing to explain the shiver of anticipation that raced over her—much less the smile that curved her own lips as she slowly began unwinding her braid.

The battle might have been lost, but the casualties hadn't been counted. Not yet. The line had been crossed and she'd let it happen. However, if she was going to suffer anyway, she was damn well going to make it worth the pain.

Chapter 17

Sebastien paced his rooms like a caged animal. One hour left, then he would claim her as his own. *Mon Dieu*, what a spell she had cast upon him. He had never been like this, the anticipation alone all but destroying his control. He had enjoyed the affections of many women, yes, but always he was the one in control, he the one seducing, the one dictating the course of pleasure.

Until tonight.

Yes, he had directed what had happened at the store. Lord knows she'd been a more than willing receptor to his advances, so much so he'd almost lost himself right then and there. But since leaving her, the waiting—and truth be told, the worrying—was killing him. Would she come with him? Would she run once again? Did he dare attempt to find her again if she did?

Never before had these kinds of concerns plagued him. His women had always been willing. His biggest concern was getting them to leave when he was through with them, not worrying if they would show in the first place.

He flung himself down on his bed with a growl of frustration, then jumped right back up again and resumed pacing. Even if Jamie refused him, there would be no other companion joining him in her place.

He sat abruptly on the end of the bed, feeling as if the wind had suddenly left his sails. Here he'd been the one mounting the campaign, and yet she was the one with the victory. She'd managed to capture all of his attention. And there was no one else he'd care to share it with, were he to reclaim it.

Ah, foxed and be damned. He dragged himself upright and went downstairs to the courtyard. The night air was thick and redolent with the scents of the nocturnal flowers that were opening beneath the full moon. The rich earthiness of it all did little to settle his nerves.

He tortured himself with thoughts of what she would smell like when he took her in his arms, what her lips would taste like when he tipped her chin up and kissed her once again.

With a groan, he sank into one of the chairs and contemplated the pale moon above. He had boldly decided to disregard his personal rule by being with her. He wondered if there really was some cosmic penalty for what he was about to do. It would not stop him. Or he would have not taken her into his arms in the first place.

He rubbed his hands over his face. He wanted to possess her so badly—what was becoming of him? Even in his days of plundering with Dominique, he'd never needed the victory or required the spoils. It was the chase that roused him.

Was that her allure? That she had not fallen victim to his charms so easily? That she resisted them even when he knew he was weakening her will?

Non, that was not it at all. Yet it was damn hard to admit it. The image of her face swam into his mind. He saw the sparkle of wit, the flash of temper in her eyes; he heard her voice in his ears, bold and direct. He pictured her movement—strong and certain, always so unaware of her femininity. This went far

beyond physical attraction. Before, were he to contemplate the essence of a woman, his mind would
have instantly strayed to her plentiful, womanly
bounty, to her full, succulent lips, the sway of her
well-rounded hips and bosom, the knowing looks of
desire she'd have sent his way.

None of those things had come to his mind when
he thought of Jamie. And yet his attraction to her
was all the stronger for it. She hadn't captivated only
his body, she'd captivated his spirit, engaged his
mind, his—

He veered away from that course of thought; it was
a far too dangerous path to traverse this night.

It was time to go to her. Had he found any humor
in it, he would have laughed at the magnitude of his
own insecurities as he left the courtyard and made his
way to the bookstore.

As he drew closer, his worries only increased. Perhaps he should have come well before closing time, to
ensure she did not run off. Bah, he thought immediately. He was being a fool now. She would be there.

If she was not, he realized he'd spend the rest of the
night hunting her down. If she was going to refuse
him, then she would refuse him to his face.

That thought brought him to a full stop just half a
block away. He could see the store up the street on the
corner. The lights were still on inside. He looked to
the upper floors and found her apartment dark. He
knew her bedroom was the corner room. He'd sat
in it, watching her sleep, that long first night after
they'd met.

He'd spent too many nights dreaming about the
soft pile of pillows and the thick duvet that tumbled
across her bed. More specifically, he'd dreamed about
tumbling her into that soft pile.

He shifted his weight but didn't resume walking.
He stopped thinking about his needs for a moment

and thought about Jamie's. Another path he'd never taken before. Had he taken advantage of her? Unjustly swayed her to accept his advances? She'd made it clear she was attracted to him, but she'd made it equally clear that she was not ready for involvement with anyone. He had spoken truthfully that he thought she was, but had that been his own desires speaking for him? Blast and damn again! This was too bloody complicated, and he was damned if he needed the aggravation. It would be easier all around if they both did as she initially bade them—which was to steer clear of each other.

After all, he could hardly promise her anything, certainly not a future together. That thought alone sent another series of shocks through him. Had he planned on promising such a thing? Even in his mortal life he'd never been compelled to do more than promise another evening of delight. Beyond that, he remained eminently unpromised to anyone. In any way. So why in hell had he thought it?

He knew why, though it brought him no comfort. Because she was not like any other woman. She had a strong heart and a generous soul, both of which spoke to his in a way no other woman ever had. He was compelled to talk to her, explain himself. He found himself wanting—nay, needing—her approval, her understanding. It should have been mortifying to admit, but it wasn't. It actually felt . . . good. This need to be needed. By her.

Yet she had been hurt, and badly, by cads who had taken her heart then tossed it aside like refuse when they were through with it.

Was he such a cad as well? Would he unknowingly take her heart with his actions tonight? And could he live with damaging that heart further when it was his time to go?

It was all too much to contemplate! Never had any

woman been worth this amount of aggravation. He rubbed his temples, then started when someone tapped him on the shoulder. He whirled around—and found Jamie standing there before him, still dressed in her work clothes, grinning like a cat who'd just trapped an unsuspecting bird.

"Finally!" she crowed. "I didn't think it was possible to sneak up on you. You looked a million miles away."

"That and more," he muttered, thinking he'd never felt more unsure and out of place. A definite anomaly for someone living the rather fantastical life he did. One look at her and his entire body leapt in anticipation. Just the reality of her presence both calmed him and sent his heart racing. She hadn't run.

"Why have you come looking for me?" He ached so badly to touch her that his tone sounded far more tense than he'd intended.

Jamie's smile faltered somewhat and she shifted under his scrutiny. He did not avert his gaze. If she was to be his this night, he had to know she was doing so with full knowledge and responsibility for the decision. It was the only way he could protect her, shy of leaving her. And that he simply was not strong enough to do.

"I . . ." She cleared her throat and stood taller. "I believe you said you wanted . . . um . . . wanted to . . . see me. This evening. I was closing the shutters when I thought I saw you down the street. When you didn't seem to notice me approaching, I ducked across the street and came up behind you." The corners of her mouth quirked slightly. "Sorry, I just had to do it. Have I ruined the mood now?"

Had Sebastien not been such a roiling mass of uncertainty, he'd have laughed at her brassy inquiry. As it was, he could not muster even a smile. He stepped closer and shifted toward the building, silently beckoning her out of the path of the evening's pedestrian traffic. She followed but said nothing more. Under his steady gaze, her smile vanished once again.

"The mood has shifted," he said softly, "but not to a lessening degree of need." He saw the spark of desire leap to her eyes then and finally felt some semblance of his control return. This he understood, this he could deal with. And yet there was so much more driving his desire for her. Was it the same for her?

He watched with great interest as she mastered her own needs and possible insecurities and looked him straight in the eyes. "Then why are we wasting time here on this sidewalk?"

Ah, but she was his match. Hadn't he always known that? It seemed so at this moment.

She went to turn back toward the bookstore, but he stayed her with a hand to her shoulder. She looked back at him questioningly.

He lifted a long lock of her unbound hair.

She ducked her chin, then looked up with a half shrug. "You said you wanted—"

"I know what I said. Thank you." He let the strands filter through his fingers. "Finer than spun gold."

She cleared her throat and laughed a bit nervously. "Is this where I'm supposed to do the clichéd your-place-or-mine thing?"

"I care not where we go," he said quietly, not taking his eyes from hers. "Whatever brings you the most comfort."

He felt the finest tremor pass through her at his earnestly spoken words. So tuned to his touch was she! Ah, but the ache between his legs—as well as the one in his chest—grew to new proportions.

"Then I think I'd like to go to your place. If that's okay." Her voice deepened slightly and took on a rough edge, as did the look of need in her eyes.

He did not release her. Instead, he turned her fully toward him. "It is more than okay. I would be honored with your presence in my home, and in my bed."

Her eyes flared again, and he actually thought he felt a hitch in his knees. Oddly, he enjoyed the sensation.

"Then . . . let's go."

He lifted his free hand to her other shoulder and pulled her a scant inch closer. Just feeling the strong muscles of her shoulders flex beneath his hands excited him. She was strength and steel, both in body and in spirit. Yes, his match, like no other. He could barely stand still for want to begin their adventure right away. But first things first.

"There is something I must ask you first."

She took a breath. "Okay."

Again, the fine trembling registered beneath his fingers. *Mon Dieu*, but she had him harder than a mainsail mast. He had a scant moment of doubt that his performance would be marred by an inability to control himself, but that only served to make him redouble his efforts to maintain a firm grip upon it. By damn, this would be a night like none that had come before it. He'd let nothing mar that.

Yet first he must have her answer. "We have discussed at length your reasons for not wanting a liaison with me." She began to speak, but he spoke over her. "I am accustomed to taking what I want and damn the consequences. I must know that you are fully aware of the consequences of this path we are about to embark upon."

"Which consequences?" Then she nodded in understanding. "If you mean am I concerned about your previous partners, well, I did take one little precaution—" She started to reach in the pocket of her shop pants, but he stopped her.

"This is not about our health, although I can assuage those fears. One benefit of my everlasting youth, apparently, is my immunity to disease."

Jamie's eyes widened and she let out a short laugh. "Okay. Well, how convenient for you. And for me, I suppose. But I want to use these anyway."

"Whatever pleases you."

Her eyes went all dark and her smile turned just a bit shy, but she kept his gaze firmly when she said, "Thank you."

He nodded. "There are other dangers."

"Being?"

He tapped a finger above her breast. "Your heart. I do not wish to damage it further."

Now he saw the flash of temper he had come to adore. "I can take care of my heart, thank you very much. I'm a big girl."

"You are a woman who has perhaps given her heart unwisely. And there could be no worse choice than myself."

She cocked her head to the side. "Are you trying to talk me out of this? Because, for a man who basically stated this morning that I was his next conquest, you sure aren't acting like the pirate you claim to be."

Sebastien did find his smile then. "Trust me when I say my desire to complete this quest hasn't diminished in the least."

"Then the answer is, yes, I'm aware you're not future life material. Did it ever occur to you that maybe I realized that is what makes you the perfect match for me? For the moment anyway."

That set him back. Not her reason for her change of heart—it did make perfect sense. What set him back was the immediate disappointment he'd felt.

Absurd! He should be rejoicing. Wasn't his main concern that she not be hurt? For him to feel such a sense of disappointment because she wanted nothing more from him than this was ridiculous. And yet the disappointment existed. Damn, but he wanted too much—and even then it was not enough. Perhaps he should be examining his own heart for fear of wounding it, rather than worrying about hers.

"Was there anything else you wanted to warn me about?"

When she grinned at him, he pushed aside the remainder of his misgivings and all of his confusion. It was no light load.

He framed her face with his hands, delighting in watching her smile dip as her eyes came alive. "Just this: The possibilities of this night we are about to share threaten to overwhelm me." Never had he spoken a truer statement. "But I am eager to explore every one of them." He dipped his head closer. "And I plan to. One at a time." He moved closer still, tipping her chin up until their lips were almost brushing. "With great and deliberate thoroughness." She shuddered, and his body responded in kind. "And I will begin with this."

He pulled her tightly against him, heedless of the passersby. "Come here, Jamie," he murmured. "Take my mouth and teach me how you like to be kissed."

Jamie gripped his shoulders, certain that she was about to dissolve into a puddle of need right there on the sidewalk. "This is insane. No one has ever made me feel so . . ."

"Desired?"

She shook her head and pulled back just enough to look into his eyes. Suddenly this very moment had taken on enormous proportions, and she refused to rush through it. She wanted to savor it, somehow knowing it would be a moment she would want to look back on many times and recall each and every second of. "I was going to say that no one had ever made me feel so much a partner."

"Perhaps that is because this is not a seduction, but an adventure. One to be shared equally if we are to enjoy it to the highest potential."

Any doubts Jamie had about this step she was about to take with him were pushed far into the background. For once she was with a man who wanted to enjoy her company and make damn sure she enjoyed his.

A slow smile curved her lips. She took enormous delight in the dark need that flickered in his eyes in response to it. She lifted her hands to his face and tilted his head just a bit to one side.

"This is how I like to be kissed." She pressed her closed lips to his. "And then I like a little of this." She moved her mouth over his, delighting in the shudder she felt ripple through him as she slowly opened her lips and pressed her tongue into his mouth. She heard him groan deep down in his throat, but he continued to let her dictate the kiss. And she took full advantage of the opportunity, reveling in how wonderful it felt to know with certainty you were pleasing your mate.

Mate. Her mate.

Now it was her turn to shudder.

And then with a growl, he wrenched his mouth from hers and pulled her up into his arms like she weighed nothing more than a feather. Which she most certainly did not.

She squealed in surprise, then found herself laughing as he strode down the street and around the corner, impervious to the stares and hoots of approval he was getting from the other pedestrians.

"You're putting on quite a show," she said, half amazed that he seemed to expend very little effort in the task of carting her about. The other half of her was equally amazed to discover . . . she kind of liked it. Very much.

"You said I wasn't behaving enough like the pirate for you." He swung into a shuttered doorway and dropped her feet to the ground. Before she could draw breath, he backed her into a corner and pressed his body full length against hers. Drawing breath became impossible.

He pushed his mouth below her ear and sunk his teeth gently into her earlobe. "Perhaps ravishment is more to your liking."

She wanted to say no and nod yes all at the same time. Surely it wasn't at all politically correct to want him to—

He tugged her chin around and took her mouth, fully plundering it, much the way he had earlier in the shop.

It was a toss-up, Jamie decided, with what few functioning brain cells she had left. As much as she enjoyed establishing her mastery over his desires with her kiss back there, there was definitely something to be said for letting the man have his way with her as well.

"Maybe . . . maybe we . . ." she murmured when he drew his lips from hers, only to begin an assault on the sensitive skin at the crook of her neck. "We should . . . dear God, that feels amazing."

She felt him smile against her now damp and heated skin. " 'Tis only the beginning."

"I might not last through the next five minutes if you keep doing that. I just realized it might be possible to expire of supreme pleasure."

"Then come expire with me, Jamie." He lifted his head, his dark eyes all but glowing. Stroking one finger down the side of her face, he spoke in French to her. It was better than all her fantasies combined.

"My French is rusty." As was her voice at this point. He scooped her up in his arms and made his way down the street toward his courtyard with long, confident strides. "Rather than tell you what I just said, mademoiselle, let me show you."

Chapter 18

Sebastien let Jamie's feet slip to the ground so he could open the gate to his courtyard. The inch of space between them now was an inch too much. He pushed the creaky gate open, then held her gaze as he swept an arm gallantly in front of him. "*Entrez vous*, mademoiselle."

Jamie returned his smile and slipped inside the gate. She walked steadily through the courtyard, no hesitation. Sebastien wished he felt her unfettered confidence. He caught her hand as she entered the loggia. It was full dark inside the stone hallway. The open, arched windows let in the night air and heavy scents of the courtyard but none of the moonlight.

He pulled her to him. Ah, but the lean length of her conformed more exquisitely to his body than the most voluptuous of women. The sensations that ripped through him were stunning. He dipped his head, needing to taste her.

Jamie groaned and let her head tip back as he trailed his lips along her neck. "Oh, Sebastien."

"*Mais oui*, Jamie. It is me." He lifted his head and searched for her eyes, despite the darkness. "If I had my way, it would always be me."

She stilled at his declaration. It had shaken him as well. He had no leave to say such things. It was bad enough that he was thinking them. "We will not dwell upon what the future holds," he said, as much to reassure himself as her. "We will think only of tonight." He ran his hands the length of her back and cupped her hips to his. They met and matched. She shuddered, as did he. "Agreed?"

"Agreed." Her voice was rough with need, a need he intended to appease.

She took matters into her own hands, tugging his head to hers. "Stop wasting time."

He was laughing as she kissed him. He returned it with equal passion, then grinned at her squeal of surprise when he abruptly ended the kiss and put her over his shoulder.

After a gasp or two, she managed to thump his back. "What do you think you're doing?"

"I'm a pirate, you will recall. This is the most efficient way to get our women where we want them." He made his way quickly inside and climbed the stairs. "Have you a complaint?"

He expected to be told directly, and in great detail, exactly what she thought of his treatment of her. She surprised him yet again. He thought her muffled noises were swearing, but he soon realized she was laughing.

"Can't you climb any faster?" she asked.

His responding battle cry echoed down the stairwell as he took the last several risers in a bound. Once in front of his bedroom door, he swung her around to slide down the front of his body. Their laughter died abruptly as their bodies came into intimate contact.

"You're wearing way too many clothes," she managed, finding his eyes in the dimly lit hallway.

"As are you." He reached behind him and turned the doorknob, then pulled her into his bedroom. He maneuvered her toward the bed, their limbs and lips in a tangle. Her shirt was yanked from her trousers and left behind them on the floor.

His bed was high, requiring a footstool to climb up onto it. He disengaged himself long enough to lift Jamie onto the bed, then stepped onto the stool so that he stood between her legs. She sunk into the thick down covering, and he wanted nothing so badly as to sink himself right down into her. But he had waited too long to rush.

The moonlight cast her in deep shadow. He reached over and switched on a small bedside lamp, filling the room with a soft glow. She smiled and reached for him.

He wasn't sure where his immediate responses tugged the hardest: in his loins—or in his heart.

And yet he did not accept her bold invitation. "Now that we are here, I find a swift ravishment does not suit my needs. Nor, do I believe, will it suit yours."

Jamie quirked her eyebrows, then slowly let her hands drift over her head to rest on the bed. "Is that so?"

He nodded. Her position was at once that of a supplicant and that of one quite in control of the situation. Her pose strained the fabric of her simple cotton brassiere. Her nipples pressed at the white fabric, beckoning his lips to come and discover the treasure that awaited him.

"I know," she said dryly. "It's not exactly a Victoria's Secret fantasy. But, then, I figured if I'm going to get involved again, this time around I'm going to be myself. So I'm admitting up front, I'm not much for sexy lingerie."

She thought him unaffected? He smiled at that and lifted his gaze back to her eyes. "I find nothing wrong with your attire, beyond that you are still in it."

She smiled then and reached for her belt, but paused. "You first."

Sebastien laughed at that. "So bold, and yet so demure." It summed up her allure exactly.

She flicked off her shoes so that they dropped to the floor on either side of the footstool. "There. Your turn."

"Ah, a temptress, to be sure." He removed his shoes and socks. "I believe the next move is yours."

She slid her belt from her pants and flung it over her head with great abandon. "Next?"

"Quite the tease, are we? Two can play at that." He grinned at her and slowly unbuttoned his shirt. He relished the slip of control he witnessed in her eyes. He slid the soft fabric off his shoulders and felt his own body leap in response to her obvious reaction. He knew he had a pleasing form, but never before had he been so aware of its impact. Never before had he so wanted to please.

"You definitely have far more experience in the teasing department," she managed.

"I wouldn't be so sure of that." He knelt on the bed, his weight sinking him down beside her. He traced his fingers along the edge of her bra.

"I told you," she said. "Victoria's Secret I am not."

"I do not know this Victoria you speak of, nor do I care to learn her secrets. It is yours I crave to discover." When she started to speak, he pressed a finger to her lips. "It is not what covers your skin that I am interested in."

Again, desire flared in her eyes. Again, he felt the insistent tug of response grow inside him. *Merde*, but if he were to grow any harder, he'd burst. He unfastened her pants and slid them down her legs. Legs that went on for centuries. She was lithe, finely muscled, and perfectly molded. The very idea of those strong legs wrapped around his waist—

And he'd thought he could not become any harder.

"Your turn." She nodded at his pants and smiled. "I'm being demure and demanding again."

"Uh-huh." With a grin, he rose and unbuckled his own pants and let them fall to the floor. A small strangled sound from her brought his head up.

"Is something amiss?" He held his arms out to the sides. "You find something not to your liking?"

She propped herself up on her elbows. "At the risk of enlarging your . . . ego . . . I will baldly admit to spending some quality time fantasizing about you. However, I guess I'd never gotten around to wondering if you were a briefs or boxer man. But even if I had, I don't think I'd have ever figured on bikinis. Much less red ones. Is that what the fashionable pirate is wearing these days?"

Now Sebastien felt that twinge of disconcertment she must have felt when he'd disrobed her. "You do not find them appealing?" He looked down and turned to either side.

"Oh, they're . . . incredibly appealing. Amazingly so."

He grinned then, enjoying her sudden hard swallow. "I thought these were a grand discovery. Quite comfortable."

"And red."

"*Mais oui.* A bold color, don't you think? However, I do find them rather . . . limiting at the moment."

Jamie's gaze couldn't help but shift downward to observe the limitations he spoke of. "I, um, can see what you mean. As you said earlier, it's not what you wear on your skin that attracts me."

He grinned and knelt beside her on the bed, enjoying the widening of her eyes as he did so. He stretched out beside her. She trembled just slightly as he rested a hand on her abdomen then moved it upward to cup her breast. "And yet, there is an allure to that which has yet to be uncovered."

She reached for the center clasp of the bra, but he pushed her hands away. "No hurrying this." He winked at her. "Sometimes a plunder is best done slowly." He smoothed his hands over her body, enjoying the shuddering reaction he felt beneath his questing fingertips.

"Slow plundering is good," she said faintly. "I like slow plundering."

He opened his mouth to tease her in kind, but the words that came out were not lighthearted and carefree, but heartfelt and sincere. "Ah, Jamie, you are built more finely than the sleekest sailing vessel." He smoothed his hand down her hips and over the length of her thighs. "Your lines are long and cleanly sculpted." He shifted his flat palm up her other hip and across her belly until he once again cupped her breast.

She only gulped in air, making her chest rise briefly beneath his touch. He teased his fingers along the edge of the brassiere, then moved his hand to her shoulder and slowly slid one strap off, then the other. Her breathing seemed to have all but stopped.

"Never have I wanted so deeply, Jamie. Never has a discovery been so sweet." He slid the front clasp open and lifted her brassiere from her skin. Now it was his fingers that trembled. Who could have predicted what the sight of her perfect, rosebud nipples would do to his equilibrium? "Such perfection," he murmured.

He dipped his head, first to her mouth, and took his time there, until he felt her begin to move insistently against his hand. Her lips were wet and full when he finally left them and journeyed downward to finally take one firm bud into his mouth. His body clenched tightly, almost painfully. He heard the groan fill his throat and issue forth as he caressed her nipple with his tongue. So soft, so delectably sweet.

He smoothed his fingertips over her other nipple, murmuring in French when she whimpered and arched more violently into him. "*Mon coeur*," he whispered against her heated skin.

She wove her fingers through his hair, pulling it free from its queue until the ends brushed across his bare shoulders and onto her skin. She tugged at his head, holding him to her. She writhed beneath him, searching for more. He drove her higher, faster. Her hips bucked off the bed. She cried out as he shifted his mouth from her nipple to her throat, then abruptly shoved at his shoulders, catching him off guard and sending him tumbling to his back.

She took quick advantage of the situation and pushed him down, her hands pressed against his chest. "My turn," she said, her breathing uneven.

It took amazing restraint to keep from hauling her astride him and taking her right then and there. "I don't believe I was finished. Was I not being thorough enough?"

She shook her head, her breathing gradually slowing. "You know exactly what you're doing."

"I told you I would not be rushed this night."

She smiled. "Which is exactly why I pushed you off me."

"Ah."

"I think it's only fair I have some plundering time of my own."

He grinned and shifted his hands until they rested on the bed above his head. "Be free with me, mademoiselle. I am at your tender mercy."

Her own smile had a touch of the wicked in it. "Be careful what you ask for. I'll have you know I've played this exact scenario out in my mind once or twice."

"Oh? And how does it end?"

He thrilled to the hot blush that stole across her neck and across her cheeks. But she didn't look away, nor did her smile diminish. If anything, her shoulders squared a bit, her chin lifting as well. Yes, she would have done well onboard ship, his pirate queen.

"As a certain Frenchman once told me," she said, " 'I'd rather show you than tell you.' "

"Please, then. I am all for being enlightened."

"First, I fear you're rather constricted here."

She slid her fingers beneath the elastic waistband of his bikini briefs. He inhaled sharply. His lapse of control only served to further build her confidence, which she made clear with a grin that was quite carnal. And yet there was a level of eroticism in submitting to her that he'd never before encountered.

She carefully freed him and slid the briefs off. With a smile that could only be described as brazen, she tossed them over her shoulder.

"Now whatever shall be done with me?" he asked, his tone as innocent a one as he could manage.

"Do you fear for your safety?"

He grinned again, unable to recall ever enjoying himself this much. He found himself wondering just how many days—and nights—he could keep her here. "I have no fear," he replied. "However, I do feel at a slight disadvantage, being completely naked and at your somewhat-more-clothed mercy."

"Is that a challenge?"

He loved the gleam in her eyes. "*Oui.* I believe that it was."

She sighed a little and said, "I wonder how many women you seduce with your accent alone. You could make a fortune in the phone-sex industry."

"Phone sex?"

She opened her mouth, then shut it again. "Some other time."

He winked at her. "I will not forget."

"No, I don't believe I'll let you either."

Perhaps it was the playful gleam in her eyes or that he'd never felt so thoroughly satisfied with life, but he could wait no longer. Sebastien reached for her and pulled her, laughing, down to him, so that she lay half across his chest. He grew serious and, slowly, so did she. He felt her heart pound against his own. "Truly, you are like no other woman, Jamie *mon amour*." He rolled her to her back and leaned in to take her mouth.

He kissed her deeply, until both their bodies writhed and shone with sweat. She arched beneath him every time he plunged his tongue inside her mouth, and he could torture neither her nor himself any longer.

"If you wish protection, retrieve it now. I want to feel you wrapped tightly around me, Jamie. And I want to see it in your eyes as I claim you this first time."

She surprised him again by reaching between them and taking his rigid length in her hand. "And I want to see your eyes as you enter me. Every time."

He almost spilled himself into her palm right then. He took her mouth again in a kiss that could only be termed ravishment. "Find them, Jamie," he said, his voice raspy and thick, then kissed her neck and once again found himself tasting her sweet, engorged nipples. "Cover me. Now."

She groped behind her, holding his head to her with her other hand. He heard the rustling of something, then her swearing. He lifted his head in time to see her tear the small pouch open with her teeth.

He grinned wide. "I love a woman with ingenuity."

She only pushed at his shoulders. "Here. I don't think I can do this. My fingers are shaking too badly." Her laugh was a bit shaky as well. "Damn, I have never been like this. It's worse than the very first time."

He slid the slippery latex from her hand and finally worked it on, his own hands trembling like they never had before. He pulled her beneath him and felt his own breath hitch when the tip of him brushed her thigh. "This is *our* first time. And that makes it perfect." He pulled her thighs up over his hips, then cradled her head in his palms and looked into her eyes. "You asked to watch me." He leaned in and kissed her, then shifted back just enough for them to look eye to eye. "Watch me now."

She gasped, but it was in obvious pleasure, as he pushed the very tip of himself inside her. He groaned deep within his throat. His hands and arms began to shake under the effort of maintaining a slow pace.

"Deeper, Sebastien," she demanded, her own voice more ragged than he'd ever heard it. "I want all of you." She reached for his shoulders and lifted her hips as those strong legs folded around his waist. "Now. Fill me up."

She pulled him another torturous inch inside her. He found a smile, even as he groaned anew. "Perhaps," he ground out, "if I make love to you often enough, we'll eventually follow *my* plan."

She tugged him in deeper. "What plan?" she grunted, then moaned and arched beneath him as he moved just slightly deeper.

"To . . . go . . . slow." And with that he let out a long, hoarse groan and pushed fully inside her.

There was nothing slow after that.

She would hardly let him retreat before bringing her hips up to force his next thrust. He met her pace and matched it easily. The bed, large and heavy as it was, rocked beneath them. Everything thundered. Perfectly matched, they moved together as if their bodies had been joined for centuries, just like this. Her head arched back and her eyes slid shut, as did his own.

He felt her tighten and begin to convulse against him, just as he, too, felt the sudden rush of completion surge within. He forced his head forward. "Jamie," he said on a rasp. "*Mon amour*." She opened her eyes just as he leaned into her and thrust fully inside. "It is now that I make you mine."

She climaxed around him, clenching so tightly that he came instantly, almost violently.

He barely held himself from collapsing on top of her. She kissed his damp neck and pulled him down on her anyway, bearing his weight almost needfully. She stroked his back, his shoulders, his hair, the side of his face. As if she couldn't bear to not be touching him even as he was still fully inside her.

Her actions made him feel . . . necessary. An odd choice, but exact in describing his emotion. *Necessary.* It was a first for him. And astonishing in the power it wielded.

"Sebastien."

It was barely a murmur but so steeped with contentment he thought his heart would fill to bursting with what it made him feel. Like a confirmation. He nuzzled the sweet skin beneath her ear as their labored breathing finally slowed, their heated bodies began to cool.

He had only one thought as he worked his way slowly to her mouth and kissed her deeply, sweetly, almost reverently.

He wanted her always.

If only there was some way to keep her.

Chapter 19

Jamie fought for the last vestiges of slumber as they left her. She struggled to stay in her dream world, stay in the hot, decadent dreams that had filled her night. She arched and stretched her body fully. God, her dreams had been so realistic that her body even had twinges of soreness, as if she really had spent the night with Sebastien buried inside—

Reality came rushing in. It hadn't been a dream. She'd really—

Jamie opened her eyes to find Sebastien beside her, propped on one elbow, watching her.

She said the first thing that occurred to her. "I have bed hair, right?" Then she blushed. *Great, and so smooth too.*

His smile was slow and devilish. "My woman should always appear in such satiated dishabille when the sun arises."

My woman. Her throat went dry. Dear Lord, what had she done? She should open her mouth this instant and lay down ground rules, explain that if they were going to continue this . . . this . . . dear God, this heavenly pleasure. Oh, what the hell, who was she kidding? Right at that moment she was totally and completely his and perfectly satisfied with that arrangement.

"Has the sun come up already?" she managed. She

turned to find that it had arisen indeed—some time ago, from the looks of things. "Oh, no!" She grabbed at the sheet, intent on yanking it off, but a heavy hand on her stomach kept it pinned firmly in place. "I have to go to work."

He tugged her gently back into the bed. "*Non*. You are free for the day, this whole beautiful day."

She rolled to her back and stared up into his face. His amazingly beautiful face. And she made a decision right then and there: All her reasons for not wanting to end up in the very place she was right now, feeling all the things she was feeling, were banished. In exile. To be dealt with at some later time—preferably never.

And this was way better than dreaming.

"What do you mean, I'm free?"

"I awoke some time ago and after contemplating you as you slept, I've decided that I'm keeping you."

Jamie's heart felt as if it had burst wide open. Dangerous, she knew. But she sent those fears into exile as well. "And what if I don't want to be a kept woman?" As if she had a hope in hell of pulling off that lie.

"I considered that."

She smiled now. "Did you really? Unsure of your charms all of a sudden?"

His grin was decidedly wicked. "Hardly."

She laughed. "Okay, now I know I'm not dreaming." She couldn't have dreamed something this perfect.

He traced a finger along her cheekbone and looked at her with such . . . She couldn't bring herself to form the word, even in her mind.

"Why am I not working today?" she managed finally, through a throat suddenly tight with emotion.

"I called Jack," he said idly, still stroking her skin, pushing her hair from her face. "He agreed to cover for you today. I hope you do not mind my interference."

Mind? If it wasn't for the heavenly feel of his touch on her skin she'd have gotten up and done a victory dance right there on the bed. But no sense in giving him too much of an edge. "Um, no. I suppose that's okay." Her nonchalance was totally ruined a moment later by the wide, satisfied grin that split her face. "Thank you."

He grinned then too, and she squealed in surprise when he suddenly rolled to his back and tugged her on top of him. She straddled him easily, her body already naturally aligned to his after just one night. "How could things be this perfect?"

It wasn't until he answered her that she realized she'd spoken out loud. "I'm uncertain of this myself. Perhaps all the stars in the night sky managed to find the perfect alignment. I do not question these things." She squealed again when he rolled her beneath him. "Especially when they work in my favor."

Jamie laughed, then moaned as she felt him insistently pushing against her thighs. Her hips shifted automatically, seeking once again what he had so generously proved he could give.

"Let me have you once more this morning, Jamie *amour*."

"Only once?" She didn't even care how pathetically needy that sounded.

Especially when he laughed and said, "Greedy wench. I think you're my perfect match." He nudged inside her, prompting her to agree with him. Wholeheartedly.

"I cannot ever imagine a time when once will be enough," he murmured into her ear. "I have plans for us today, but I find I cannot leave this bed without once again feeling your body tighten around mine."

Plans. Jamie wanted to ask him what plans, but then he was inside her, and all she could think was that a lifetime of this would not be enough.

࿈

"Sailing? Like, on a boat? With sails?"

Sebastien laughed as he held the car door open for her. They had enjoyed their walk back to the store. "I believe that is why they call them sailboats, mademoiselle."

The sun was high above the horizon now, but the breeze was light and the temperature perfect. He could not recall a moment when he had been happier or more content. He had thought that moment had come only when he was deep inside Jamie and newly spent. But he was discovering that this contentment had little to do with physical appeasement. His soul was appeased just having her with him, her sunny smile aimed in his direction, her quick wit matching his so effortlessly, her—

"I don't sail, Sebastien."

He laughed. Her sharp tongue, never too shy to tell him her thoughts. Yes, he loved even that.

"Ah, *mon amour*, and I am about to correct that sad state of affairs."

"I'm perfectly happy with that sad state of affairs."

Sebastien merely stood with his hand on the open door. Jamie grumbled, but she climbed into the driver's seat. He closed the door behind her. Even the prospect of folding his body into this small car and allowing her to propel them headlong down a crowded roadway did nothing to dampen his spirits.

She said nothing for several long minutes, then finally he heard the low sigh. He smiled and relaxed. "It won't be so bad as all that. I promise."

"I didn't see anything wrong with what we were already doing today," she mumbled.

"*Ma chère*, have you ever made love on the deck of a sailing ship, the water rocking beneath you?"

Jamie took another corner at a speed that had him grabbing for the dashboard. But it was the wicked smile she aimed his way that had his heart rate spiking.

"Maybe sailing does have one or two things to recommend it, after all."

Sebastien laughed and settled back in his seat. As much as he could, anyway. "I do not understand why you choose a conveyance of such narrow parameters."

"Now who's grumbling?"

"They make larger vehicles, this I know. You were gifted with genetics that made you tall and strong. I simply do not understand why you chose—" He was forced to swallow the rest of his words as she swerved into the parking lot of the marina they'd visited before. His hand was still pressed to his heart even after she turned off the ignition.

"Big baby."

He looked at her. "The same might be said of your fear of sailing."

"I never said I was afraid."

"I don't believe I mentioned fear either. Merely my discomfort with the size of your car."

She reached over and peeled his hand from the dashboard. "Uh-huh."

He tried to think of a snappy retort, but wasn't fast enough. "Okay, I'll strike a bargain with you," she said.

Amused—which he could afford to be now that his life was not in immediate danger—as well as intrigued, he lifted a brow. "Oh?"

"You feel this need to get me on a sailboat."

"I just wanted to share—"

She lifted a hand, stalling him. "I agreed, don't push it. Now, since I'm making the supreme sacrifice of abandoning all my principles of speed"—she pretended a shudder—"for sailing, well, I think it's only fair you make a sacrifice too."

"I believe I got into this automobile willingly this morning. Is that not sacrifice enough?"

She smiled but shook her head. "I think you would be far more understanding of why I chose this car if you knew how to operate it."

Sebastien opened his mouth, then closed it again. Thankfully, since he'd most likely have embarrassed himself.

"I will sail with you, if you'll let me teach you how to drive my car." She leaned over and kissed him on the cheek. "Come on, a big, bad pirate like you? What have you got to fear for?"

"My life?"

"Well, your immortality will come in handy, then, won't it?"

She was out of the car before he could respond. Would that he could have.

His immortality. It was the first either of them had spoken of the improbability of this newly forged bond working for any length of time. But she had done so jokingly. And although he had to admit now that those fears had been hovering just below the surface of his consciousness since the moment he'd awoken this morning to find her still beside him, her hand folded within his, he would not give it a foothold in his mind. Not now. Not today.

He climbed out of the car, watching her as she walked into the rental office. The sun glinted off her hair as it swung across her back. Her long legs, beautifully showcased in her white shorts, handled the sway of the dock with certainty. She turned just then and waved at him, then curled her finger, beckoning him, her smile an obvious taunt. His heart swelled painfully in his chest. No, he would not think beyond today. He could not bear to.

He crossed to the docks, idly wondering if he kept her out on the water long enough, she might forget about the second part of their bargain.

As he stepped onto the dock, she tossed him her car keys. "Here, hold on to these. You'll be needing them later."

He laughed then and once again accepted his fate. This time, far more willingly.

෧෮

Jamie leaned back against the prow and unabashedly watched Sebastien man the wheel. The wind had unbound his hair long ago and plastered his shirt to his chest. She felt something tender and raw fill her as she continued to watch him. This was his home, this was where he truly belonged, mastering the water with his own strength and power. She knew this because she saw the joy in his eyes. For the first time she felt as if she was seeing the man. Not the pirate, not the genie, but who he really was. Her eyes watered and she tried to blame it on the wind, but she knew differently.

He chose that moment to look at her. He motioned to her with a toss of his head. "Come on, it's time you learned her feel."

Jamie laughed. "I'm feeling her just fine right here." She'd be the last to admit it, but she did feel the power of the water and the movement of the boat—and she liked it. It was more elemental, less man and machine against the water, more man and boat moving with the water.

And she *was* dying to try the wheel. The only reason she was still sitting here was because she wasn't sure she could manage it without embarrassing herself.

She was entranced enough—both by the effect the boat had on her, as well as the one Sebastien was having on her—that she didn't want to do anything to alter that perfect balance. The whole day was perfection; why ruin that?

"Now who's being the big baby?" he called out.

Well, okay, so there were some things she couldn't ignore. She stood and made her way toward him. The pitch and roll of the boat was very different from the ones she'd grown up on or raced. But it wasn't unpleasant. Not at all.

"Enjoying yourself, *mon amie*?"

She tilted her face up, squinting in the sun. "Yeah, I guess it's bearable."

He laughed and pulled her in front of him, positioning her hands on the wheel, keeping his hands on top of hers, his chest pressed to her back. She quite liked this little setup, but she'd be darned if she'd tell him.

He leaned down and kissed the side of her neck. "Do you like the feel?"

"Mmm-hmm."

He grinned against her skin. "I mean the boat."

"Handles just fine."

He took his hands from the wheel, and the whole boat suddenly took a violent pitch to one side. "Whoa!"

Sebastien's laugh could probably be heard over the water as far back as the dock. He covered her hands again and quickly had the boat back under control. "A bit of a challenge?"

"Shut up." But she was smiling. "I'll get the hang of this. Besides," she leaned back against his chest, "if sailing means we can stand here like this, I'm all for staying out here as long as it takes."

He chuckled and kept his hands next to hers on the wheel. Keeping his voice low and in her ear so his tone matched the gentle swell and pull of the water, he explained how to work the wheel, how to feel the water and gauge the wind. Jamie felt lulled and energized at the same time.

"I guess I have to apologize."

"For what, *ma chère?*"

"For assuming speed equaled power." She felt the wind and the water pull at the sail and shifted the wheel accordingly. A thrill of accomplishment filled her. "I felt it!"

"Yes, just like that. It is a good feeling, is it not? Instead of man against the elements, it is man working with them."

"I was just thinking that earlier, while I was watching you."

"What else were you thinking?"

"That you belong out here. I could see how much this meant to you, and I'm sorry I gave you a hard time about coming out here."

"No need to apologize." He was quiet for a moment, then said, "I missed this."

"Seeing you out here, I can't imagine you stayed away." She craned her neck around to look at him. "Why did you? If you were near Pontchartrain for this many years?"

She felt his shrug. "Perhaps I could not bear it. The longer I put it off, the less I allowed myself to think about it. Then it seemed as if that time in my life was meant to stay in my past."

"I don't think I could have stayed away," she said quietly. She hadn't thought he'd heard her over the wind, but he lowered his head to kiss her neck again.

"Would that I had found you sooner, *ma chère.* I believe all things happen for a reason. Perhaps we were meant to make this rediscovery together."

She said nothing for several long minutes, then finally spoke what was on her mind. "Were you afraid?

Afraid that sailing again might make your . . . your new life harder to bear?"

There was a long pause and she felt him stroke her hair. "Perhaps." He stroked her hair again, and again. "And perhaps you understand me better than I do myself."

She shook her head. "I think we are a lot alike, that's all. When I gave up racing, it was a long time before I trusted myself to take a boat out."

"You feared the water would lure you back to life on the racing circuit?"

"Exactly."

"But there is no life for the water to lure me back to. This is no longer the man I am."

Jamie smiled. "You might not be a privateer any longer, but that doesn't mean you're not a sailor. That can be in your heart forever."

"Maybe. I suppose I simply felt as if fate had yet again told me to leave one life for another. Maybe it was easier to just make a clean split of things."

"Or maybe keeping this bit of yourself would have helped you make the transition."

"Transitions. I have had enough of those. I suppose I have always felt as if I were cast in a role not of my own making. I've learned to make the best of what life has handed me, but to be truthful, I've always felt somewhat . . ."

Jamie let the sentence dangle for several moments, but when he didn't continue, she shifted around until she almost faced him, letting him command the wheel. "Somewhat . . ."

He looked down into her face. "Misplaced. *Oui,* that is as best as I can explain it. As if I have never truly had a home but have merely fostered myself in the homes others have provided. Or forced on me."

"Have you ever gone home?"

"I'm not certain I truly have one." He looked beyond her, out over the water. "Maybe you're right, though, about the water. Maybe this is as close to feeling at home as I can imagine."

"I meant home to Corsica, to . . . I don't know. Find your people, your relatives, your real family."

Sebastien kept his gaze on the water. There was a very long silence, and Jamie's heart ached inside her chest. "I'm sorry," she said softly. "I wasn't trying to make you feel bad."

"I cannot find my family," he said, his voice rough.

"There are all kinds of sophisticated search engines now that help—"

"*Non*, Jamie. I cannot find them, for I do not know who they are."

"What do you mean? How?"

He turned her back around and pulled her close to him before taking the wheel in both hands again. "Valentin is not my own family name. It was assigned to me by my first captain. His cabin boy before me had been a Valentin, and it was simply easier for him to remember."

"You said you were a boy when they pressed you into service. Eleven."

"You have a good memory."

She could have told him that she remembered every word he'd ever uttered, so strong was his impact on her. But that revelation in and of itself kept her silent.

"Isn't eleven old enough to remember your real name?"

"That time in my life was harrowing beyond description. I did not leave my family willingly, and the life of service I was pressed into killed many who were older and stronger than I. I had a younger sister . . . I think." He stopped abruptly and shook his head. "I don't have much recall of any of those early years." He paused for a moment, then quietly added, "And I'd like to keep it that way."

"I'm sorry. Truly, I never meant—"

"Family is what you make of it, Jamie. Just as you have made a family of Jack and your friends."

"But I have a father."

"And where is he?"

Jamie knew that he wasn't asking for a geographical location. "He is there for me when I need him."

"But you understand me?"

She nodded.

"I have no tangible memories of Corsica. Maybe one day I will go back there. But that does not pull at me, and neither does the prospect of tracking down people who have no real direct connection to the man I am now." He laughed, but there was no humor in it. "Such as that man is."

Jamie turned again, gently pulled his face toward her, and gazed deeply into his eyes. "You are more a man than any I have ever met."

"And yet I am not enough of one to give you what you so deserve. What I would wish to give you, if I could."

Jamie did not want to think about what he could not give her. Not today. "I'm sorry I brought it up. This day was to be ours, and I won't ruin it with talk of tomorrow or the future."

He smiled ruefully. "Now you're sounding a bit like me."

"I don't happen to think that is such a bad thing." She turned back around and took the wheel from his hands. "Now, let me see what I can do with this ragtop."

❧

They said nothing as they turned in their paper-work to the rental office. Just as they'd said nothing beyond what was necessary for her to learn to man the helm all the way back in, which she'd managed to do without bodily harm or permanent damage to the boat. She did owe Sebastien a debt of gratitude for saving that buoy marker, though—as did the bird living in the nest on top of it.

But his moping had gone on long enough. She stopped before they left the dock and turned to him. "Thank you."

"You're welcome, mademoiselle." He smiled, but it didn't reach his eyes.

"I enjoyed sailing." She laughed, forcing real humor into it. "But God help you if you ever tell anyone, hear?" She'd be damned if she'd let him waste even one more moment of their day together. She ignored the little tug of desperation that thought brought on. It was that same tug she knew he'd felt out there on the water—fear of what happened when this day came to an end.

"So," she said brightly, determined. "Got the keys?"

He groaned. "Please, Jamie, not today. Can't we retire home and spend our next several hours—"

"Which reminds me," she broke in, a devilish smile on her lips. "You owe me another sailboat ride. We never did manage to . . . you know."

"I'll promise you anything if you'll agree to forgo the rest of our bargain."

"Not a chance." She took his hand. "Come on, it's not all that bad. In fact, I bet by the time we get back to your place, you'll be talking about what kind of car *you* want."

He swore at length under his breath.

"Very . . . creative. And I don't even understand French. But it's not getting you off the hook." She tugged him across the parking lot. "There's an old shopping center near here that's all closed up. The parking lot is more weeds than pavement at this point, but it has lots of room." She grinned up at him. "Just think of it as a paved ocean."

ᣟ

Sebastien swore for the millionth time as he popped the clutch yet again. "Jamie, I cannot do this, and I wish to end this experiment. I have lasted well over a century without learning to man such a cursed contraption as this, and I don't—"

"That's only because you can't get past second gear. Trust me, once you open this baby up, you'll be totally sold." Jamie had to admit that she wasn't sure he'd ever get out of second gear either. He was not the easiest student, and she told him so. "It would help if your heart was in it a little more."

He looked at her directly, teeth clenched. "I have no heart for this."

"Now, now. I said the same thing about sailing, and look how well that turned out." Okay, so mentioning their time on the water was not a good idea. His eyes got all stormy again, and she thought for a moment that he was going to get out of the car altogether.

She blew out a sigh of defeat. "Oh, okay. You win. Maybe some other time. I didn't want to make you angrier, I just thought it would be fun. Just because I went sailing, you don't have to humor me if you really don't want—"

"Hold on," he snarled. With a growl of the engine, the car lurched forward, almost stalled, lurched again as he shifted, then lunged forward. He pressed down on the gas, lurched again as he shifted, then lunged forward again at an even greater speed.

Jamie clutched the dashboard and started praying.

"I think I am beginning to understand," he said, real wonder in his tone.

"You're heading for a building."

"This is not so bad."

"You're heading for the freaking building!"

"No need for panic," he said calmly. Then he laughed as he turned the wheel and almost set the car on two wheels.

Jamie managed not to scream, but only because she felt as if she'd swallowed her tongue.

"Does it have higher gears?"

"*No!*"

He spun them around again, almost doing a one-eighty. Rubber burned.

"You're killing my Pirelli tires."

"I will buy you new ones." He let out another laugh and raced across the parking lot yet again.

"Dear God, what have I done?" She began to pray in earnest.

He spun the car around and braked suddenly, almost sending her through the windshield. Thankfully, the engine conked out when he took his foot off the clutch. Jamie lunged for the steering wheel and all but yanked out the keys.

Sebastien sat back and folded his arms over his chest, looking very satisfied with himself. "What, you do not wish for me to drive you home?"

Jamie glared at him, still incapable of speech.

Sebastien reached over and turned her head toward his with a finger beneath her chin. "Now it is my turn to thank you, Jamie *amour*." He was smiling now as she hadn't seen him smile since . . . since right before she'd been stupid enough to bring up his past out on the water. Seeing him happy again . . . well, for that she was thankful, very, very thankful.

But not enough to let him drive again. Ever.

"You're welcome," she said, finding a smile. "Now can we go home and finish the day as we started it?"

"*Mais oui, ma chèrie.*"

"Thank you, God," she whispered.

Sebastien laughed and kissed her. In an instant the

moment shifted. The anxiety of the past hour and the painful emotions from the boat ride all dissipated.

Another emotion rose to take its place. And Jamie was terrified to put a name to it. She simply gave herself over to it.

"Take me home, Sebastien."

"When I kiss you, I feel like I'm already there."

Jamie knew it was love right then. Because she actually gave him the keys.

Chapter 20

*J*amie opened her eyes to find Sebastien beside her, propped on one elbow, watching her. Unlike the morning before, his expression was unreadable and did not change even when she smiled tentatively at him.

It was not a good sign.

She slowly pulled the sheet up higher on her chest. "Morning." Inane, but she was suddenly at a loss for what to say. She didn't know what she expected, but . . . well, she did know what she expected. She expected him to be like he had been yesterday morning.

But yesterday was over in more ways than one.

A chill raced over her skin.

"*Bonjour,* mademoiselle."

His voice was rough and sexy and made her shiver again, this time in remembrance of just how it had sounded last night as he'd whispered to her all the things he planned to do to her. And he had. Yet she could find nothing of her bold pirate in his eyes this morning. He appeared moody and withdrawn.

"Is something wrong?"

"I am not entirely certain."

Oh, great. This was definitely sounding like the beginning of the end. Only she wasn't ready for this to end and she had every intention of figuring out how to make it last. Maybe she'd grown after all. "Can I help?"

He was looking at her, but she wasn't certain what he was actually seeing.

Abruptly, he said, "Tell me about your husbands."

More than a little surprised at the demand, her first instinct was to fling back the covers and stalk out of the room. But she didn't. In racing, she had always fought hard to the bitter end, because she knew she was good enough to win if she worked hard enough. In relationships with men, she didn't have the same confidence—her track record certainly hadn't bred any. But running away hadn't solved anything before. And what she discovered right now was that, for the first time, she didn't want to run. She wanted to stay and fight. For him. For them.

"Pardon me for sounding a bit confused, but I'm having a bit of a hard time figuring out what went so terribly wrong from when we finally fell into exhausted sleep a few hours ago and now."

"Nothing has gone wrong." He seemed honestly confused. "Do you not wish to discuss your husbands? I did not ask to anger you. I merely need to understand—"

"Why would you be thinking about them now? What could you possibly need to understand about my husb—" Her eyes widened. "Oh, wait just a minute. You had better not be planning on bringing up that whole matchmaking thing." She tossed the covers back. "Because after what we have shared, I cannot believe you would dare think about finding me anyone—"

A strong hand clamped down on her arm, stopping her escape. "That is the very last thing I'm thinking about at this moment."

She looked back at him. Damn, but he was too sexy in the morning. Hair rumpled, a morning shadow of beard lining his jaw, his bare chest looking hard and tan against the white sheets, his eyes so dark and deep she felt she could tumble headlong into them. Her anger dissolved, leaving only the confusion. "Then why do you ask?"

"Come back here and I'll tell you." He tugged her back into bed, and damn if she didn't let him. She rolled to her back, coming to a stop in the crook of his arm, her body aligning all too well with his. Her fears began to dissipate. A little.

"So, what is it about my failures as a wife you'd like to know?" she asked dryly.

"First of all, I do not believe you failed as a wife. Did it occur to you that perhaps the men you married failed at being a husband?"

"Yes, well, they definitely didn't win any awards either, but still . . ."

He brushed the tangled strands of hair from her face. "I asked about them because I want to understand the mistakes they made with your heart." His deep voice thrummed a responding chord deep inside her. She'd never seen him so serious. "So I don't repeat them."

She melted. "Why?" She immediately saw the hurt and realized he'd misunderstood. "I didn't mean I don't want you to try, I just meant that how . . . You know . . . we can't . . . you . . . I . . . Damn." This was too hard. "Can't we pretend it's still yesterday?" Her throat tightened at the look in his eyes. She all but begged him. "Just for one more day?"

He pulled her abruptly to him and kissed her mouth. More rightly described, he possessed it. She submitted instantly, only he was not satisfied with her submission. As he had every time they'd made love, he demanded her active participation. And as she'd eagerly discovered, equal partners in passion can produce amazing results.

She was completely without breath and reaching for more when he lifted his head.

"Maybe we should find a way," he managed roughly.

That stopped her. "Find a way . . . to what?"

Now it was his turn to look away, to sigh in frustration. "Never mind. You are right, I am spoiling this morning we have together." He turned back to her and stroked his fingertips down her cheek. "I apologize. I have lain awake for hours and I haven't properly wished you good morning."

Despite the tumble of confusion and alarm she felt, she found a smile. She clung to it almost desperately. "Oh, I think that kiss was pretty much a great good morning for me."

His lips quirked, but his eyes still looked concerned. "I'm sorry I didn't begin with that, then. I do not wish to waste a moment with you."

"I don't wish to waste time with you either." She worked hard to keep a lock on the fear, fear so great it threatened to swell up and choke her.

Jamie looked up at Sebastien to find him studying her again, but this time there was only heat in his eyes. Heat and need. This she understood. She shared that need. And, God help her, she would not walk willingly away from it.

Yes, there would be pain. Crushing heaps of it. Eventually. But right here, right now, she could honestly say she wouldn't give the last two days back even if she could.

"What are you thinking?" he asked. He smoothed a fingertip across her brow.

She found a smile, a heartfelt one, and focused firmly on it. He was right. They shouldn't waste any of what time they did have. "I am thinking that it's Monday and the shop is usually pretty quiet until the afternoon. Do you have any pressing engagements this morning?"

"I believe I could make myself available." As if taking her cue, finally the devilish grin resurfaced, all the way to his twinkling dark eyes.

Jamie relaxed and allowed the buzz of anticipation to build within her. "Then why don't you show me again how you hunt for buried treasure?"

He ripped the sheet from the bed and tossed it to the floor, a very piratical gleam in his eyes. "Aye-aye, *mon amour*." He laid a large, warm palm flat on her belly. "I believe I left off the last hunt right about here." He kissed a tender spot just below her navel.

She twitched at the tickle of his morning beard. He immediately lifted his head, eliciting a whimper of disappointment from her. That quickly turned into a squeal when he rolled her into his arms and slid off the bed to stand at the foot of it.

"You have this plunder-and-ravish thing down." She wrapped her arms around his neck. Being carried in the arms of a man was even better when they were both naked, she decided.

"I may not be a privateer anymore, but I was once quite good at what I did."

"Trust me, you're still quite good at what you do."

His grin widened. "I believe a warm shower is in order. You have tender areas that need ministering to."

"And you have a beard that needs taming."

He raised his eyebrows. "Am I to trust you with a blade at my throat?"

"I believe that is how we met, was it not?" In the very instant she said it, she wished she could take it back. Reminders of anything having to do with the origins of their relationship were exactly what they didn't need.

But he didn't even blink. "And you wielded it beautifully, my pirate queen." He pushed open the door to the adjoining bathroom, a decidedly larger one than hers. He let her slide down the front of his body, both of them shuddering with a low groan as she settled upon his erection.

"And you . . . wield things quite well yourself." Her voice was tight and she squirmed on him. "Oh, Sebastien."

He pushed the door shut, then shifted so her back pressed against a towel that hung from the back of the door. "Wrap those legs about my waist, Jamie," he said hoarsely.

She did and exhaled on a long, needy moan as he slid inside her. "Oh, yes." She groaned. "This is definitely the perfect way to minister to my tender areas."

"I cannot stay here," he murmured against her throat. "I am not protected."

She held him more tightly, her legs wrapped firmly about his waist, her arms clamped about his neck. "Don't leave. Not just yet."

"If it were within my power, I'd never leave." He kissed her throat and shifted more fully inside her. "You hold me as if made for me, Jamie."

She blinked hard to keep the sudden tears from escaping. He said the most wonderfully amazing things to her. She buried her face in his neck so he wouldn't see. "I know," she said, hoping he took her hoarseness for need. She did have immense need. A bottomless pit of it. And she never wanted to crawl out. "I know."

She tightened around him and he groaned, his hips beginning to move. "Jamie, we—"

"It's okay," she murmured against his ear. "It's not the right time for me. I won't get pregnant." She wrapped her legs even more tightly. "I want to feel you—like this—in me." She wanted to feel him come inside her. In fact, she could never remember something being this important.

He shuddered at her words, then abruptly shifted her off him. She groaned at the sudden loss but let her feet drop to the floor. Sebastien gathered her close and rested his forehead against the door, eyes shut.

"This is insanity," he said heavily. "We lose control, you and I, too easily."

She stroked his hair and turned his face to hers. "It would have been okay. I don't take unnecessary risks." She tried a smile. "I gave up life in the fast lane, remember?"

But he didn't find a smile in return. "We want— *Non. I* want this too much. It is too dangerous for us to continue like this."

She sighed, hating this. She supposed if she'd been honest with herself, she'd have known there was no avoiding it. They couldn't pretend things hadn't changed between them now. "You knew about the danger. You warned me, remember? And I understand danger, better than perhaps anyone."

He framed her face and looked intently into her eyes. "Tell me, is this how you thought it would be? Will you be able to just walk away afterward, your heart unscathed?"

She wanted to lie, to tell him what he wanted to hear. But what did he want to hear? Truth, honesty. She'd promised herself that much, and she owed that to him as well.

"No. It's more. Much more. I don't want it to end. But we both knew it would have to at some point. I don't want it to hurt either, but it will. More than I even knew. And that's only going to get worse the longer it lasts." She looked into his serious eyes. "But if we both understand that, and are still willing to—"

"I don't know that I am willing."

Jamie knew her heart was involved, but only when she felt the giant, rending wounds his words opened deep inside it did she really learn what pain was. "I'd—" She had to stop and clear her throat. "I thought I had matured enough to handle something like this. I thought I could keep it all in perspective."

"Mine is already lost, Jamie."

She nodded, feeling the burn of tears behind her eyes. This time she let them surface. What was the use of hiding them? "Mine too. It wasn't supposed to be this bad. I wanted—" She looked into his eyes, hers so blurred with tears she couldn't read his expression. "I wanted, for once, to enjoy something without having a price to pay for it. Stupid me."

"*Non*. It was foolish, perhaps, for both of us to underestimate the power of our union. I would not give up a second of the time we had, Jamie. And not just this weekend, but all the seconds that came before. You have taught me that I have a heart that is capable of—" He shifted his gaze from hers and took her hand in his instead. He kissed her palm and curled her fingers tightly over it. "Keep this. It is everything I feel for you and cannot say."

There was no stopping the tears now. Silently they tracked down her cheeks. "This is really it, then?" He stepped back, but she refused to retreat. Right there, with both of them naked and standing in a cold, tiled bathroom, she was not retreating. "There must be a way, Sebastien. You said yourself you don't know all the rules."

He smiled then, but there was no joy in it for either of them. "You believe in what I am. I have at least gotten that from you."

"When I am with you, I do. You overwhelm me, and everything seems possible."

"And when we are apart?"

Just hearing the word *apart* tore a bit more at her already ragged heart. Could this be the last time she would see him? Her voice was a bit shakier when she continued. "When we are apart, I guess I try not to think about that part at all."

"You would want to stay with me, then, even thinking I am a man plagued by delusions?"

She should have hesitated at it being put like that, but she didn't. "Yes, I would stay with you."

His eyes grew fierce. "I would have been honored to have a woman such as you by my side. I only wish my path had crossed yours centuries ago."

She felt her legs begin to shake. He was really ending this. Right now. And she was very afraid there was nothing she could do about it. "I am crossing your path now. Why can't we just continue as we began last night and see what happens?"

"What will happen is that I must make my last match. And once I do, I will leave you—whether it is my wish or not. I do not think we should go on, only to compound the pain of that inevitable conclusion."

She stepped forward and took his hand, trying to quell the desperation she felt, but she was not quite successful at it. "So what if you don't match Jack right away? Is there a rule that says how much time you have?"

"It won't be Jack, Jamie."

That stopped her. "What? I thought you agreed to try and see if—"

"I can't explain it. I just feel it. I know what I am supposed to do. I will match him if you like, but that is not my destiny."

"So, then, you're saying—What?" Her throat went so dry, her next words were hardly a rasp. "You have to match me? With someone else? But you said—"

He reached for her hand, but she snatched it away. Suddenly she felt cold, and very naked. She snatched the towel from the hook and wrapped it around herself. A certain kind of calm descended over her, possibly more of a protective shield. Without it, she'd have shattered into a million pieces. She turned and looked at him. "I won't be matched, Sebastien. Not with anyone. I will not accept anyone else into my life right now. I wasn't even going to accept you. And look where that got me!"

She turned to leave, but his quiet voice stopped her.

"There is something else I must explain to you."

She wasn't certain she could will herself to stand there a second longer. "What?"

"When I am done, and the sword is returned to you, you will not recall my role in your life."

She spun to face him. "What? You think I'll just forget you?"

He shook his head. "I didn't say that. You will remember me as someone in your life. But you will have no memory of my function while I was here, that I was the matcher of souls."

"How can that be?" She began to shake again. It was too much, all of it, too much. Not only was he taking himself away, ripping her heart out, and planning to try and foist it off on another—She couldn't even finish the thought. But now he thought to rob her of what they had shared as well? She should be angry enough to embrace that pronouncement, but she wasn't. She was . . . she was devastated.

"I cannot explain. Other than to tell you that when I have come back in the past and sought out matches I had made, to see how they were prospering, they remembered me as an old friend in their lives, but that was all they remembered. The sword and its properties, along with my role, were lost to them. Perhaps to maintain the sanctity of the sword's function. So that it cannot be corrupted."

"Then you're saying I will remember you as a lover, but . . . but what?"

"I am not certain. You know more of me than I've

ever revealed before. But I do know you will have no recollection of the sword, of how we truly met, or of my true function here."

She couldn't even begin to assimilate it all. Only one thing swam to the surface. "Will I forget the pain, then?" she asked, tears clogging her throat.

"I do not know. Pain isn't usually associated with what I do. But I will forget nothing."

She wrapped her arms around herself, clutching the towel as if her life depended on holding on to it. "It all seems rather cruel."

"I had never believed so before." He stepped closer. "I feel different now."

He went to reach for her, but she couldn't allow it. She was holding on by a very raveled thread. "No. Don't."

The pain in his eyes almost undid her completely. "I'm sorry," he said quietly.

"You know the worst part? This time I finally thought I'd found something worth fighting for." She opened the bathroom door. "I have to go. Right now." He followed her into the bedroom and watched her gather her clothes. She made it a point not to look at him, standing there in all his naked glory—watching her walk out of his life. "I'd really prefer it if you didn't come around anymore. Do whatever you have to do, but keep away from me and my friends. Understood?"

"Jamie—"

Now she did look at him, not caring how ravaged her tear-streaked face looked. "If you could do one thing for me, then this is all I ask. Stay away."

He could only nod. When she was at the door, he said, "I must fulfill my role. No matter what you or I feel about the matter." His voice was choked now too. "I have no choice."

"I don't plan on making it any easier for you."

"I will make you a happy future, Jamie. I will give you that much."

She turned then, eyes burning, cheeks flushed. "I wanted you. After I said I would never allow myself to want again, I wanted you anyway." She swiped a hand across her cheek. "The only thing I want now is my life back."

For the third time in her life, she walked away from a man she'd given her heart to, stepping over the broken pieces of shattered illusions. Only this time it was far worse than anything that had come before. This time she was fairly certain his heart was broken too. There was no redemption in that. Only more pain.

Chapter 21

Jamie didn't care about the men anymore. They came into the shop, bumped into her at the market, jogged by her on the Moon Walk. She never gave them a second glance, much less a second thought. It should have been a relief.

"Sugar, we have to talk." Ree settled her elbows on the counter and pushed a glass of iced tea at Jamie.

Jamie sighed. "That's the last thing we have to do."

"So you say. But how am I supposed to go around enjoying this delicious love affair I've embarked on, when I feel guilty even mentioning his name in front of you."

Jamie just eyed her. "Oh, so this is all about *you*. Well, guilt isn't going to work. I really don't want to talk about Sebastien. But please feel free to talk about Angel all you want." She picked up the glass as a truce sign. "I truly am happy for you, Ree. And for Marta as well." She took a small sip. "And please, tell her it's okay to send out the wedding invitations. I won't crumble just because she's blissfully happy. I'm not that self-centered." She put the glass down and sighed again, this time more plaintively. "Am I?"

Ree patted her hand. "No, sugar. In fact, that's half the problem. You bury yourself in work, and the rest of the time you're either out racing across the lake or upstairs in that attic."

"You're saying I've adapted to heartache too well?" She lifted an eyebrow. "That's a new approach."

"Sweetie, we're just wanting you to be as happy as we are. You know damn well neither Marta or I ever thought we'd find something like this. It's hard to remember why it seemed so impossible now, you know? Just when you think you don't have a prayer, your prayer is answered. So it's only natural that we want you to have it too."

"Well, you can't have everything. You'll just have to settle for being wildly in love with a guy you used to despise."

"Not that again."

"No, I'm sorry. You know I don't mean it. Maybe I'm not handling my problems as well as you think. But I'm trying, Ree. And it would help if everyone else would just carry on like I'm not made of crystal or something."

Just then Jack burst into the shop. He scooted right over to the counter and hopped up on it, legs crossed at the knee. "Guess what happened to me?" He took a rose from the counter vase, clamped it between his teeth, and leaned back in a dramatic pose.

"You won the lottery?" Ree guessed.

"You were propositioned by that big, preposterously muscled dancer whose hair you did last Thursday?"

He took the rose out and swatted Jamie across the shoulder. "Neither. I was having a drink last night at Bobby's and ended up in an all-night conversation with his roommate's cousin. He's in from St. Louis on business."

A sick ball of dread began to well up in Jamie's stomach. She couldn't speak for fear it would rear up and gag her. Sebastien had done it. He'd matched Jack. If her plan had gone right, that meant— Sebastien was gone.

Or that he was actively seeking her mate right at

that very moment. She didn't know which idea she hated more.

Jack tucked the rose behind his ear, his smile wide, eyes dancing. "I'm telling you, this is nothing like I've ever felt before. He's thirty-four, drop-dead gorgeous, and recently out of a long-term relationship. He wasn't looking for anyone in his life and, frankly, neither was I. Girls just want to have fun, you know," he added with a naughty wink. "But we really clicked. I can't even describe it." He laughed. "Listen to me, I'm babbling." He grabbed Ree's wrist, his excitement palpable. "We're going out of town. He has a business trip to San Fran. I'm going with him."

Ree pulled him close for a tight hug. "That's so wonderful!" She sat him back, her expression turning serious. "Now, because I love you, I have to warn you—"

"Yes, Mother," Jack interrupted. "We've already swapped medical tests and we'll use protection. Now, can I please be excused? I have some shopping to do." He was out the door as quickly as he'd appeared.

Ree fanned herself. "My Lord, I've never seen him like that. I sure hope this works out. Of course, with the way things have been working out lately . . ." She turned to Jamie, and her hand dropped to her side. "What's wrong?"

Jamie instantly tried to smooth her expression into a calm, smiling one. "Nothing. I'm happy for him."

Ree's eyes widened. "Oh, Lordy. I'm an idiot. You said Sebastien was going to match him up." She reached for Jamie's arm, sympathy and concern brimming in her eyes, but Jamie moved out of reach.

"I'm okay," she lied. At that moment she didn't even know what okay was. "And he already told me this wouldn't affect his . . . whatever. His mission."

"So he's not . . . gone. Or whatever happens to him when he's done matching three people up."

Jamie's stomach pitched. And her head hurt. "I

don't think so. Not that it matters." *Liar.* She had promised herself she'd never see him again, but there was some tiny, masochistic element of comfort in knowing he was still out there somewhere.

"Sure it does. We've talked about this, Jamie Lynne. You believe in him."

"No, that was you who was all ready to jump in."

"You do too. No more lying to yourself. I think a part of you has believed since that first night. Admit it, he's a hard guy to doubt."

Jamie didn't want to admit anything.

"Sure, it makes no rational sense, but neither does the idea of me and Angel being head over heels. And hell, honey, it's hard to ignore proof like that." She reached out and touched Jamie's arm. "And besides," she added gently, "if you didn't truly believe he was going to disappear on you after making his matches, you'd have made his exit from your life a hell of a lot more difficult. You *have* changed, Jamie."

Jamie wanted to argue, but she was just too tired. Tired of it all. Tired of pretending she was okay when she wasn't, tired of pretending she didn't mind sleeping alone in her bed when she did, tired of pretending she could imagine spending the rest of her life never seeing him again when that was all she thought about.

Ree stepped around the counter and took Jamie's half-empty glass away from her. "Honey, why don't you take the rest of the afternoon off? Marta will be here in a little bit, and I can hold down the fort until then."

The thought of facing an entire afternoon alone, with nothing to keep her company but her anguished thoughts, was not appealing. But neither was looking into Ree's sympathy-filled eyes. "I'm telling the truth when I say I'm okay with you and Marta finding happiness. Jack too. I'll get my own act together. Please, just go on and enjoy what's happening in your life. I promise not to be a wet blanket."

"It's a gorgeous day outside. Why don't you take my car so you can put the top down? Take a long drive, maybe out River Road or something. Get some fresh air, clear your head. Crank up the tunes, sing out loud. It will make you feel alive again." She wagged a finger. "No speeding tickets. Unless, of course, the cop is a cutie."

Jamie rolled her eyes. She wasn't sure she was in the mood for a long drive, but racing over the lake hadn't done it for her. It had only made her think of the times she and Sebastien had been out there. Running made her think of walking the streets of the Quarter with Sebastien. Hell, everything made her think of Sebastien.

"Maybe it will help." She'd said it mostly to appease Ree, but the more she thought about it, the more the solitude appealed to her. At least she wouldn't be torturing anyone else with her morose thoughts.

Ree tossed her the keys, and Jamie leaned in and gave her a quick hug. "Thanks. You know, for caring." She stepped back. "Even if it's not necessary."

Ree nodded and waved.

Jamie grabbed her wallet and headed out the back. Ree's little BMW was even smaller than her car. Folding herself into the tight space made her think of— *Stop it. Enough is enough.* Fresh air, good tunes, clear head. That was her sole focus for the next several hours. Even if it killed her.

She put the top down, revved the engine, popped a Stones CD into the player, and edged out onto the street. There was no one around, so she cranked up the stereo and belted out "Satisfaction" along with Mick as she laid rubber all the way to Esplanade.

❧

Sebastien watched Jamie exit the alley behind the bookstore. The little black car took the corner with a squeal. He stepped from the shadows of the corner doorway as she sped out of sight. Another piece of his heart disintegrated as she once again, albeit unwittingly, raced out of his life.

Fool! But the self-recrimination no longer served to punish him. He'd called himself a hundred worse names in the weeks since Jamie had walked out of his bedroom. He still believed he'd done the right thing in not prolonging a doomed relationship. But, *mon Dieu*, for a man who had tried to avoid more pain, he'd failed miserably. And from the determined look on Jamie's face every time he'd spied her these past weeks, she was faring little better. There was no ego gratification in that knowledge. Only more pain. He should never have touched her.

Dear God, but how was he to go on without ever touching her again?

He slapped the brick wall next to his head and turned to walk down the street. He had found Jack a mate. He should feel rewarded by the joy he'd brought to someone, and he *was* happy he'd been so successful with relative ease. But he'd done it for selfish reasons, which was something he'd never done before. He'd wanted to return to the sword, to the anguish-free haze of limbo. He'd matched Jack in the vain hope that perhaps his feeling about it was wrong. But Jack was falling in love—and Sebastien still roamed the earth. His mission had not been completed.

Which was why his stomach rebelled and his skull felt three sizes too big for the skin wrapped about it. He had to find Jamie's soulmate.

It made him want to smash something. It made him want to howl. The very idea of another man touching her, tasting her, making her laugh—hell, even making her swear. *He* wanted those privileges. He'd postponed beginning the search, thinking if he never matched her, at least he would have the pleasure—pain of watching over her.

But that was not how it worked. He understood now, as he never had before, that he was not only ordained to fulfill his mission, he was compelled to. He could not simply roam this earth, putting off his calling until such time as he saw fit to fulfill it.

This time would be no different from any other. There would be no reprieve. For himself, or for Jamie.

Which brought him to a new frustration: He could not analyze exactly how he determined his matches. He simply studied his selected soul, then went about finding a compatible mate. There was never any doubt of his success. Perhaps he did have some sort of otherworldly power, as Jamie had thought him to possess. Some matches had taken him some time and quite complicated maneuvering, but he had always had a notion of what he was looking for. He merely searched until he found it.

Until now. He was faced with matching the soul of a woman he knew better than anyone he'd ever matched before. And yet he could not discern where to begin, who to look for, or what in the hell he was going to do about it.

He should never have touched her.

It had clouded his thinking beyond repair. And yet he had to find a way to part the clouds, to divine what he was to do next. For his own peace of mind, and for hers. He had no choice. He could not sleep. He could not eat. He felt as if his insides were eating him alive. What manner of curse was this eternity he'd been cast into? Never before had he suffered from it. Perhaps this was the penalty he'd feared would be levied against him for taking his mistress to bed. And yet, even looking deeply inside his own black soul, he could not honestly say he truly regretted a single heartbeat of the time he'd spent with her. Maybe that was the worst of it. He should never have touched her—but he cherished the moments when he had.

Now he must find her a mate, find some way to create some element of rightness in all this. If she were happy, wouldn't that be right? Perhaps that would comfort him during the long, empty years ahead.

And yet he could not imagine this ache in his heart ever lessening, much less leaving him. Nor was he certain that he was man enough to look upon her in the arms of another and feel anything but fury and heartrending loss. He could only do as he'd been cursed to do—and hope.

"Sugar, you look like you lost your best friend."

Sebastien turned to find Ree Ann standing in front of him, arms crossed beneath her ample bosom.

"I have always credited you with being very intuitive," he replied, his jaw set firmly.

Her full mouth turned down at the corners, and the amused twinkle left her eyes. "Oh, honey." She reached out and patted his arm. "Here I was all prepared to read you the riot act for breaking Jamie's heart, and your heart looks more than a bit battered itself."

"I do not know of this riot act you speak of, but never fear, I have castigated myself often for this turn of events I've landed us in."

She rubbed his arm, then gestured for him to continue walking. Despite her high heels, she fell into step easily beside him. "Well, if you're miserable, and she's miserable, what in God's name are you doing apart?"

"You know of my background, mademoiselle, *oui*?"

"Yes, Jamie told me."

"Then you understand that I should never have dallied with her, should never have risked her heart as I did." He scowled. "I know my role here, and it is not to involve myself with my mistress."

"Honey, we all do foolish things when we are in love."

That stopped him cold. He turned and stared at her. "I feel much for Jamie, do not misunderstand. More than any woman has wrought in me. But true *amour*? *Non*, I am not capable of that."

"Oh, sugar, of course you're capable. We're all capable. A few months ago I'd have been first in line to agree with you, but not now. And you, of all people, should understand that the heart is always vulnerable."

"Not mine. It is why I was cursed with this life. I respect love and all its mysteries, but never have I been in danger of succumbing to its demands myself."

"Not until the one person comes along who can change all that."

"Yes, that would seem to be true, and well I know it. But in hundreds of years, many women have crossed my path. Certainly if it were to happen, it would have by now. I daresay it cannot happen. Not to me."

"Then why are you mooning all over the Quarter like an abandoned puppy?"

"I do not 'moon,' as you so eloquently state. I simply cherished her company; we shared many views and found we were alike in many ways. Kindred spirits perhaps. And because of this I taunted myself for a time with the possibility of basking in that shared bond." He heard his own words and knew he was rationalizing. But to believe anything else was too dangerous. "I realized too late it was a risk I should never

have taken. Jamie's heart has been dallied with unwisely in the past. I, of all people, should have stepped
back, remained objective."

"She told you about her marriages?"

"I am aware of them."

"So she didn't tell you." Ree slowed down a step or
two, then turned an assessing eye to him.

"*Non*. Not in detail." He stifled a sigh and slowed
his pace as well, until they were stopped and staring at
each other. Well, he was staring at a point past her
shoulder, but he could feel her gaze squarely on him.

"Would you like to know about them?"

He looked at her and found that her expression
had turned harsh.

"You know, maybe it would help you search for her
perfect mate."

He could not hold her accusing gaze.

"Of course, why you think you need to look beyond
your own mirror I don't know. Whoever said love is
blind sure as hell knew what they were talking about."
Before he could respond, she suddenly grinned and
added, "Oh, and I forgot to thank you, by the way."

He narrowed his gaze. "For?"

"Angel."

He actually felt heat rise in his cheeks. "I was
merely a catalyst. I did nothing more than play guide.
You weren't to know."

"Yeah, well, some rules are made to be broken. Or
badly bent, anyway. Speaking of rules, you have to
'guide' Jamie now, right? I mean, I hear Jack is
matched, and you're still here. So you have no other
choice?"

"Had I another option, I'd have taken it." Ree had
that relentless look in her eye, and Sebastien realized
how she'd become such a success. "I hope that Angel
has opened his mind enough to allow you to assist

him in his business. You two will do quite well as a team."

Ree laughed openly, causing several people to look their way as they passed by. "Oh, sugar, you have no idea." She gestured at the next corner for them to cross. "I have to circle back to the shop. Marta's holding the fort and I can't leave her for long."

He nodded and crossed to the opposite corner. Part of him wanted to quicken the pace and end this interlude. But a greater part wanted to slow down and prolong it as much as possible. He stifled a groan. Had he become so pathetic that he longed simply to be close to any acquaintance of Jamie's?

He said nothing as they wandered down another block, but when the shop loomed ahead at the next corner, the question was torn from him. "Will you tell me? About the men she married?"

Ree Ann sighed dramatically. "I thought you'd never ask."

"If you were so determined, you simply could have told me."

She shook her head. "I had to know it was important enough to you to ask yourself."

He sighed deeply, not hiding his frustration. "It has been centuries of time and even that has not been long enough for me to unravel the vagaries of the female mind."

She smiled up at him. "Which is just the way we like it, sugar." She pulled him to the side of the walkway and stepped into the recessed area of a gated alleyway. "Now, listen. Jamie's daddy is a race-boat driver, as was Jamie for a number of years."

"This I know. We have been on the water together. It is in her blood." As it is in mine, he almost added, but caught himself. One look in Ree's considering eyes told him she'd seen it anyway. *Damn female.*

"Well, she was young, just out of college, and on the international circuit herself for the first time. Her daddy let her race a little as a youngster, but after she passed her high-school equivalency with a tutor, he made her come back here to get a degree. Something to fall back on, you know. Anyway, she was young and quite a daredevil when it came to racing. It's a very testosterone-driven sport, and Jamie had always been a tomboy. 'One of the guys,' if you know what I mean. Being a tomboy was the only way to be taken seriously."

"I understand this."

"She had confidence oozing from her pores when it came to climbing on those death traps she raced. But where men and relationships were concerned . . . well, she wasn't quite as certain of her feminine wiles. In fact, she was pretty certain she didn't have any at all."

"This I can also understand."

Ree raised an eyebrow. "Oh?"

Sebastien saw a flare of protectiveness rise in Jamie's friend, and he relaxed somewhat. Ree would be there for her always. "Jamie chose her friends wisely." When Ree merely nodded, he went on. "When I first met her, I was not drawn to her in the ways I am usually drawn to a woman. She is not . . . overt, in her sensuality."

"But?"

"The fire is there," he said quietly. "Always there, for the one who knows to look for it."

Ree fanned her neck. "Why, yes, you do understand a little about women."

He smiled. "I offended her initially, though unintentionally. I was clumsy in explaining my attraction to her."

Ree smiled as well. "Apparently you eventually worked that out."

There was both pleasure and pain in his response. "*Oui.* That we did." He cleared his throat. "Tell me of this first man in her life."

Ree snorted in disgust. "He was the darling of the racing world. Blond, blue-eyed Swede. Sexy, cocky as hell, and a damn good racer. But he lost his sponsorship with an Italian conglomerate because he ran a little too fast and loose for their corporate tastes. So he was looking for new sponsorship dollars."

"He sought to get them through Jamie? Through her father?" Many things fell into place at that moment. "Why not go directly to her father?"

"Because he knew he needed to settle down—or at least appear to—if he was going to get anyone to pay serious attention to him. By marrying Jamie he achieved that goal and got the sponsorship from her daddy. But he never had any intention of really slowing down his playboy ways. He merely intended to be more discreet." She paused, her eyes reflecting both the anger and pain she felt on her friend's behalf. "You know, I don't think it was finding him in bed with two of his racing groupies that really did her in. It was when the ass tried to explain to her that he really didn't think she could handle his rather abundant needs and should be grateful he didn't put the demand on her alone." She snorted. "The bastard basically told her she was incapable of satisfying a real man. Jamie was too mortified to break the guy into a million drownable pieces. She left him and took her dad's sponsorship with her. She figured it was the only thing she had that he ever really needed. They divorced fairly quietly."

Sebastien felt twin surges of fury and pain. He wanted to hunt down the bastard and kill him for what he'd done to Jamie, and he wanted to go to her and make her understand just what an idiot the man had been. But, then, he realized she knew that now.

She was well aware of just how satisfied a man could be in her company. She'd learned that with him. Somehow, knowing that didn't make him feel the least bit better. "What of the other one?"

Ree seemed a bit taken aback at his rougher tone, but she went on without comment. "It was several years later. His name was Steve. He was a bit older than Jamie and a friend of her father's. He was a racer as well, but money didn't appear to be an issue and he truly seemed to be interested in Jamie."

"What happened?"

"He had been married before, which Jamie felt made him even more compatible. Apparently, his wife had left him for a younger man. Well, ex-wifey came back into the picture about six months after Steve and Jamie were married. Appeared she didn't much like life off the circuit and wanted her old life back, complete with her old husband. She went after him, guns blazing."

"And the bastard chose her over Jamie?"

Ree nodded. "He offered her a generous divorce settlement, which Jamie promptly tossed back in his face." She studied him for a moment, then said, "So you can see why she was a bit wary of starting another serious relationship. You're the first man since Steve that she's been remotely interested in. And I'd say her interest in you was far from remote."

Sebastien didn't know what to say. He'd never felt so acutely that he'd let another person down. He'd done that and more to Jamie. Shame for his cowardice filled him.

"She didn't fight to keep either of those men. I think she knew then they didn't deserve her loyalty or her commitment. Much less her heart."

I wanted you. After I said I would never allow myself to want again, I wanted you anyway. Her words echoed in his head, in his heart. *This time I finally thought I'd found something worth fighting for.*

Ree rubbed her hand over his arm again, her voice gentling when she spoke. "She doesn't want anyone else, Sebastien. If she can't have you, please, just leave her alone."

He looked into her earnest eyes and felt an anguish, a bleakness, that he had never felt before. "I cannot."

Those eyes flashed instantly to anger. "Then do something about it, dammit. Go after her. Fight for her, for yourself, for both of you. Someone sure as hell should."

"I can promise her so little. My fate—"

"Is not determined until you have exhausted all the possibilities. But you didn't, did you?" she demanded.

He knew the truth was on his face. All his rationalizations were so much refuse, littering the ground beneath his feet.

"You don't even know what the hell all the possibilities are," she accused, with deadly aim. "At least if you fail in the end, you'll know you did everything in your power to keep her. You'll know she was worth trying for. And for once, so will she."

Chapter 22

*I*t was dark but still sweltering when Jamie finally turned into the alleyway leading behind the bookstore. Her car was there, which meant Ree had either gotten a ride from Marta or she was with Angel. Jamie would bet money on the latter.

"Good for her," she murmured, but couldn't help feeling the teeniest bit jealous. Okay, she was green. Through and through.

Ree had been right: The drive in the country was a good one. The summer air was hot enough that she'd kept the top down as the sun set and the stars began to rise.

Out on the winding River Road, she had almost convinced herself that everything would be okay. She had her friends, an occupation she derived a great deal of satisfaction from, a fulfilling hobby, and a home to furnish and settle into. All in all, she'd made the transition from the racing circuit to the real world pretty painlessly. And she was happy with her life. Truly. Her father had been right. He'd seen what the circuit was doing to her, both emotionally and physically. She'd always crave the excitement of racing over the open water, but she didn't miss the rest of it. This was what she needed.

She'd even almost gotten herself believing that her brief interlude with Sebastien should be seen as a sign of hope. Her heart wasn't permanently out of order, and maybe, just maybe, one day in the distant future, fate would be kind enough to hand her a man who wouldn't bust it into a million jagged little pieces.

Tears suddenly burned behind her eyes. She blinked hard a couple of times to keep the tears at bay, then got out of the car, put the top up, and locked it.

Okay, so she really didn't believe that last part yet. But she was working on it. That was good, right? She'd gone into this relationship with her eyes open and had taken her chances, knowing what she risked. That it had ended in disaster was only a minor setback. It felt incredibly major, but if she kept telling herself that it was merely a stumble along the path to maturity and wisdom, she'd eventually see it that way.

Sebastien stepped from the shadows just as she fished out her door key. "Jamie."

Jamie jumped. For a split second she honestly thought she'd conjured him up. But he stepped forward then, the moonlight glinting off his dark eyes. She could feel him viscerally, just standing there, several feet in front of her. As if she'd been invaded. Her senses certainly had. He was no delusion come to call.

It took everything she had to steel herself against doing what she most wanted to. Which was to launch herself into his arms and beg him to stay. Just for one night. Then for as many more as she could shamelessly persuade him to agree to. But the one thing she'd managed to hang on to in all her previous relationships was her dignity. Even with her heart and hopes in tatters, she'd never groveled, never begged, never cried.

She'd already figured out that was because the others weren't worth begging. So what did that say about her, that she still felt like begging Sebastien to give them another chance?

"What are you doing here?" Her voice was harsh, but it was the best she could do.

"We have to talk."

"No, I don't believe we *have* to do anything. I've said everything I wanted to say." *Except I love you.* That little revelation sealed her throat over.

"I need to talk with you, Jamie. Please, allow me to come upstairs."

Oh, no, she thought, panic filling her. Upstairs was too intimate, too personal. She'd never be able to rid herself of his presence then. "No," she managed. "I asked you for only one thing."

He stepped closer. "I know, but—"

Suddenly it was all too much. The depth of her feelings for him, the confusing emotions ripping around inside her—it was all too much. "I can't go through this again." There was desperation in her tone, but she couldn't help it. She *was* desperate. "I'm still not doing so well from our last good-bye." She looked up into his eyes, knowing the vulnerable picture she painted, but damned if she could do anything about it. "This isn't a game to me, Sebastien." Her voice began to break. "I can't play with you anymore."

She tried to push past him, but he stopped her with a hand on her arm. Her heart leapt in foolish response, overjoyed that he hadn't let her go. Her head pounded a fierce tattoo of pain as she tried to realign her resolve to leave and not look back. "Please don't," she whispered, not sure if she was appealing to him or to herself.

He turned her very gently to face him, tipping her chin up when she wouldn't look at him. Whatever he saw in her eyes, she thought, might be mirrored in his own. Pain, heartache, anguish. It was all there. It undid what little resolve she'd managed to muster.

"Please, don't leave me," he said.

It was like a knife plunging into her heart, the pain was so clean and swift. "I'm—I'm not going anywhere," she whispered, unable to do more than that. "For the moment." She found she had some dignity left. A tiny shred, but she clung to it.

"I failed you," he said. "Horribly."

She looked at him then, confused. "You mean . . . because you haven't been able to match me?" She freed herself and walked several feet away, reaching in vain for some semblance of control. "Well, I told you to save your energy."

He stalked up behind her and swung her around, the rage and fury in his eyes shocking her into silence. "When you needed me to trust you, I failed you. Despite all the souls I've brought together, when it was most important I did not understand the true fragile nature of a heart. Not yours. Not mine."

She started to speak, but he spoke over her words. "Your heart has been sorely mistreated in this life, and I am the worst offender of all, because I should have known better. Where those before me never cherished what you had to offer, I did. And yet I handed it back to you as if it meant nothing."

Slowly, Jamie began to understand. He knew about her husbands, what had happened in her marriages. Now the anger pulsed, and she welcomed its warm embrace. "Who told you? Never mind, it doesn't matter." She poked a hard finger into his chest. "And now you're here because you feel guilty. Because when the choices got tough, you bailed out, just like they did. Well, you know what? I don't need your damn guilt, and I sure as hell don't need any pity."

He gripped her wrist and pulled her up close, his eyes blazing into hers. "I don't give a damn about those men. I know they weren't worthy of you. And this isn't about pity, because you damn well know they didn't deserve you. This is about us. *I* should have been worthy of you, Jamie. *I* was the one who should have realized what was at stake. *I* was the one who should have fought for you."

She pulled from his hold, terrified that if she let him touch her a moment longer, she'd crumble when he stopped. "I don't want to be fought for now." A lie for certain, but she had to protect herself. "You made your decision. I got over them. I'll get over you."

That stopped him. If he'd sliced into her earlier, she'd just returned the favor tenfold, judging by the pain filling his eyes. He stood there and stared at her, feet braced apart as if to withstand the blows of the sea, hair tossing wildly around his head in the night breeze, eyes stark and empty.

When she couldn't bear the anguished silence a second longer, she turned toward the house.

"What if I don't want to be gotten over?" he asked hoarsely.

Now it was her turn to go still. Her heart made a small leap of life even though she ruthlessly sought to quash it. She turned back to him. "You said you had nothing to offer me. Your life is not your own to give. When you match me, you will be gone."

He crossed the small space separating them, his expression so fierce and determined she almost backed up a step. Almost.

"Maybe I cannot find you another mate. Maybe there is no one else. Only me."

Now her heart stopped leaping about. In fact, it stopped altogether. "What are you saying? Are you saying you're not really—"

"I am what I claim to be. You do believe that, don't you, Jamie?"

She nodded. "Yes. I think maybe I always have. I've wanted to believe almost anything else. Maybe because I knew from the moment I saw you in my attic that—"

He touched his fingers to her lips, then curled

them into his palm as if he couldn't bear to do only that. "That what?"

Too much was happening, too many things had to be figured out before she was ready to tell him what she felt. She shook her head. "Why did you let me leave? I was willing to stay, to try and find a solution."

"Because I didn't believe in myself. I didn't trust this new feeling I have enough to fight for it. I thought I was doing the right thing. I truly did not believe I was made to feel this for anyone, the way I see men with women every day of my life spent on this earth. You deserved more than that."

"What changed your mind?"

"I have spent these past weeks—how did Madamoiselle Broussard phrase it?—'mooning all over the Quarter like an abandoned puppy.' "

"You've talked to Ree?" Jamie blew out a harsh sigh. "So she told you."

"She only wanted to see to your happiness. But it wasn't just learning of your past. All that did was help me put my own actions and decisions into perspective." He stepped closer. "But I already realized I had done the wrong thing. I missed you. More than I thought a man could miss the company of a woman." He began to pace. "I realized I could not tolerate the idea of anyone else having you. I want your smile, your laughter, your temper, your moods." He stopped and sighed. "I want you all for myself. When I told you it was over, I thought I did what was best for both of us. But in truth, I was afraid. Afraid to trust that what I felt was worthy, was good enough, to risk more pain. But, *mon Dieu*, there can be no deeper pain than this."

Jamie didn't know what to say.

"Unlike those before me, I cherish you. I have never stopped wanting you, never stopped wishing it could be different for me. For us."

Jamie's heart pounded so hard that she couldn't hear herself think. "You're still what you are."

Now he did close the space between them. "*Oui.* But now I am willing to try to discover if there is a way for this to work." He reached out to stroke her face, but she stepped back a pace and he dropped his hand to his side. "Have you given up on me, then? Have I lost you because I was too afraid to trust in my own heart?"

Jamie pulled back another step. "I don't know what I feel." She did know. She'd fallen deeply in love with him. But that was the last thing she could tell him right now. More false hope was the last thing either of them needed.

"You said you would have fought for me," he said. "For us. Do you no longer consider this a worthy battle?"

"I thought so when I was in your arms, in your bed. I thought I wanted you to come charging to the rescue and pledge your undying love to me." She looked at him, letting him see all the pain and confusion that was in her heart. "I want you, Sebastien. More than I've ever wanted anyone."

"Then why the sadness in your eyes, *mon amour*?"

"This is supposed to be the happy ending, right? Boy gets girl, loses girl, then discovers he can't live without her. Girl rejoices. Boy and girl live happily ever after." She paused, unsure how to explain, then simply said, "How come this doesn't feel like happily ever after?"

"Jamie—"

"No, listen to me. Your future hasn't changed. Maybe you were right all along. I thought I could handle a relationship with you even knowing that our future was uncertain. After these past weeks I'm not so sure I would survive it. I don't think I can do happily until he has to leave."

"Are you so certain it would end that way?"

"Can you believe otherwise?"

"You believe that I am what I say I am. Why not believe anything is possible?"

"Because if I do and I'm wrong, then what happens?"

"You'd rather be alone." He made it a statement. "You'd rather I didn't finally question my continued existence on this earth and perhaps find a way to end it."

"How can you? Without ending it completely?"

"I don't know. But for the first time, I want to find out." He didn't let her escape this time. He came and pulled her into his arms. "I have to find out." He cupped her face. "Don't you understand? I can't continue in this altered existence. I want to live my life with you."

Jamie's heart nosedived right to her toes. He was everything she'd ever wanted, and it scared her to death. A man who wanted her for herself, who wanted her so badly that he'd give his life for the chance to be with her. A man she in turn wanted so badly that she was willing to let her soul be destroyed just to be with him again. Her defenses were so mangled, she no longer knew how to keep them up. She ran a trembling hand over his cheek, bone-numbing fear and radiant joy all twisted up inside her gut. "I understand completely."

"Then let's try to find a way. Let me find a way to give you happily ever after."

Chapter 23

Jamie wasn't certain she believed in happily ever after. That it was possibly staring her in the face made it seem even more improbable. "Is there any such thing for us?"

"Fight with me, Jamie," he whispered roughly. "Help me find a way to keep us like this, with your heart beating against mine."

She couldn't speak for the lump in her throat. This was real, and yet it seemed every bit as fantastical as Sebastien's existence. It would be so easy to say yes. In that moment she would have given anything to ensure that they would be together forever. And yet, when she nodded and pulled his head down to hers, it was the single hardest thing she'd ever done. "I'll fight for you, Sebastien Valentin," she murmured against his lips. "But you'd damn well better make sure we win."

His laughter, rich and full-bodied, filled the sultry night air. "*This* is the pirate queen who stole my heart." He swung her up into his arms, ignoring her squawk of surprise as he kissed her.

They both laughed as he maneuvered her around so she could unlock the door. "I can walk, you know," she said as they locked the door behind them. She wasn't entirely certain it was the truth. Her body shook with the need to have him inside her once again. The very idea that they would claim each other in her bed, where she'd spent night after night trying to ignore that very fantasy, all but undid her.

"Carrying you gives me pleasure."

She hated to admit it, but it gave her a great deal of pleasure too. "I suppose you'd enjoy knowing that I could rather get used to this."

"Indeed. I love to feel you in my arms," he said as he climbed up the stairs. "I never thought I would again." He was barely winded when he slid her to her feet inside her bedroom doorway. He looked from her face, bathed in the moonlight streaming through the curved front window, to the bed. "I have so longed to have you here. I have longed to see your hair spread upon the pillows, your arms lifted in welcome to me."

Jamie slid the band from the end of her long braid and slowly began to untwine her hair. A devilish smile curved her lips. "Your wish is my command."

His grin was so wicked it took her breath away. "I rather like this reversal of roles." He stepped closer to her and lifted his hands to the buttons of her polo shirt. "How many wishes do I receive?" He leaned down and nipped gently at the curve of her neck.

"And here I thought racing was a good adrenaline rush," she murmured as he continued his assault, shifting his lips to the sensitive spot at the nape of her neck.

He pushed aside her heavy mane of hair and nibbled his way around her neck as he moved behind her. She felt his chest brush against her back and gasped. She'd had no idea that her spine was such an erogenous zone.

"I like that I make your heart pound," he whispered, brushing his lips toward her other earlobe. "Just the taste of your skin makes my pulse race like that death-defying automobile of yours." He circled back in front of her. He lifted her hand and kissed her palm very gently, but with definite purpose, then curled her fingers around it. "You carry my heart right there," he said.

Her own heart skipped a beat, and a lump formed in her throat. She would fight for this man, for the happiness he could give her. Life didn't hand out guarantees on time. Any time they had together was worth whatever toll it took. He was worth it. And looking into his smiling eyes, she knew for certain that she was worth it too.

Jamie shook her hair loose, the unbraided waves cascading over her shoulders. "How many wishes should I grant you?" she asked, feeling suddenly lighthearted and free. Freer than she'd ever felt, even when racing across the wide open water. Now she had something important to race toward. A finish line that could reap rewards she'd never even dreamed of. "You've already used one. And I believe the standard is three."

"Then I will take the other two. With pleasure."

Her smile was bold this time. "Use them wisely. Because then it will be my turn."

"Perhaps my wish will be to grant you more wishes."

"Oh, no, it doesn't work that way."

He immediately captured her hips and held them firmly in place when she tried to move away. "*Non?* Then why don't you show me how it works."

She took the challenge and began to unbutton his shirt. The task was made all the more erotic when he refused to release his grip on her hips. She was forced to lean back to get to them all, which only served to press her hips all the more intimately into his.

"Your turn," he said as she slid the shirt down his arms and let it drop to the floor. "And I wish to see you more clearly. Turn on your bedside lamp."

"That's wish number two," she said, her voice a bit

shaky as his fingers slid beneath her shirt and pulled it over her head. He held her tightly enough for her to arch over and just barely reach the switch on the lamp. He lifted her upright, the tips of her breasts just brushing against his chest. "One wish left." She moaned aloud when he bent his head and captured a nipple through the cotton cup of her bra. "But please," she managed, "take your time."

"I plan to take all the time allowed me." He bent her gently onto the bed.

He followed her down, and there was no escaping her deep groan of satisfaction when he settled his weight on her in all the right places. "Pants," she gasped. "We have on too many pants."

He chuckled, the action making his lips vibrate against a particularly sensitive spot just above her navel. He'd somehow managed to slide down her body, his mouth doing all sorts of interesting things to her stomach. She lifted her head just as he managed the tricky maneuver of unbuttoning her pants with his teeth. Their eyes caught and he winked at her, teeth bared with the fabric of her pants clutched firmly between them. He lifted his head so the zipper slowly opened, then released her pants and looked intently into her eyes before dipping his head down, apparently intent on the elastic waistband of her panties.

Dear God, she thought dazedly, he was every woman's pirate fantasy. Only he was no fantasy.

Her head lolled back on the bed. She felt the night air brush her skin as he slid her pants down her legs, with his hands this time. His mouth was now finding all these interesting paths along her thighs. Who knew the knees were erogenous zones? Hell, with this man, there was no such thing as a nonerogenous zone.

She felt his weight leave the bed, and she opened her eyes to find him standing at the edge of the mattress between her now-bare legs. He lifted her feet and placed them on his chest, then pressed one foot to his mouth and began to tease her with his lips and teeth, working his way slowly toward her knee. He watched her all the while. She was hot and edgy, wanting him to move faster, to hurry. It was all she could do to keep her hips on the bed when what she desperately wanted was to buck and writhe as he continued his slow and thorough assault. "Sebastien, please—"

He lifted his head. "I have one wish left, then you may begin making your demands of me."

She groaned and dropped her head back on the bed, accepting her defeat willingly.

He unbuckled his pants and she heard the whisper of fabric as they slid to his feet. She had to look, then immediately wished she hadn't. Torture. It was sheer torture. And naturally he was grinning.

"I see you approve."

"What, bikini briefs weren't . . . brief enough?" Her voice sounded more like a croak.

"At the moment, any restraint is too much." He stripped the indecent scrap of black cotton off.

And she'd thought the torture couldn't get worse. The man was gorgeous. Everywhere. She truly hadn't . . . well, magnified his gifts during their time spent apart. There was no stopping her from squirming now. Her body knew what awaited it, and it wanted it right now, dammit.

He slid her panties down her legs and she wrestled to take off her bra. Not nearly as seductive a maneuver as his disrobing, but it accomplished her goal. Which was to feel as much of her bare skin pressed against as much of his as soon as possible. "I can't wait any longer. I'm dying."

He smiled and moved his body over hers, sliding

her farther up the bed as he did so their feet didn't dangle over the edge. His body teased hers unmercifully, every contact point screaming with almost painful arousal. He brushed against her but didn't enter her.

"Sebastien," she groaned, shamelessly lifting her hips.

He kissed her deeply, thrusting his tongue into her mouth and himself into her at the same time. She arched violently against him, taking all of him, wishing only that they could be even more closely joined.

He took her hard, and she pushed him even harder. She rode the wave fierce and fast, wanting to climax right then and simultaneously wanting to stay right on that blissful crest forever.

His mouth was on her neck, his hands full of her hair. "Now it is time for my last wish," he ground out. "Hold on tight." He rolled to his back, taking her with him, until she was straddling his hips.

He was still hot and deep inside her, even more deeply now. She gasped at the sensation of it, her hands braced on his chest while she adapted to all the new sensations rocketing through her.

"Look at me, Jamie."

She raised her eyes to his, her body already moving on him, unable to remain still.

His hands were on her hips, then he slid one hand along the inside of her thigh until he was touching her just above where they were joined.

"My wish is for you to come to me, Jamie. Come to me now." He moved his fingers and thrust inside her at the same time.

The pleasure was blinding, the release explosive. It crested and crashed down all over and through her. She bucked helplessly on top of him and rode it for all it was worth. Only when she collapsed onto him, still shuddering and quivering, did he carefully roll her back beneath him. He kissed her as he began to move inside her again. Amazingly, the wave began anew.

"Come with me this time," he demanded, his body establishing their rhythm this time.

She complied. Fervently.

He took her deeply and she rose to every thrust. His body tensed and he reared up above her, groaning loud and long as he climaxed. The pleasure of watching him, hearing him, knowing she had given him such satisfaction, drove her over again seconds later.

She pushed her fingers through his damp hair and kissed him on his temple. He responded by kissing her beneath her ear, then in the crook of her neck. It seemed impossible, but those gentle kisses stole more of her heart than the pulse-pounding moments just before. She felt cared for, cherished.

He rolled to his side and took her with him. Their arms and legs locked effortlessly, and she tucked her head against his shoulder. They fit so perfectly, she thought, her mind still recovering from the spin it had just taken. It was as if their bodies had been dancing like this for eternity.

She wanted to tell him how he made her feel and why she loved him. She was still trying to find the words when sleep claimed her.

Chapter 24

Sebastien knew the instant she left the haven of sleep. He'd been watching her for the past hour or so and had been perfectly content to continue forever. Now that she was awakening, he felt his pulse begin to speed up, his nerves tightening along with it. He was determined to have this morning proceed far differently from their last one.

He also knew today would be a day of reckoning unlike the other. Their true battle had only just begun. However, this time their adversary was his past, not each other. She would have to be strong and willing to trust him. He thought of the night they had just spent together and knew she had that inside her. Today they would face adversity. But he was determined that they would face it together.

She awoke slowly, sweetly. She turned her eyes to him and there was no surprise in them, no sudden shock of awareness. This time her entire consciousness had known he was there beside her. He took a measure of strength in that knowledge.

"Good morning," she said, sleep making her voice husky.

He bent down and kissed her forehead, then her eyelids, her cheeks, and finally her mouth. When he lifted his head so he could look into her eyes, he was immensely gratified at the emotion he saw shining in them. "Good morning, *mon amour.*"

She shifted and snuggled against him. He thought he felt his heart actually stop for a beat before resuming, so right did she feel nestled there. Her hands slid around his waist, and he pulled her more tightly against him and stroked her hair.

"I must say I recommend this as a way to start a morning," she mumbled against his chest. "In fact, I think it would be a fascinating way to spend the afternoon and perhaps the evening as well."

He continued to thread his fingers through her hair, smiling at her drowsy words even as his heart turned to more-serious revelations. She was precious to him. How had he ever thought to live without her? He knew he would do anything to protect her and keep her safe. He had to smile at that. If he were to reveal that last thought, he was certain she would make it understood that she could take care of herself. And that also gave him a sense of peace. She was a strong, smart, resourceful woman. He liked knowing that she wasn't helpless or frail. Yet he wanted to protect and coddle her nonetheless. Should make for an interesting partnership, he mused with a welcome sense of delight.

Partnership. How was it he'd never seen a woman in that light before? He settled her more closely against him. Because, he thought, he'd never met his soulmate before.

And that revelation shocked another thought, an alarming one, into his suddenly clear mind. If he were to tell her this, tell her of his love for her, that would fulfill his obligation to the Sword of Hearts. Would he disappear?

Just then she kissed the skin that pulsed over his heart, making him wonder how on earth he could last even the next five minutes without saying those words to her, so urgent was his need. But it was a risk he could not take. Not yet. He had forged a plan in the predawn hours. He must adhere to it.

"I want to show you something," he said quietly.

She smiled sleepily up at him. "I believe I've seen everything at this point."

He smiled, his heart full of emotion. How was it he'd survived never truly feeling this? How did he have the audacity to match the hearts of others without knowing the true power the heart wielded? Would this revelation make him a better matcher of souls?

The very idea of returning to that existence brought a stab of pain. He resolutely turned his thoughts back to her.

"Can you take the day off work?" he asked.

Now she looked intrigued. "You're so serious all of a sudden. What exactly do you have in mind?"

"A short trip. We will need your car. There is a place I want to take you."

"Can you tell me?"

He shook his head. "I will need your trust, Jamie."

She studied him for a long moment, then scooted up and kissed him deeply. "You have it. You have it all, Sebastien."

He could sense the words of love he so wanted to say himself forming in her mind before her lips began to move. He kissed her to keep them where they were—felt but unspoken. He refused to risk it until they were there.

"Get dressed," he urged when he finally lifted his head. "Or I will detain you here for hours."

"And I'm supposed to be motivated to leave by that?"

He smiled then. "We will have more time, Jamie. That is what today is all about."

Now she turned more serious. "Sebastien, what is it you're planning to do? Maybe we should discuss this first."

He slid from the bed and gathered his clothing. "I am asking for your trust. Please." He came around to her side of the bed and pulled her up and close. "I let you down once before, but that is a mistake I will never make again."

She nodded. "I know you would never purposely hurt me. It's not in your soul."

He grinned at her, his heart lighter, more certain than ever that there was solution out there for them. There had to be. "I believe there is time in our agenda for a shower. Although I suggest we conserve time and share it."

"Did I mention I adore your overdeveloped sense of logic? You're like Mr. Spock. Only sexier."

"Who is Mr. Spock?"

Jamie laughed and pulled him toward her tiny bathroom. "I'm not so sure I can explain that one. Come on, I'll tell you after I get you all wet and soapy."

Sebastien laughed and allowed her to pull him along. "Your wish is most assuredly my command, mademoiselle."

&

Jamie followed Sebastien's directions out of the Quarter and away from New Orleans. They were heading south.

"Exit here," he said.

She did, but glanced over at him. "Barataria?"

He nodded but said nothing else.

Jamie didn't push it. He'd been incredibly attentive and playful in the shower. He'd spent more time staring at her over breakfast than eating.

Ree had been disgustingly giddy on the phone

when Jamie told her why she needed to take the day off. She'd tried to apologize for the last-minute notice, but Ree wouldn't hear it. Of course, she'd want to hear everything later. Right now, even the prospect of one of Ree's interrogations didn't bother Jamie.

Her thoughts were focused on Sebastien and this mission they were on. He'd been quiet since they left the Quarter. His eyes had stayed on the road ahead, but his hand was on her thigh, or her shoulder, or mindlessly twiddling strands of the hair she'd left down this morning. His touch was a constant reassurance when her mind wanted to race off in all sorts of terrifying directions. Somehow this was all going to end up okay. Whatever he had in store, she wouldn't disappoint him. Or herself.

It was a revelation, this partnership they'd forged. Unlike any she'd ever entered into. Her smile faded as her thoughts turned helplessly to their future. What lay in store for them?

"Turn here," he directed.

"This leads back to national park land."

"I know."

Jamie didn't know much about Barataria, other than it was threaded with swamps and bayous and home to a still-thriving fishing community. It was also originally famous—or infamous—as the place where the Laffite brothers had created their pirate den. She swallowed hard and her hands tightened on the steering wheel. No way was this a coincidence.

The entrance to the park loomed ahead. "Do I go in?"

"Oui." He pointed. "Follow the signs that way."

She wove the car around and through the park until they were in the farthest corner.

Sebastien directed her to the side of the road. "Park there."

Jamie cut the engine before turning to look at him,

but he was already getting out of the car. "Can you tell me now?"

"*Non*. We are not there yet. Follow me. Be careful."

Jamie didn't argue. Panic was gaining an edge, and she focused on his path to keep her thoughts from pushing her over the edge. She quickly realized why he'd insisted that she wear her rubber boots. He entered the woods and brush, walking confidently along an unseen path. The ground was alternately boggy and muddy. He held out his hand occasionally to help her over the worst of it. They ended up at the end of a bayou in an area of the park that looked as if no one had ever visited it before.

He took her hand and led her to a particularly huge cypress tree. "This is what I wanted to show you."

She stared at him. "A tree?"

He shook his head, then smiled. She wasn't as reassured as she'd like to be. There was still worry in his eyes, and a trace of fear.

He pulled her to him for a kiss. It deepened quickly and almost went beyond control before he finally managed to disengage. They were both breathing heavily. He leaned his forehead on hers, clutching her shoulders tightly. "I've never brought anyone here. Well, not since . . . not for many years," he said.

"Since when?" Jamie hadn't missed his pause. "Who did you bring here last?" She felt a shiver race over her skin despite the thick humidity.

"I will explain, but first I want to show you this." He turned to the tree, and moments later a large piece of the trunk was removed. Sebastien reached inside the dark, musty interior and drew out a cloth-covered box about the size of a large shoe box. Jamie couldn't help but gasp when he tossed the oiled flaps of the cloth back to reveal a jewel-encrusted box.

"My God," she whispered. The metal was tarnished and black, but the jewels shone brightly even in the dappled sunlight that filtered through the trees. "Where did you get that?"

"My last run with Dominique. To what is now Haiti. We encountered a brigantine on our return. We were victorious and brought back its spoils." He looked at her. "Guns, gems, foodstuffs. And men and women bound for slavery."

"What?" She lifted her gaze from the box to him. "Slavery? What did you do with them?"

"This was my share," he said, refusing to answer the question. "This box. I had hiding places for several of my rewards. The rest I kept with Jean and his men. But we all were well aware that the political climate changed with serendipitous rapidity. It was always wise to have something to fall back on were we to be raided." He looked at her. "This and several other stores are still in their original hiding places. When I come back, this is how I fund my time here." He opened the box to reveal a small pile of coins. "I sell one or two of these to a coin dealer. They weren't worth as much originally, but now it usually doesn't take more than one or two."

Jamie tried to take it all in. "And no one questions how you came to own them?"

"They aren't as rare as that. Many a story can cover their history. I generally say they have been passed down through time in my family. Not so far from the truth." Again he smiled, but there was sadness in it.

Jamie picked up several of the coins and examined them, then put them back and turned her attention to him. He seemed to be waiting for her reaction, so she gave him one. "If you brought me here to prove that you are what you claim to be, it was unnecessary. You know that."

"I do. And that wasn't the reason, although I did want you to know about this. In case—"

Now she was alarmed. "Don't. I wouldn't do anything with this." She gestured to the box. "It's yours, and it will remain safe here as it has for hundreds of years."

"There is more I must explain."

Jamie breathed out a sigh. "I'm not so sure we need to do this, Sebastien." She raised her hand. "I know, I know, you want me to trust you. I do. But if you could just explain the big picture here, it would greatly alleviate a lot of panic I'm trying really hard to pretend I don't feel."

He motioned to a fallen tree. "Sit. Please."

"Only if you'll sit beside me." She had an almost desperate need to keep him close. As if being able to reach out and touch him at any given moment provided security of some kind.

He covered the box and set it on the tree, then knelt in front of her, taking her hands in both of his. "I have spent most of the night trying to divine a way to ensure that we have a future. A future together."

Now her heart went into triple time. "I want that too, more than anything, you know that, but—"

"Please let me talk, Jamie."

She nodded, but it was a hard-won silence.

"This was the last place I was on this earth as a normal, mortal man."

The heart that had sped up so stopped completely for one beat, then another, before resuming a shaky cadence.

"We had made plans to return the people on the ship to their homes, the ones who wanted to go. There was one, a young woman, Yolande, who wished to stay here." He looked into her eyes. "With me."

Jamie felt her throat tighten. "Did you love her? Or think you did?"

"*Non*. But she fancied herself a future here with me. A future I repeatedly explained would not happen. I did not want her permanently in my life. My life was not one conducive to home and hearth—at least, I could not envision myself in such a lifestyle. I brought her here, away from the others, to explain."

Jamie's eyes went wide as she put it together. "Oriane. The priestess you said cursed you. Yolande must have been her—"

"Daughter. *Oui*. And her. *maman* was quite upset with her plans to stay with me. I was unaware then that Oriane was a tribal priestess back on their island, very powerful, and was grooming Yolande to take her place. She came looking for her daughter."

"And found her here, with you."

He nodded. "I was brash and quite bold, and Yolande was very determined. I thought her quite the experienced seductress and I wanted her badly, but I'd made it clear we had no future and she had finally agreed. She told me she would return with her mother, but she would go back on her own terms. And those terms included having me once before she left. I saw no harm in complying with her wishes."

Understanding dawned on Jamie. "Her mother really *found* you. Together."

He nodded again. "Oriane was outraged that I had defiled her daughter. I had no idea Yolande was a virgin until it was too late."

"You're lucky Oriane didn't kill you."

"In a manner of speaking, she did just that."

Jamie squeezed his hand then. "Oh, Sebastien," she whispered, her throat burning.

Sebastien held on to her hand just as tightly. "She claimed that I took the body of a woman, with no thought to her soul. She told me I was incapable of understanding the true value of what is supposed to be between a man and woman. Therefore, my eternity would be spent creating situations whereby men and women would forge these bonds. It would be my responsibility to see to it that they be happily ever after in love."

"So your punishment was also meant to be a learning experience."

"I suppose, although I must say I didn't see it as such. Certainly not in the beginning." He looked at her. "Perhaps not until now."

Jamie didn't know what to say to that. "But you did eventually find happiness with your fate."

"*Mais oui*, I did." Sebastien smiled, and this time Jamie was heartened to see it reach his eyes. "But through all those years and all my escapades, my heart remained intact, mine to direct at will. I honestly thought it impossible that I'd ever lose control of it." He cupped her face. "Until you played pirate queen and released me from my sword. I think a part of me knew that very night that I was facing my destiny."

Jamie smiled in return. "And I thought you were a lunatic left over from Mardi Gras." She wanted so badly to join in the pleasure of this moment, to tease and laugh and revel in the blossoming of their love for each other. For although he hadn't said it, she knew without doubt what his feelings were. But she couldn't relinquish the hold on the dark cloud that seemed to hover just above them. They weren't carefree lovers in the throes of new love.

She grew more serious, and he did as well. He pulled her to a stand. "There is something else I have to tell you. If I thought withholding it would change things, I would."

She tried to pull her hands free, panic beginning to rise. "What are you talking about?"

He held her hands tightly, almost too tightly. "Jamie, listen to what I am about to tell you, and hold it close to your heart always, for I cannot predict what will happen the moment I am done."

"You're scaring me. If you think what you're about to say will change things for the worse, then don't say it. I know everything I need to know. I lo—"

He stopped her with his lips. His kiss was hard and desperate and did nothing to assuage the terror building inside her. She broke free from the kiss and tried to pull her hands away, but still he would not let her.

"Let's go home," she said, knowing the panic was as clear on her face as it was in her voice. "Everything will be fine. We'll be together and we'll figure out what you're going to do with yourself and—"

"Jamie, hush."

She did, but her eyes burned with unshed tears. "Don't do this," she whispered. "Please."

"We can't simply return to New Orleans and pretend everything is normal. It isn't. I was brought here by your summons to match three souls. I have matched two of them."

He looked intently into her eyes, and Jamie felt her heart grow heavy in her chest as the realization of what he was saying washed over her. She held on to him. "No!"

He nodded. "Yes. You are my third match."

"But . . . what will happen? You can't make a match with me and just disappear. I mean, how is that happily ever after?"

"I don't know." He looked as bereft as she felt.

It was all she could do not to throw herself to his feet and beg him to somehow change the course of his destiny.

He pulled her to the tree, then reached inside and retrieved another wrapped parcel. This one was much bigger and longer than the jeweled box. She knew with a certain dread exactly what it was even before he unwrapped it. "No, I don't want it! You can't make me take the sword back."

He pulled the cloth free. The glorious scabbard gleamed in the shards of sunlight. "I must present this to you, *ma maîtresse*."

Tears burned their way past her eyes and streamed down her face. "How can you do this? You said you'd never hurt me. You are destroying me."

His own eyes burned with a fierce need that all but undid her. "Do you think I don't bear the cost of this too? Do you think that if there were any way to leave my business on earth unfinished that I wouldn't?" Color rose in his cheeks, and a sudden breeze lifted his hair in a dark halo around his head. "I could do that only if you remained unmatched." He looked directly into her eyes. "Can you tell me truthfully that your heart is not matched to mine?"

Tears tracked a steady path down her cheeks. She shook her head. "No. I love you, Sebastien. With all my heart and soul, as I have never loved anyone."

She hadn't known his eyes could reflect more emotion than she'd seen in them a moment before, but they did. He took her mouth in a kiss that left her feeling branded to her soul. And perhaps she was. Had been, since that first kiss they'd shared the night she'd summoned him forth.

He trailed his fingers down her face in a lingering caress, then pushed the tip of the scabbard into the soft ground beside her feet.

Jamie wanted to yell, scream, and defy this moment to the end. She wanted to hurl the sword and its damned curse into the murky depths of the bayou, never to be seen again.

But she was riveted to the spot on which she stood, held there by the power of his gaze. "You said the people you match don't remember your role in their lives. You can't mean to tell me that I'm going to forget you." A sob rose in her throat, threatening to choke her. Surely the fates would not be so cruel as to rob her of everything, including her memory of him?

He pulled her into his arms. "I do not know what is in store for either of us. But I do know this." He pulled back enough to look at her. "These are words I have waited a lifetime to say. Several lifetimes." He bent and brushed the softest of kisses to her lips, then gazed steadily into her eyes. "You are my one and only. A soul to match that of a man who didn't believe he had one. Only with you would I find eternal happiness. And if I were to die in this instant, I would know and cherish into all eternity the blessed gift of your love for me." His voice grew hoarse, his eyes glassy. "I love you, Jamie Lynne Sullivan. With all my tarnished heart and soul."

Jamie flung her arms around his neck, as if she could prevent whatever was to happen next by the sheer force of her physical strength.

His arms came around her as well, and she poured her heart and soul into believing the strength she felt there, firmly anchoring her to him, uniting them against the fates.

In the next instant, a bolt of light descended from the cloudless sky. It struck the hilt of the sword and bathed the entire length of it in a brilliant blue light.

Chapter 25

Jamie and Sebastien clung to each other as the impact rocked the ground beneath their feet. The light grew until they were both forced to look away.

When the glow faded, they turned to look once again.

A short, dark-skinned woman stood several feet away.

"Where did she come from?" Jamie whispered. But she was afraid she knew the answer. She wanted to look at Sebastien, but she couldn't take her eyes off the woman.

She was clothed in a sarong-type outfit of brightly woven orange and red fabric, shot through with gold threads that caught the sun and reflected it back like sparks. Her hair was wrapped in a turban of similar fabric. Her skin was very dark and smooth, so that her eyes were almost luminous as she stared at them. And yet Jamie knew this was not a young woman but a very old one.

"Oriane." Sebastien turned toward the woman, keeping his arm tightly around Jamie's waist.

The woman nodded. "It is me, returning to you once again." The musical lilt of the Caribbean colored her voice.

"But how—"

She waved a graceful hand. "Ask not how, Sebastien Valentin. You of all men know there is more to this world than what you can see or touch."

"Why do you return?"

She nodded toward Jamie, who found herself standing taller, not loosening her grip on Sebastien's waist. They had come this far together; she would fight to the end to ensure that they stayed together.

The woman smiled, her teeth a surprisingly white slash that matched her eyes in luminosity. "You are a strong one, mam'selle," she said, nodding in approval. "I suppose I should not be surprised that Sebastien would settle for one such as you. He will need your strength just now."

Jamie shivered, certain that the woman had read her thoughts. "He has it, and my love and devotion."

Another approving nod. And yet Jamie didn't feel the threat lessen.

Oriane turned to Sebastien. "My Yolande didn't have the strength or fortitude of character such as this one. I knew that. She never understood." She stepped closer, and Jamie gripped Sebastien's hand and held her ground, as did he.

Oriane pulled the sword from the ground and ran a loving hand down the scabbard. "I did not curse you to punish you, Sebastien. Or to punish my Yolande, foolish girl that she was." She shook her head, and suddenly the look in her eyes made her look every year as old as she most likely was. "I had such hopes for her. But it was when I looked upon you, saw the magic in your old soul, that I knew it was you I was destined to teach, not her."

"Teach me?" Sebastien said with a touch of disbelief. "You have odd methods of schooling, if I may say so, madame."

"What I had to impart I knew you would not listen to in any other way. You had to learn yourself to open up your heart to the possibilities that exist between a man and woman." She smiled then, and it was as surprisingly beautiful this time as before. It reached her eyes and made Jamie feel warm, as if the sun shone only on those Oriane looked upon. Ridiculous, but she could not shake the feeling.

"Yes, child. I have the power." She nodded to Sebastien. "And so does he. He thinks his gift is merely that of knowing the ways of the men and women he has matched with their soulmates. It is not so." She turned to Sebastien. "You never questioned your success. Did you not think it unusual? So many successes with such relative ease? Did you not understand that you could see into their souls, divine their needs even when they themselves could not?"

Sebastien laughed, but even Jamie heard the tension underlying it. "Love did not seem so great a mystery to me then."

"Ah." She grinned widely and laughed. "'Then,' the man says." She clapped her hands. "And now? What say you now, Sebastien?"

Sebastien turned away from her and looked into Jamie's eyes. "I say I had no earthly idea of the power of true love. Until now."

"It has taken you long enough." Oriane clapped her hands again. "Far longer than I had anticipated. But even I should have known that there are things that cannot be rushed. And love is one of them. Even if it takes centuries." She held out her hands. "Come to me, children, and take my hands."

Sebastien looked at Jamie, who nodded.

They stood before Oriane. She took Sebastien's left hand, then Jamie's, and crossed them one on top of the other and held them joined between her own. "You were to have helped me in my journey, Sebastien. I, the teacher, you the pupil. And yet, through all these years, you have also been the teacher."

"How have I taught you, Oriane?"

"With your open soul. For a man who thought he could not love, you embraced and shared in the love of others with joy and abandon. Sometimes too much abandon," she added with a look, even though her eyes twinkled. "But I do not condemn you for that."

Sebastien grinned. "*Merci,* madame."

She turned serious. "You have a great gift, Sebastien. Greater perhaps even than mine. Perhaps your powers will heighten with your new knowledge and insight. To rob the world of them would be a sorrowful waste."

Both Jamie and Sebastien frowned. Jamie could feel his hands tense in hers as Oriane continued to hold them.

"What are you saying, Oriane?"

"I am saying that I planned today to take you back with me, to teach you the rest of what awaits you, now that you understand more of what lies within you."

"No!" Jamie demanded. "You cannot do this." She tried to pull her hands free, unsure if it was to grab hold of Sebastien or to put them around Oriane's throat.

With seeming effortlessness, Oriane held her hands in check. She turned a dark eye to Jamie. "You would rob the world of his gift for your own selfish pleasure?"

Jamie shook her head. "I won't deny that he has given me something that I never, ever, thought to have. But after all he has done for those countless other souls, he has finally found his own. How could you rip that soul from him? How will the world benefit from a man who has finally found love, only to have it taken away from him? Why would he want to share his supposed gift with anyone, then?"

Oriane said nothing in response to her outburst. She turned calmly to Sebastien. "And what say you? Do you think it is more worthy to devote yourself to the love of one, rather than to the happiness you could bring to many?"

"What I know, Oriane, is that without Jamie I would be worthless to you. Whatever I have inside me can only be called a gift now because of Jamie. I would never have understood the real power of love without her."

Oriane studied them both at such length that Jamie thought she'd lose the tenuous grip on what was left of her control.

"Please, Oriane." She was begging now, but she didn't care. She would do whatever she had to. "I love him. He loves me. Surely whatever happiness we create within our lifetime is a worthy enough contribution to mankind."

Oriane smiled then and looked to Sebastien. "She is well and truly the one whose soul is meant for yours. A fierce protector of those she cares for. You are a fortunate man. She will love you well, Sebastien." She lowered her voice and fixed him with a hard look. "You will do no less for her."

Sebastien turned to look at Jamie, the emotion that filled his eyes closing her throat over. "I will love her for the rest of my days." He looked to Oriane. "We will be worthy of the forfeit. Surely you have others besides me to continue on with your work."

"I do. They will have plenty to keep them busy. However, your work is not done." When they both started to argue, she shushed them with nothing more than a look. "You have taught me that life never reveals all her plans in advance. I believe together you will bring more happiness to others than you would apart. Now, if you will bear with the ramblings of an old woman, I will bless your union." She raised their joined hands high above her head.

Oriane bent her head and began to chant. It was part invocation, part song, all beautiful. When she was done, she opened her eyes and blessed them with a beaming smile.

She released their hands and picked up the sword. She handed it to Sebastien. "A symbol of where you came from, and of what you are meant to do in your future."

"What do expect me to do now?" Sebastien asked.

"I expect you to return to your home in the Quarter and make this woman proud that she fought so hard for you. Make yourself worthy of her love. You will continue as a mortal, for I cannot keep you in the other realm now that you are promised to her."

Jamie took Oriane's hand and leaned in to kiss her cheek. "Thank you, Oriane. We won't disappoint you."

Jamie wasn't entirely certain, but she could have sworn the older woman blushed. Even as she had the thought, Oriane stood straighter and cleared her throat. "You have the sword, and I understand you are powerful enough to wield it if necessary."

Jamie's mouth dropped open, then shut again as she realized Oriane was making a joke. She laughed. "I think I like you, after all."

Sebastien leaned down and took Oriane's hand. He pressed a courtly kiss to the back of it and offered her a bow. "The sword will grow tarnished for lack of use, I assure you."

Oriane nodded, obviously pleased. She turned and walked back to the spot where she first appeared. "Enjoy your life, Sebastien and Jamie. When you reach the end of it, we will meet again." Before either of them could question her, she winked—and was gone.

Chapter 26

*A*fter several long seconds of silence, Jamie said, "So I don't guess you want to explain that last part, do you?"

Sebastien pulled her into his arms and kissed her soundly. "I don't have time to concern myself with the hereafter. It will take all of my considerable attention to make certain you are happy in the here and now."

Jamie smiled, the smile growing to a grin, then to laughter as she finally began to allow herself to believe what had happened. "Is it real? You and me? No more souls to match? No more disappearing back into the ether?"

He nodded. "Your soul and mine are the only ones I must concern myself with for the rest of our time on earth."

"Mine's already yours. I love you, Sebastien."

"I love you, Jamie." He grinned. "I rather enjoy saying that. I hope you don't mind."

"Go ahead. I dare you to make me tired of hearing it."

"That is a challenge I accept with full enthusiasm." He swung her up into his arms.

"Take me home, my pirate."

He kissed her until she was breathless, but his grin was devilish when he lifted his mouth from hers. "I have other plans."

Jamie lifted her eyebrows. "Not here. Sorry, I'm not *that* adventurous."

Sebastien looked surprised, then laughed. "No, mademoiselle, that is not what I had in mind. However, I do enjoy the workings of your mind. I will have to think on that suggestion a bit. I'll get back to you on it."

Jamie threw her arms around his neck. "Then exactly what plan did you have?"

Sebastien let her feet slide to the ground and, with another lingering scorcher of a kiss, reluctantly released her and turned to the sword and jeweled box. He rewrapped both carefully, then pulled a rucksack from the tree.

"Quite the locker you have there. Not a bad nest egg either," Jamie said.

He smiled at her. "We pirates are a resourceful lot." He finished storing everything, then closed the sack and hefted it over his arm. He stood and scooped her right back into his arms.

"You know, I should get really annoyed with how you toss me around like a rag doll."

"Are you annoyed?"

"Not in the least. I'm a discredit to the feminist movement. I'll explain that later too," she added, seeing the question forming.

"If the rest of your afternoon is free, I have a suggestion on how to spend it."

"My life is yours. At least until tomorrow morning at ten." She could only imagine Ree's reaction when she gave her the good news. "Where are we off to?" she asked as he started back through the woods.

"To plunder and pillage."

"Ah." She smacked her forehead. "Silly me."

They reached the car and he swung her down once again. She caught his pointed look and stared him down but finally gave in with a resigned sigh—and a small prayer. She dug the keys out of her pocket and slapped them into his palm. "Keep it under seventy-five."

"For a woman who enjoys speed, I don't understand this sudden restraint of yours."

"Yeah well, as it turns out, I do better taunting death when I'm behind the wheel."

He leaned down and kissed her cheek. "Trust me, *ma chèrie*, for I would never risk something I cherish as much as I do you."

Jamie merely snorted.

Sebastien laughed and went around to open the passenger door for her.

Once they were both inside—and she had securely buckled herself up—Jamie asked, "So, what is this about plunder and pillage?"

"This was not the only place I tucked away my . . . well, resources. From one summons to the next, I never knew what might still be around." He pulled her close. "Have you lost your taste for uncovering buried treasure?"

A thrill rushed through her at the very words. "Treasure hunting? For real buried treasure? You've just granted my fondest wish. Well, one of the remaining few that you haven't already fulfilled."

He rubbed his chin. "Well, there is the matter of a ring. I believe, if it hasn't been discovered, that I have a diamond and ruby ring that once graced the hand of a certain member of Spanish royalty. Unless you are averse to wearing a piece of my ill-gotten gains as the symbol of our betrothal, it would look lovely on you."

"Depends on why she gave it to you," Jamie said dryly.

Sebastien threw back his head and laughed. "*Mon Dieu*, but I love you. I shall let you choose your own jewel from whatever treasures we reclaim this day. We will have it set in a ring of our own design. It will be yours and yours alone."

Jamie took his left hand in hers and kissed his ring finger. "I don't want jewels. I think something like a simple band, maybe two bands entwined together. One for you, with a matching one for me. A symbol of our souls, matched and eternally wrapped around each other."

"Is that your wish, *mon amour*?"

His eyes sparkled, and she could only think of how deeply she'd come to love this man. Her so-called normal life would never be dull or boring. She couldn't wait to see what happened next.

"That is my wish, my former pirate genie."

He pulled her into his arms and lowered his mouth to hers. "Your wishes will forever be my command."

She wiggled her eyebrows suggestively. "Well, *that* could get very interesting indeed."

"I'm counting on it. Now, kiss me."

She granted him his wish, then sighed in satisfaction. "*Now* this feels like happily ever after."

"Indeed it does." Sebastien grinned, leaning in for another kiss. "Indeed it does."

About the Author

Born and raised in Maryland, Donna now lives in Virginia with her husband, sons, and growing menagerie of dogs and birds. She can be reached online at www.donnakauffman.com or by mail at PO Box 541, Ashburn, VA 20146.

THE ROYAL HUNTER

"You're lying." Archer knew it, just as he knew they'd run out of time.

Her eyes flew to him, the bright spots in her cheeks heightening further, her eyes getting glassy. "No! I don't know anything about what you're telling me."

"You recalled something just now. What?" He took her arm. "Tell me."

Baleweg shook his head and smoothly released her arm from his grasp. "Archer, really. Not all things can be solved with your bullying ways. And here I had heard stories of your prowess with the fairer sex. Propaganda, I'm beginning to believe."

Archer tossed him a look. "This isn't a seduction, old man."

"I should hope not. You'd be going about it all wrong."

"This is why I always work alone," Archer muttered.

Baleweg turned his gaze to Talia. "We need your help. The queen needs your help. It is time for you to return and take your rightful place."

"I'm not a . . . I can't—"

Whatever Talia might have said was drowned by the sudden wail of sirens. Two vehicles spun into the side lot. Men in blue uniforms poured out of the doors before the rolling vehicles had come to a complete stop, all of them shouting commands.

"Come, Archer," Baleweg commanded. "Our time is up for now." He closed his eyes and Archer saw the triangle begin to open behind him amidst the hedgerow.

Archer pulled Talia around to face him. Her dazed gray eyes finally locked on his. "You will help us, Talia Trahaern. We will be back."